Maestro w[illegible]

Maestro dispatched an apepi as it slithered toward one of the myriad bystanders too stupid to realize they should run in terror. As his banishing sword sliced the giant snake in two, the slimy creature exploded into a ball of smoke. One handy thing about most demons: when banished, they popped back to their personal hell without leaving behind an enormous mess. Made it easier to deal with the local constabulary. Also meant they occasionally hunted down their killer for revenge.

Speaking of which, Maestro spun and skewered one of Azidahaka's three heads, pulled the blade free, and sliced off the other two, sending her back to a very, very hot place.

How had the kid managed to create a dimensional portal *this* bloody powerful? Maestro knew the "kid" had been born in the 1940s, but nearly everyone held in magical stasis at a particular age maintained the maturity of that stage. Spook would be seventeen forever.

Assuming he learned to watch his own back and managed to survive the night.

Maestro sliced through a ghast behind Spook, who spun quickly enough to see it evaporate with a high-pitched scream. He glanced at Maestro in embarrassment at letting down his guard and threw out the first thing that came to mind to cover his humiliation. "And you just happened to have a couple of banishing swords in the back of your Mystery Machine?"

His surface thoughts were easier to read than stereo instructions.

"And you don't?" Maestro raised an eyebrow.

Behind Spook, a ghoul chased a middle-aged woman in a housecoat. Maestro intoned a spell. The ghoul evaporated.

Spook stared like a groupie. "Your eyes. . ."

Maestro grabbed him by the shoulders and turned him around just in time for his rising blade to slice a ghost in half. "Yes, yes, yes," Maestro muttered. "They glow purple when I cast that spell. It's very cool. Now you need to get centered and *close that portal*."

Also by John Robert Mack, available or forthcoming on Amazon.

The Tango Triptych
Tango with a Twist
Whiskey Tango Foxtrot
No Tengo Tango

Tales of Mystery and Woe: a comedy
Tales of Mystery and Woe: a comedy
Witches Grow in Threes
Call Me Angel

The Zen Bastard Adventures
A Consequence of Folly
A Consequence of Desire
A Consequence of Hubris
A Consequence of Valour

Third Testament
The Gospel of John
The Acts of St. Michael
Nativity
The Apocalypse of John
Apocrypha

The Danny Decker Adventures
Danny Decker and the Horribly Unlikely Space Adventure
Danny Decker and the Suspiciously Inevitable Quest
Bobby Decker and the Ridiculously Commercial Crossover

Zen Monsters
Zen Monsters: Book One
Zen Monsters: Book Two

Avalon Redux
Once a Future King
Avalon

Convergence
Where everyone meets and the universe ends. Again.

Tales of Mystery and Woe

a comedy

John Robert Mack

Tales of Mystery and Woe: a comedy
This book is an original publication of Zen Monster Press.

Edited by Lauran Strait.
www.linkedin.com/in/lauranstrait

Visit the author at
www.johnrobertmack.com
email: john@johnrobertmack.com
www.facebook.com/johnrobertmack

Contact the author for information regarding volume discounts for classes, studios and other organizations. Bring the author to your live event, in person or online.

Cover by JRM
Cover model Travis Greene.

For Sarah, inventor of alpacas, Mother, and other flights of fancy.

Episode One: Origins

Spook

Austin, Texas
Thursday, 10:00pm

Spook was dead.

He'd been killed back in 1961 at the age of seventeen but never stopped walking around and shooting off his mouth. Or so his brother, Ross, liked to say. For the record, Spook hated the word "zombie."

He stood in his basement, arms raised and eyes closed, reciting a spell of demonic summoning. "*O Fortuna. . . velut luna. . . statu variabilis. . . semper crescis. . . aut decrescis.*" Dust motes sparkled in the light of a hundred blood-red candles and swirled inside the arcane containment circle painstakingly inscribed on the bare concrete floor.

Spook's "**Ye Olde Booke of Shadows**" had called for "**thee blude of a styll-brything mongrel poured unto the colde, colde stone whilst it screamed its fynal cries of terrour after its throat was verily slitte.**" But that was impossible, since an animal with its throat slit couldn't cry out in terror anymore. Spook had a deal with the butcher down the road who sold him farm animal blood at cost, just to get rid of the stuff. Close enough.

He continued his spell as he dribbled the cow's blood into the concrete, which ate it up greedily with faint suckling sounds.

Spook hung out with a Goth crowd that'd taught him how to dress the part at a place called Bitter Sweets on Austin's east side. All these years of spell casting and hunting creatures of the night, and Spook had never realized the importance of image. His short black hair rose in a spikey mess. His normally dark, Mexican skin was made up pale and kohl surrounded his eyes. He wore black leather pants, knee high black boots, a black velvet shirt and a burgundy cowl with the hood down so it wouldn't mess up his hair.

Who'd have known it'd take so much effort for an actual life-challenged American to blend into the death-becomes-us crowd?

He opened his eyes and raised his voice. "*Vita detestabilis... nunc obdurate... et tunc curat. Ludo mentis acie...*" His voice dropped an octave and reverberated with a cavernous echo. "*Egestatem... potestatem... dissolvit ut glaciem.*"

The dust motes swirled into a vortex within the protection circle and a column of light ignited, bright enough to drive away the shadows and expose the clutter in Spook's basement, pushed to the walls to make room for spell casting.

The illumination revealed the usual assortment of old—but still perfectly serviceable—chairs and tables, a collection of demon banishing swords and daggers laid out for easy access, boxes of clothes bound to come back into fashion someday, a standing mirror of soul capturing, and a *Hello Kitty* lamp.

An ethereal breeze stirred the various flags, banners, and drop cloths. Faintly, in the background, a chorus in three-part harmony rose up to support Spook's voice.

The spell was working.

He could feel it.

The power started as a tickle at the base of his spine and spread through his nervous system, which was nothing more than a conduit for magical energy since his death and reanimation. Warm. Tingly.

Oh yeah, it was working.

"*O Fortuna... velut luna... statu variabilis... semper crescis... aut decrescis.*" Soon, the gate would open and his own personal demonic companion would step through the dimensional rift and shuffle up this mortal coil to—

A happy violin riff cut through Spook's chant. Someone had rung the front doorbell.

He faltered, as did the unearthly chorus. But only for a moment.

Ignoring the distraction, he raised his voice and focused. The chorus rejoined him and the spell continued. "*Vita detestabilis. . . nunc obdurate. . .* damn it."

The violin music broke in again, joined by a heavily accented little girl's voice. "Hello Kitty, come outside and play!"

"*Et tunc curat Ludo mentis acie. . .* crap."

The theme song interrupted itself to start over.

Person at the door impatient much?

The chorus cut out. Spook lost his place in the spell. "Blast!" His voice still held all the reverb and echo of a demonic overlord.

The maelstrom in the center of the room suddenly and rapidly swirled down into a tiny spot on the floor like water down a toilet in fast forward. The last of the magical energy disappeared into the concrete with a pathetic "thwip."

The *Hello Kitty* theme repeated itself.

With a disgusted snort, Spook glared at the ceiling in the direction of the front door. He pulled at his sleeves and headed for the stairs.

"That had better be pizza."

As he tramped up the stairs, his Goth boots thundered to suit his mood at the interruption.

He burst through the door into a kitchen obviously decorated entirely from Ikea and headed toward the front door. A more traditional doorbell replaced the bright melody from his downstairs alarm. "If there's no pizza. . . there will be Hell to pay."

Unfortunately, the soft and well-padded carpet in the front hall spoiled the heavy tread of his boots, but he managed two heavy stamps on the hardwood of the foyer to get his steam back up. When the doorbell rang two or three times in rapid succession, Spook yanked the door open as abruptly as he could.

"You better have pizza!"

A middle-aged man in a grey trench coat stood with his back to Spook for a moment before turning quickly to face him, his mouth already open to speak. He did not have pizza. His mouth hung open for a split second before closing as if he'd forgotten what he was going to say or had changed his mind.

Holy Columbo!

He looked Spook up and down and then his eyes settled on

Spook's face with an expression so utterly blank, it was worse than scorn.

In the bright light of the front hall of a two-story, mid-century modern home and surrounded by furniture from Ikea, the burgundy coat and knee high boots were possibly a trifle excessive. And how much make-up had Spook actually applied?

Emotionless, the stranger extended a business card. "I just happened to be passing through your neighborhood and thought you might need some help controlling the demon you're trying to summon."

Spook sucked in a quick breath. How did he know? He grabbed the card. It read:

> Maestro
> Tell me your tale of woe.
>
> Mysteries solved.

Spook glanced from the card to the man. "What. . . demon. . . what?" He floundered. "Do I look like someone who would try to conjure—?" He glanced at his reflection in the hallway mirror, suddenly embarrassed at the get-up. With the crowd at Bitter Sweets, it had seemed restrained. Hadn't it?

The stranger, Maestro, spoke gently. "You look like a reject from a Goth *Hello Kitty* convention."

Spook wanted to disagree but searched Maestro's eyes. He was definitely a fellow mage. Sorcerer? Witch? A powerful one, whatever he was, from the complete sense of control he radiated. Other than the power in the man's eyes, though, he was so bland he'd be nearly invisible in a crowd.

Oooh. Was that just how he liked it?

Spook drew himself up. "How did you know I was summoning a demon? Could you sense a disturbance in the ethereal realm? Ripples in the—"

Maestro snorted. "You are such a little girl." He pointed up.

Spook looked at the ceiling. Nothing there apart from a few cobwebs. Time to call the maid.

The man grabbed him roughly by the arm and dragged him across the porch and onto the front lawn. He was stronger than he looked.

The front lawn needed mowing. Time to call one of his grand-nephews—

Maestro pointed up again. "Actually, the giant hellsmouth over your house was my first clue."

"Holy spit!" Spook stumbled as Maestro released him.

There, above his home, raged an enormous, swirling tornado of smoke and fire and lightning lit from inside by a sickening green radiance. Spirits and demons flew in and out of it, for all the world like fireflies swarming a lantern.

In almost sixty years of hunting supernatural evil, Spook had seen *nothing* like it. Nothing even close. He was so ultimately screwed.

Maestro smacked him on the back of the head. "Close your mouth before something evil and smelly flies in. You look like a tourist." The man calmly turned away from the giant funnel of interdimensional power as if it were nothing more than a backed-up sink. "Tell me this isn't your first ride on the merry-go round."

Spook ran to catch up to the stranger who had already opened the back of a green and white VW Microbus.

Maestro dispatched an apepi as it slithered toward one of the myriad bystanders too stupid to realize they should run in terror. As his banishing sword sliced the giant snake in two, the slimy creature exploded into a ball of smoke. One handy thing about most demons: when banished, they popped back to their personal hell without leaving behind an enormous mess. Made it easier to deal with the local constabulary. Also meant they occasionally hunted down their killer for revenge.

Speaking of which, Maestro spun and skewered one of

Azidahaka's three heads, pulled the blade free, and sliced off the other two, sending her back to a very, very hot place.

How had the kid managed to create a dimensional portal *this* bloody powerful? Maestro knew the "kid" had been born in the forties, but nearly everyone held in magical stasis at a particular age maintained the maturity of that stage. Spook would be seventeen forever.

Assuming he learned to watch his own back and managed to survive the night.

Maestro sliced through a ghast behind Spook, who spun quickly enough to see it evaporate with a high-pitched scream. He glanced at Maestro in embarrassment at letting down his guard and threw out the first thing that came to mind to cover his humiliation. "And you just happened to have a couple of banishing swords in the back of your Mystery Machine?"

His surface thoughts were easier to read than stereo instructions.

"And you don't?" Maestro raised an eyebrow.

Behind Spook, a ghoul chased a middle-aged woman in a housecoat. Maestro intoned a spell. The ghoul evaporated.

Spook stared like a groupie. "Your eyes. . ."

Maestro grabbed him by the shoulders and turned him around just in time for his rising blade to slice a ghost in half. "Yes, yes, yes," Maestro muttered. "They glow purple when I cast that spell. It's very cool. Now you need to get centered and *close that portal*."

Suddenly, Spook spun out of Maestro's grip, stabbed forward into a ghoul and then quickly flipped his blade backward into a second as it zoomed out of the hellsmouth. "Yeah. . . centering here. Totally peaced-out and chill." He pulled a dagger from his belt and tossed it into the center of a cresil chasing a dachshund with obvious lascivious intent.

Maybe the kid wasn't utterly hopeless, after all.

Then he grinned like a puppy eager for a pat on the head, which completely ruined the effect.

"We're kind of on a clock here," Maestro reminded him. "Reporters and cops on the way."

Spook frowned and turned his back to Maestro, bringing his hands together. "Not helping."

With a quiet mutter, Maestro banished the giant hellworm inching toward Spook. "Civilians gonna start dying soon." He let his sword drop to his side for a moment and watched energy swirl and collect about Spook.

"Helping even less," the lad complained. But he did focus better. His energies stabilized into a gentle globe around him.

Spook needed someone directing him. Not good. He'd spent so many years as part of a team, there was no telling how badly he'd screw up on his own. And the fact that he'd tried to summon a demon in the first place meant he'd started down a dark and lonely path.

Which, although Spook would never know it, was the real reason for Maestro's visit. He'd seen what he needed to see. Spook couldn't be left alone. Maestro had watched him from a distance for years. It was time to step in.

"Tourist," Maestro teased. He raised his banishing sword and tossed it from hand to hand in a rapid figure eight around his body. "*Lorem ipsum dolor sit amet.*" He spun twice, whirling the sword over his head. "*Duo nonumy legimus dignissim.*"

He grabbed it in tight fists as it glowed bright white, switched his grip so the point faced the ground. With a guttural shout, he drove the sword up to the hilt into the pavement, dropping to one knee as he did so.

"*Quidam!*"

Lightning crashed into him. A sphere of white light, centered on the quartz crystal in the hilt of Maestro's sword, expanded in a flash out to a distance of about a hundred yards, instantly banishing anything supernatural it touched. Dozens of creatures exploded.

Stupid bystanders applauded.

Maestro focused hard to keep the spell from destroying Spook as well.

The kid staggered as the hydra he'd been fighting suddenly ceased to exist. He turned to Maestro with shock and awe all over his face. "Who the hell are you, and how have I never heard of you?"

Maestro's grip on the sword tightened as the blade began to vibrate. Uh-oh. "Kinda hoping you'd hurry up." Sweat trickled down his forehead and into one eye. The ground trembled.

"Oh. . . right." Spook raised his arms and the echo returned to his voice. "*Sicsercedtau. . . sicsercrepnessilibairavutats anultulevanutrof o*!"

Maestro closed his eyes. Please let it work. He could do it himself, but didn't want to play that card just yet. Please let Spook be able to handle it.

The clouds churned.

The demons screamed.

The giant cyclone of arcane energy swirled into the roof of Spook's home like water down the drain of a toilet. Great billows of smoke and lightning sucked into the house, and Maestro opened his third eye and shifted his gaze to Spook's ridiculously cluttered basement.

The entire maelstrom whirled into the center of the summoning circle on the floor and vanished with an anticlimactic "thwip" that barely managed to blow out the ridiculous and unnecessary assortment of candles.

Apparently, Spook's magic had worked. Good.

Maestro loosened his grip on the sword and let himself breathe. The giant glowing bubble faded like so much steam. With the thunderous roar of a demonic gate silenced, the car alarms, the weeping, and the distinct sound of police and fire sirens rose to fill the void.

Damn. No rest for the wicked.

Before Spook could start in on some foolish "we saved the day" ritual he'd no doubt had with Percy and Ross, Maestro left the sword in the road and rose to his feet, motioning the lad closer.

Spook wiped his forehead and hurried forward, smiling.

Maestro reached for the boy, who grinned even more and opened his arms for a celebratory hug.

Maestro snorted. "Don't be ridiculous." He spun Spook around so they were back to back. "Don't move. Our work isn't done."

Maestro pulled out what most anyone would mistake for an iPhone. When he touched the screen though, a 2-D hologram popped up above it. He tapped the image.

"*Harkle barkle Beelzebub*." Hopefully, his words were good enough to fool Spook into thinking this was spellwork. Sometimes alien technology just worked better, but he couldn't let the little ghoul know about it.

A faint light pulsed out of the device and flashed across the neighborhood, blanketing the block in something not unlike the vapor from dry ice.

Maestro closed his eyes and sent his gaze outward and upward to look down on his handiwork.

In a slowly blossoming wave, every person, animal, and insect settled to the ground as if needing a nap. Cars crawled to a halt. A cat about to pounce on a mouse gently fell asleep, the mouse dropping only an inch from its paws.

Opening his eyes, Maestro clicked his tongue at the eerie muting of sound from this particular app. He shoved the device into a pocket before turning to Spook, who walked away and spun a slow circle. Disgusted with Spook's touristy amazement, Maestro slipped his sword from the pavement and hurried to relieve Spook of the second banishing blade.

"That's why you haven't heard of me," Maestro explained. "They won't remember a thing when they wake up."

Spook gestured at the spouting fire hydrants, the crashed cars. "But how do you explain all this?"

Maestro yanked open the back of his van. Damn, it did resemble the Mystery Machine. "A gas main blew up and knocked everyone out." He tossed the swords into the back and slammed the doors.

"Gas main? Really? You expect people to buy that?" He tapped a sleeping mailman with one toe.

Striding directly behind Spook, Maestro reached over his shoulder and pointed at the nearest yard. "Abracadabra." He tapped the device in his pocket.

The lawn exploded in a carefully controlled ball of fire. Before ringing Spook's doorbell, Maestro had set the explosives against just such a necessity.

"Jeepers!" Spook rocked back into Maestro.

Maestro pushed him gently but firmly away. "I do expect them to buy that."

People woke up and the sirens roared back full volume.

How did everything look? Mayhem and destruction, yes, but no one had been seriously injured.

The hellsmouth had been closed.

No civilians would know how close they'd come to the Apocalypse.

And Spook would never guess why Maestro kept an eye on him.

This incident belonged in the "win" column.

"You. . . are a rock star." Apparently, Spook agreed.

Without offering him the satisfaction of a response, Maestro dragged Spook back into his house, released him, and wandered into the living room. Spook would close the door behind them.

Spook leaned against the closed front door.

What. the. hell?

His unusual visitor wandered around the living room. He seemed to dismiss most of the furniture but paused to touch the ratty afghan over the back of Ross's old recliner, the only piece of furniture that wasn't new.

Spook's brother loved that chair. He'd passed out in it a thousand times over the years after nights of cocktails when he was too drunk to drive home to Lana and the kids. It'd been Percy's before. . . and that old man had been the closest thing to a father Spook and Ross had ever known.

And now Ross was an old man and he'd die, too, just like Percy.

Maestro moved to the fireplace and examined the photos on the mantel.

Spook left the safety of the foyer and joined his guest in the living room.

Standing there in a rumpled overcoat, the man radiated nothing. As average and boring as anyone on the street, but the power he'd shown had been incredible.

Was there any chance he'd be willing to work with Spook, train him? Spook had been alone longer than ever in his afterlife. It blew.

Maestro turned his disquieting gaze on Spook. Okay. Kinda intense.

Russ's recliner called Spook, so he moved to it and worried one corner of the afghan. "Don't the cops ever notice there's a VW microbus at an awful lot of gas main explosions?"

"I change cars fairly often." He didn't look away, and his eyes held no emotion. Geez.

Why was he still here if he was just going to be Mr. Standoffish? There had to be some way to connect with this guy, but he was so intensely distant.

"Why the demon?" Maestro demanded.

Wait. What?

"What?" Spook asked.

Maestro didn't respond.

"Oh. . ." Spook wasn't about to admit the truth, so he stalled. "Why does anyone summon a demon? Power."

Maestro finally broke eye contact. "Seems like you have a pretty nice setup here." He glanced around the room before leveling his laser beam gaze on Spook once more. "Why the demon?"

Spook smoothed out the afghan. "I told you. . . I wanted more power."

Maestro shoved his hands into his coat pockets, cocking his head to one side. He needed a fedora. "If I thought that were true, I'd have let my banishing spell take you out as well. People could have been hurt tonight. They could have died. If you were delving into the dark arts just to satisfy a craving for power, you'd already be lost." He adjusted his coat. "Why the demon?"

Spook fled the safety of Russ's afghan and moved to the fireplace. "You won't believe the truth." A photo drew him in: Ross, Spook, and a very perplexed-seeming Santa Claus. Ross had been much older than the dime-store fat man.

Maestro plucked the photo from the mantle. "This was taken recently and I note a suspicious lack of ridiculous Goth apparel. Something changed." He handed the photo over. "Why the demon?"

Geez. What was his deal?

The photo felt heavy in Spook's hand. "There's nothing ridiculous about Goth apparel." Ross had grown so old.

Maestro leaned against the fireplace. "Ordinarily, I'd agree with you, but on you, it's preposterous. It's like Elvis Presley drag. Not everyone can pull it off. I ask one last time, and then I simply walk out the door." He took the photo from Spook and replaced it. "Why the demon?"

Spook stared at the photo. What could he say? It seemed idiotic now that he needed to explain it. When he'd been on his own last night, looking up spells and drinking Jim Beam, the whole plan had seemed so logical. Tonight? Under the scrutiny of a mage who made Spook's own ability seem feeble? Idiotic.

With a grunt, the other man pushed himself away from the fireplace and headed for the foyer.

Damn it. He'd leave forever if Spook didn't tell him the truth.

Was he that desperate? Yes.

"I was lonely."

Maestro stopped but didn't turn around.

Spook picked up the photo. "Ross was the one who found me after... after this happened to me. We were seventeen." Those first days had been full of terror and despair and Ross had held Spook together through it all. "He's not... biologically, he's not my brother, but we fought supernatural evil bastards for so many years. We sort of adopted each other." Even after Ross had married and had kids, the two of them would go off together whenever Percy found something to kill. Then Percy died.

"Then Ross got old." Spook replaced the photo and faced Maestro. "And one day, he's going to die. And so will his kids. And his grandkids."

"But not you?"

"I'm already dead."

"So you summoned a demon to keep you company?"

Spook shrugged. "At the time, it made a certain kind of sense." How long before Maestro started laughing? "I told you you wouldn't believe the truth."

"Oh... I believe you all right. I mean..." He gave Spook a very pointed and critical perusal. "Have you looked at yourself in a mirror?"

As Spook stepped closer, something moved in the foyer. Oh. It was him. In the mirror. Sweat had ruined his make-up. In the sharp light of the overhead lamp, he was a caricature of a zombie pretending to be a real boy playing at being the undead. Ridiculous. "I don't pull it off, do I?"

Maestro regarded him and, against all probability, he showed only the merest hint of judgment.

Maybe Spook didn't need to do this all by himself after all. "Teach me. Please!" Spook took a single step closer. "I've been fighting the supernatural a long time, but I've never known anyone who can do the kind of stuff you did tonight. . . well, except for a couple of evil demons. . ." That was one possibility he hadn't considered. "You're not an evil demon are you?"

Maestro didn't even react to the question. "I'll help you on two conditions."

"Anything."

The scary man crossed his arms. "Don't be so quick to make promises." He stared at Spook for a long time. "Condition one: get rid of the makeup unless you're going out on a Friday night. You look ridiculous."

"Done." He wiped his face with the back of one sleeve.

"Condition two: don't ever try to hug me again."

Spook grinned. "Agreed." This would be easier than he'd anticipated.

"I mean it." The man's face had returned to that spooky lack of expression worse than any amount of disapproval. "You ever try to hug me again, I will sever your soul from your body and send it to spend an eternity in the deepest circle of Hell."

Whoa.

"Can you really do that?" Spook asked.

Was Maestro going to smile?

Nope. No response.

Spook swallowed. "Agreed. For reals."

The other man's hand came up so fast Spook jumped. "Okay, there's a third condition," Maestro said. "No catch phrases. I don't ever want to hear you say 'for reals' again." He grabbed the doorknob and yanked the door open.

"Hey!" How would Spook find him? He pulled out Maestro's business card. "Your card. . . there's no contact info." He held it up as if Maestro didn't already know what was on it, or, more importantly, what was not.

Maestro met Spook's gaze. "I thought you said you'd been on this merry-go-round before." He closed the door between them.

Spook grinned. "Brass ring."

He ran up the stairs three at a time to get his laptop and start googling.

E.T.

Austin, Texas
Thursday. Midnight. . .

Well, technically, Friday.

Agent Elizabeth Turner of the Galactic Police had dressed to impress. Her four-inch red stilettos clacked loudly on the pavement as she approached the two policemen manning the crime scene tape line. Her shapely legs showed to their best advantage in a little black dress she'd fabricated from a local website that had guaranteed a beneficial reaction from the males of the dominant species.

The outfit she wore had been copied from a local copulation professional: blonde, shapely, and with the enlarged mammary glands local males seemed to enjoy.

Strangely, when she'd replicated the woman's DNA and shifted to her form, her own hair had turned out brown and her mammary glands grew nowhere nearly as large as the original's. With a little concentration, both adjustments had been easy to manage.

The two policemen turned to her and their faces changed from bland professionalism to an obvious desire for copulation. Mentally, Turner adjusted the data lens in her right eye and checked their irises, heart rate, and overall body temperature. Ah yes, the outfit and dress definitely worked. One of the males even grew tumescent.

She paused at the tape line, glanced down, then looked into their faces in an expectant manner she'd learned from the copulation specialist. "Good evening, gentlemen. If you would be so kind. . ." She held up her FBI badge.

They nearly came to blows over who would raise the tape for her.

As directed by her coach, she "winked" at the men when she passed: opening and closing her eyes slowly and deliberately with an exaggerated pinching of her facial muscles. Or was it supposed to be one eye? Well, they didn't seem to mind.

Her first goal accomplished, Turner checked out the scene. Local police agents loitered in the most undisciplined disarray she'd ever seen. The body lay covered in a sheet in the center. Blue and red lights flashed, creating shadows everywhere. While the shadows appealed to the spy in her original genetic imprint, where were the hovering flood lights?

Oh. . . yes. This planet didn't have antigravity yet.

Well, they had electricity and incandescent bulbs, didn't they?

Turner dropped to one knee by the body and pulled the sheet back. Female. African descent mixed with European impurities. Seemed right. From a pocket, she drew what hopefully looked like an iPhone and touched the screen to make it jingle as if she had a message.

While pretending to answer a text, Turner used the camouflaged Doohickey to scan the corpse. Single. No family. No friends to speak of. She had lived the last several years completely alone.

Perfect. No one would recognize Turner in *this* outfit. While the copy of the copulation professional was obviously desirable, myriad males throughout Austin knew it. She could wear the dead woman without concern about detection.

Turner pulled a vial from the small purse that hung over one shoulder. She removed a swab and shoved it into the dead woman's mouth.

Wait. Two men approached.

Turner rose.

"So I thought it might be your kind of thing," one of the men said. "You know. . . a Steven Spielberg. Probably a *Close Encounters*."

Turner knew the speaker as a leader among the local police force, a tall, blocky Mexican with the distinctive short-cropped hair that indicated he had likely served in the national military.

"Any particular reason?" a stranger asked.

Turner didn't recognize the policeman's companion. He was average height, brown hair, green eyes, and he wore a rumpled grey overcoat that was at least ten years out of fashion. Most likely no one important.

Without sparing them a second glance, Turner brushed quickly past and made her way to an alley to change outfits in private.

Maestro noticed the leggy blonde as she hurried away. Why was an FBI agent at a crime scene dressed like a hooker?

Ricardo yanked away the sheet to reveal the corpse.

Oh, drat.

A perfectly round eight-inch hole had burned all the way through her torso and cauterized. No blood. The pavement showed clearly beneath her. It had to be a laser blast. If magic had killed her, it would linger. This was definitely what Ricardo called a *Close Encounter* and not a *Poltergeist.*

Ricardo let the sheet drop over the woman's legs. "Unless she happened to wander here after being seared by a large industrial laser in a lab somewhere, I'm going to guess we have visitors with something a bit more portable."

"Heh. . . Visitors." Maestro chuckled. "I love your euphemisms, Ricardo." He finally looked at the dead woman's face.

Shit!

This was Turner. Here. Now. Dead? How?

"So what do you think?" Ricardo asked.

Maestro scanned the street for some sign of the FBI hooker. She was nowhere to be seen, but he had to find her.

"I need to see man about a dog. . . or in this case, a woman about a llama." He grabbed Ricardo's hand. "I'm on the case." He hurried off, knowing Ricardo wouldn't be offended. The cop was accustomed to Maestro's ways.

Maestro closed his eyes, centered, and cast his gaze outward.

She'd gone into the alley. Now that he knew it was her, she was easy to follow.

As he approached the corner, uncomfortable squelching sounds reached him, but when he entered the alley's mouth, the tall Black woman merely cracked her neck to one side and then the other. She wore the exact same slutty dress the blonde hooker had worn.

Yep. This was Turner.

She startled at Maestro's appearance, glanced from him to the uncovered corpse in the middle of the street, identical to her in every single way.

The wheels turned while she recognized him from the crime scene.

Her hands covered her face, and she burst into melodramatic sobs. "Oh, my poor identical twin sister, I can't believe she's gone. I came into this alley so no one would see my foolish outburst of emotion. Please go away, total stranger. I want to be alone."

"Oh, my gods," Maestro cursed, "I hope you aren't undercover. That's. . . that's just embarrassing. . . Please stop."

When she showed no signs of ceasing, he pulled a card out of a jacket pocket. A tiny hologram winked into existence in the air over the card, a 3D glowing image of a nearly naked woman sitting on a very 1950s style space rocket with a male bug-eyed alien hanging out a window staring at her.

One moment, it showed a perfectly normal woman with the caption "Buy two. . ." then the shape shifted and a third breast appeared. ". . . get one FREE!" The bug-eyed alien's eyes actually popped out of his head with a humorous sound effect. The shape shifted back and forth like a tacky neon sign.

Instantly sober, Turner grabbed the card from him. She scowled. "Where did you get this? Earth doesn't have holographic technology."

"Rapscallion Alpha."

She yanked a cell phone out of one pocket, but when she waved it at him, he recognized it for what it was.

"Your Doohickey has a nice chameleon app," he said. "Looks just like an iPhone."

Turner scowled at him again. "You're a quantum jumper."

Maestro glanced around. No one lurked in hearing distance. "Time traveler. I'm from a future after Earth's made first contact. The Primitive Planet Protection Pact doesn't pertain to me. . . personally."

She flipped the card over. "Are there many jumpers on the planet?"

"Not nearly as many as you might think, considering." He held a hand out for his card. It was a memento of a much better time. "You're new?"

She handed the card back. "Just got here."

Ah, that explained a lot. "So what does an officer of the Galactic Police want with a dead woman's identity?" Although he already knew the answer, this was their first meeting as far as Turner was concerned so he had to play it out. Time travel made relationships complicated.

She opened her mouth to protest, but changed her mind. Instead, her eyes took on that slightly glazed expression that meant she was checking the readout in her data lens.

"Any naked pictures of me in there?" He liked her mounting frustration. "Maybe a shot of me as the Vitruvius man with a digital readout of all my vitals?" He spread his legs and held his arms out for effect.

She grabbed his elbow and dragged him deeper into the alley. "I'm hoping to flush out some smugglers."

"Big?"

Once away from the streetlights, she released his elbow. "I'm not at liberty to divulge—"

"Alpaca Consortium big?" It was rude to mess with her that way, but he had so few means by which to amuse himself and such a very long time ahead.

Her eyes narrowed. "How could you possibly know that? Wait." Her eyes went unfocused again and she frowned at him. "You've worked with the Galactic Police before." Her eyes scanned back and forth as she read something on her data screen. The frown deepened. "You're psychic."

"You have a problem with psychics?"

"Not at all." She focused on him. "Only the mindreading part. . . and the future prediction thing."

Maestro laughed. "Oh, well as long as it's only that we should get along like a house on fire."

Ignoring his joke, Turner spoke to him for the first time as if he were a professional. "Did you read anything from the dead woman?"

"You're not worried I read it from you?" Maestro asked.

The Galactic Police agent scoffed then frowned and crossed her arms, most likely realizing that scoffing was a human reaction. "I'm a Shifter and a highly trained Galactic Police agent. You can't read my mind."

Okay, she was as arrogant as the versions Maestro knew. Might as well enjoy himself. He turned in the direction of the corpse he'd only barely examined.

"The sweater is alpaca wool," he lied with his sincerest voice. "Normally not a big deal, but it's almost a hundred degrees in the shade today." He turned to the agent and crossed his arms to match her. "Her left eye has a contact in it but not the right, which is also highly unusual unless she has a contact laced with tech. Visual enhancers and recording devices, I'd surmise." He nodded. "I'm guessing she was a plant whose cover got blown. The laser residue was the giveaway though—"

"You guessed." Turner glared at him.

"I guessed." He let his hands drift into his pockets. "I can't read the mind of a corpse. There's nothing supernatural involved, so I go with powers of observation and the occasional leap. Whenever alien authorities—"

Turner bristled. "Would you please refrain from using that word? If you *are* a jumper, you should know how offensive it is."

Oops. He'd lost a lot of his extraterrestrial etiquette in his self-imposed exile. "Apologies. I've been following this timeline for a while and haven't been off-planet in a few centuries. I meant, whenever *extraterrestrial* authorities get involved on this world, it almost always has something to do with the Alpaca Consortium. It *is* the Alpaca Homeworld, after all." Time to stop playing with her and make a sincere effort. "Look, let's start this again now that we know where we stand."

He offered his hands palm up in a traditional greeting recognized on nearly every civilized world. "From those who have to those who need."

Startled, Turner stared at his hands for a moment before holding out her own in the same gesture. "I have not the need but appreciate the offer." Her voice lost all of its pretension. "You haven't been off-world in centuries, but you have translator microbes?"

Maestro smiled cryptically. "It was centuries ago to me, but I was born two hundred years in the future as far as you're concerned."

She regarded him for several moments, as if trying to decide whether he was sincere. Finally, she shook her head. "You are a man of many mysteries, Mister. . .?"

With a flourish, Maestro pulled out his card and held it out to her.

She took the card and read it. "Maestro?" She looked up at him. "As in band leader?"

He acknowledged her deduction with a simple nod.

She stared at the card. "I hate mysteries."

"And what name are you using in this outfit?" he asked for the sake of it.

She startled, as if suddenly realizing she'd broken Earth protocol. "Sorry. Turner. Elizabeth Turner, FBI."

Maestro couldn't suppress a smirk. "Elizabeth Turner, the Extra-Terrestrial?" He made a point of emphasizing the first letter of each word. He enjoyed messing with ETs when they first came to Earth. They always picked stupid names.

She seemed to realize she'd missed a joke. "As I said, I hate mysteries."

Maestro stifled a chuckle. "Sorry. There's a bit of a pun there. I assume your translators kill the joke."

"I'm not using the microbes," she told him proudly. "I speak twenty Earth languages fluently; I simply have no sense of humor. I'm a Shifter, after all, and a member of the Galactic Police on a very important mission."

Of course, she was. Well, he had stuff to do, too. Perhaps this was all they were supposed to accomplish in this encounter.

"I apologize again, Agent Turner. I do not wish to keep you from your job." He turned and headed back up the alley.

"Maestro?"

He stopped and smiled. "Yes?" Maybe there was more to this meeting, after all.

"You seem to have contacts with law enforcement agents who know about your. . . more mysterious aspects."

"As you say." He turned back. Where exactly would this go?

She stared at him in obvious indecision for several moments before speaking. "I might have use for a local who isn't bound by the protected status of the planet."

Ah . . . this was the agent he'd known in more than one timeline, but he still had to check one thing. "Really? You'd stoop to using a monkey?"

Her face expressed shock at his implication that she'd use such a derogatory term. "I. . . I never used that word. . . I never would."

Calling a sentient species by the name of one of its evolutionary ancestors was the absolute worst insult imaginable in most of the civilized galaxy. The fact that he'd shocked her proved she was, indeed, the same person in this timeline that he'd met in several others.

He hurried to her side. "Think nothing of it. I was just checking." He extended his hand again.

She took it and held it a second or two longer than absolutely necessary.

He raised an eyebrow in query.

Noticing her faux pas, she quickly released his hand and controlled her expression. "Do you have a few spare minutes?"

"For an officer with the Galactic Police I can spare a full hour."

She smiled. "How about two?"

It could've been any warehouse in any star system, filed with a large number of old crates and the vague odor of vermin and the urine of vermin.

Turner wore a smart business suit with just a hint of "tacky" garnered from extensive research into the ways of wealthy Texas eccentrics. She'd changed the holographic make-up from the copulation professional, or "hooker" as the man named Maestro had insisted she be called.

He seemed rather uncomfortable, although the plain jumpsuit he wore should not have been in any way restrictive. An engine whined and the strange human jumped.

"Jumpy?" Turner asked.

"It's the jumpsuit." He fiddled with the zipper down the front. "I don't much like Kla'arkians."

Just how extensively had this human travelled? "There won't be any actual Kla'arkians," she reassured him. "Just their lapdogs. Well, lap-insectoids."

His face wrinkled in apparent disgust. "Hunters? Ugh. . . I'm going to bathe twice a day for the next year."

So he knew of the insectoid race as well. Interesting. "I will engage in all communications for this meeting," she said, hoping to reassure him further. "You're only duty is to act as a psychic recording device."

An ensign spoke into her auditory implant.

"The interface is working," she relayed to the human. "Images are bright and clear." She tapped her Doohickey and created a 2D screen for his benefit.

The screen showed the bridge of the orbiting Galactic police cruiser: a white circular deck with a central area that displayed holograms of a star ship, Maestro's vital signs, and a hologram of his psychic feed. The screen zoomed in on the psychic feed, which showed exactly what Maestro saw: rusty metal walls and some crates.

Then the display showed the hologram as Maestro regarded it.

On the cruiser, a simple rail ringed the display area and separated it from the crew circle. Several of Turner's fellow agents clustered around the central rail and a number of others worked at a variety of screens. They wore a dozen different planetary species.

She missed them. How long would she be stationed on a planet of statics? Being stuck in one shape limited their perspective in so many amazing ways.

Pushing aside her homesickness, Turner spoke to the human at her side. "No heroics, Maestro. I just need you to record the transaction.

This operation has been going on for years and has already cost hundreds of lives."

The human nodded emphatically and stared at her with wide eyes. "Just to make sure I have this right, boss, what's to stop them from tracing the neural link back to me and blowing the whole thing?"

Oh, the simplicity of the human mind. With the utmost patience, Turner explained the situation yet again. "No one can trace a neural link. It operates on a quantum level."

Maestro fell quite still. "That's right," he said, his tone quiet and more than a trifle menacing. "Shifters haven't invented a quantum trace yet in this timeline. Where *I* come from, your Doohickey would have a quantum memory core with a link to its own private universe for infinite power and storage." His face relaxed and he suddenly seemed far older than was possible for a human. "I may be from Earth, but I was born over two hundred years in your future. I think I can handle myself."

Behind him a force shield extended across one end of the cargo bay, revealing the blue and green disc of the Earth. Much closer hung the dark, grey ball of its satellite lamely named the Moon. Most humans would probably stand gape-jawed at the sight of their planet from space, and yet this man hadn't more than glanced at the sight.

Time to stop underestimating this one because his planet of origin was so backward. The man himself travelled time and, in some ways, had to be her technological superior.

The ensign in her ear saved her from an embarrassing apology. "They're on their way in."

She repeated the news to Maestro, who slumped a little and rendered himself even less noticeable. He seemed proficient in his role.

Turner had a role to play, too. Lights and shadows, hers was a ludicrous part but she'd researched it thoroughly by watching several reality TV shows, studying how the so-called "one percent" behaved.

No putting it off.

She bent over and shook out her hair, stiffening the roots and "jacking it," as one show had described, "all the way up to Jesus."

Rising to face her companion, she tapped the Doohickey and painted her face holographically with "more color than a ten-dollar whore."

From the astonishment on Maestro's face, the effect must have been perfect. Splendid.

And there was the golden shimmer that indicated a low tech transport. No time to adjust anyway.

Eight cylinders of crackling light solidified in the center of the cargo bay. The displacement created an uncomfortable thrumming sound, and the bodies actually formed in front of her, slow enough for her eyes to follow. Really, if they were going to steal their tech, why plunder old-fashioned detritus? Transporters that old were unsettling.

The Hunters didn't seem any the worse for wear, though. They stood seven to eight feet tall and resembled nothing more than enormous, armor-plated fleas. She knew the plating was a fabricated exoskeleton and quite necessary when genetically altering an insect species to this gigantic proportion. They also utilized rebreathers to facilitate oxygen absorption.

Time to start.

Turner erected her posture, planted her feet further apart, and pressed both hands into fists at her hips. "Strap me to a Harley and *fuck* me," she called out in her best impression of a Southern American. "You guys are even better than the fuckin' view up here. If I'd've known I could get *this* kind of party with a couple of low class llamas, I'd have jumped that bronco a year ago."

Maestro's mouth opened wide—his eyes even more so—and his pupils dilated. Sexually excited? Probably. Her impression had to be spot on.

The Hunters chuckled. Well, whatever they did to express amusement was translated for her as the chuckle of a human.

"How charming," the leader said. Her translator microbes rendered the sounds in a voice with a deep, British accent. Odd.

Well, in for a quark in for a great wall. . . Turner grabbed one of the enormous weapons the Hunters all carried. "Shee-ite, that is one motherfucker of a gu-un."

She almost dropped it. The last time she'd carried one she'd been a twelve foot Saurian and could have juggled three of the things with her tail. "I'd love to get me one of these for that little Chihuahua next door what never shuts up, know what I mean?"

More chuckling. Under other circumstances, the Hunter leader likely would have already vaporized her, but the cargo her character had for sale was so ridiculously valuable to the Kla'arkians they'd put up with almost anything. She needed them to believe she was a tech-drunk native until the cargo arrived.

Right on cue, the small herd of alpacas she'd requisitioned appeared in the empty space near the force field.

One bleated.

Oddly, Turner's bizarre character was actually enjoyable. She aimed the rifle on a convenient nearby crate and pulled the trigger.

A thin red beam struck the crate. It exploded in a cloud of debris that dissolved into smoke. The Hunters certainly stole a higher caliber weapon than transporter.

"Cooo-eee," Turner shouted. "Can you throw one of these sombitches in?"

The leader spoke amidst the untranslatable chittering of its companions. "I'm certain something might be arranged."

She swung the rifle around to smile at Maestro. Acknowledging assistants helped put them at ease.

Pew. Pew.

One of the Hunter underlings vaporized in a faintly smelly puff of smoke. It screamed while it dissolved.

Turner froze. Had she done that? Drat. "I didn't mean that." Had she hit the trigger by accident?

Maestro closed his eyes.

The Hunter leader chuckled. "I've been meaning to do that for months." It swung its own weapon around and another underling dissolved amid a high-pitched screech. "See? Fun for all." It lowered its weapon and regarded Turner levelly.

While expression was hard to read on an eight-foot flea with an armor-plated face, it gave the distinct impression it would put up with almost any good-spirited hi-jinks from the backward owner of an enormous heard of alpacas.

"Your merchandise is worth far more than any of my warriors," the leader said, confirming her suspicions. "Than all of them, for that matter." Without even looking, it fired the weapon again, vaporizing yet another underling.

Turner cocked one hip and rested the elbow of her gun arm on it, nodding at the weapon in her hand. Would he understand her intent?

The leader nodded once, then gestured for one of the remaining underlings to step forward. It held a metal briefcase.

Turner nodded for Maestro to take the case, which hadn't been the original plan, but she was improvising. If the Hunter saw her grab the case, why did she have the man who appeared to be a servant?

Maestro did as he was told.

"It has been a *pleasure*, people, doing business with you." Turner grinned. "And if you ever need more of the smelly critters, you know who to call, and I don't mean Ghostbusters! Am I right?"

As Maestro handed her the case, Turner glanced past the Hunter delegation. Through the cargo bay force field, the flashing red and blue lights of several Galactic Police cruisers heaved into view from the bright side of the moon. Excellent.

A moment later, and with virtually no noticeable shift, she stood once again in the alley where she'd first met her human companion.

"*That's* how you perform a transport." Turner's people, the Shifters, were the most technologically advanced species in the known galaxy. It showed.

Very satisfied with her work, she flipped her hair and let it drop down her back. She also erased the exaggerated make-up.

Maestro handed her the briefcase, stripped off the grey jumpsuit, and changed into jeans and a t-shirt. He was more athletically built than she'd have guessed.

"Thank you for your help." She extended an arm for the human to drape the jumpsuit. She ran her Doohickey over his head to dissolve the psychic link.

"Hey, don't hesitate to call if you ever need a human telepath who doesn't mind being hooked up to a neural interface and isn't subject to the Primitive Planet Protection Pact."

"Thank you. That's kind." Turner couldn't tell whether he was serious but took him at face value since that was easiest. The complexities of human sarcasm baffled her. "I wasn't sure how you felt about all this. The interface is gone."

"Thanks. It was. . . it was actually kind of nice to be out there again. It's been a while." His expression remained unreadable. "You can, of course, contact me whenever you need."

"Your card doesn't have any contact information." She pulled it out to double check.

He smiled. "Do you really need it?" Without another word, he turned and calmly left the alley, as if helping the Galactic Police was, by far, the least interesting item on his schedule that day.

He vanished around the corner.

"Doohickey?"

"Yes, Agent Turner?"

"I need everything the GP has on that man."

"Of course."

Muscle

Austin, Texas
Friday. 2:15 a.m.

Reggie Sato tossed six full bags of trash into the dumpster behind the Biker Bar. Three in each hand. To say he was strong would be like saying the Texas sun at noon in August was warm.

Everyone in the bar called him Muscle. Back home in Japan, his nickname had been *Chīsana kin'niku akuma.* Which amounted to the same thing. He dropped the dumpster lid into place and was heading back toward the bar when a kitten mewed nearby.

A little black ball of fluff sat on the pee-stained concrete a few yards away staring up at him with eyes so big they had to be computer enhanced. It mewed again.

Reggie smiled. He crouched beside the kitten.

Immediately, it leapt onto one of his massive thighs, climbed up his back, and settled on one shoulder, kneading the strip of fabric on Reggie's black tank top. It nuzzled his neck and purred loudly enough to wake the dead.

Reggie smiled and scratched the kitten gently under its chin. He would name it *Bakeneko* after the cat demons from his homeland.

Home. He lost his smile. He had been in the United States for almost a year and was no closer to fulfilling his quest. He missed the monastery and his brothers and sisters there. He missed his sensei most of all. The ancient, little man was the only father Reggie knew, and they had not spoken in months.

In the monastery, all Reggie had thought about was going off to see the world. . . now that he was in it, all he could think about was home.

Sensei would have something to say about that, so Reggie felt embarrassed to call.

The kitten bumped his cheek, reminding him of his *real* priority, and Reggie resumed rubbing the tiny chin. When the loud rumble of a purr returned, Reggie smiled once more.

The sound of a fist hitting flesh accompanied a muffled grunt somewhere up the alley, near the street. Somebody threw a small, thin man into the garbage cans.

A woman cried out. "We'll give you everything we have!"

Reggie focused and pulled the scene closer. Three men together and a teenage couple. Two of the men closed in on the thin teenage boy on the ground while the third held a gun on the girl.

Reggie rose and slipped off his sandals. At his ear, the kitten hissed. Gently, Reggie lifted the tiny ball of fluff and placed it on the dumpster. He turned to lock in the scene at the mouth of the alley and, for a moment, closed his eyes.

"Just get his wallet," the man with the gun said. "We don't have time—"

Reggie grabbed the gun arm and braced it.

"Where the fuck did you come from?" the man shouted.

The bone broke with a snap, and the gun clattered to the ground. Reggie struck the man in the jaw, and he dropped like a sack of rice.

The girl sucked in a quick breath. While the two men who had been kicking the boy rose to full height, Reggie pointed at the brightly lit street a few yards away. When the girl did not move, Reggie gently pushed her in the right direction.

"Ethan . . ." she muttered, looking down at the groaning young man.

Reggie gave her one more gentle push then faced the two men who now held guns leveled at his chest. He could only hope she chose the wisest path.

The men called to their unconscious friend with a broken arm. Apparently, his name was Jerry.

"What kind of a stupid idgit are you?" the bigger of the two said. "You think that ninja shit matters to a gun?"

Ninja? Interesting. People did not usually realize Reggie was Japanese. Unless he was angry, he resembled his Nigerian mother more than his Japanese father.

The mouthy thug fired his gun.

A slug hit Reggie in the right shoulder, forcing him back a step before he regained his balance. That made him angry. His deep growl reverberated in the alley, and he could not stop his eyes from flashing red just once before he took a deep breath to regain his composure.

The thugs' eyes widened.

"What the hell is he on?" asked the man who had shot Reggie.

"What the hell *is* he?" the other asked.

The boy on the ground groaned. How was *he*?

Reggie needed to handle the thugs. The young man might need medical attention.

Staring the shooter square in the eye, Reggie lunged one foot forward to stomp the pavement.

The concrete rumbled and cracked.

The men broke and ran into the open Biker Bar back door.

Reggie smiled for a moment before moving to the injured boy's side. The girl had called him Ethan. He had stalled out on his hands and knees, though from fear or from his injuries was hard to say.

Reggie crouched and slid one hand under the young man's bicep, lifting him gently to his feet. He couldn't be more than sixteen.

"They came out of the shadows. . ." He shook out of Reggie's grasp. "I could've taken them if—" He looked Reggie up and down. His eyes widened. "Monica. . . where's Monica?"

Reggie nodded in the direction of the street, gestured, and gave another quick nod to let Ethan know the girl had escaped unharmed. He pressed young man's ribs.

The young man winced but nothing could be broken or he would have had much more pain. Probably bruised but hopefully no internal bleeding.

Reggie steadied Ethan and examined his eyes. Could he focus?

The young man met Reggie's gaze evenly. "I'm fine. I've had

worse at my dad's gym. . . but thanks. They got the drop on me." He glanced at Reggie's shoulder and his eyes opened wide. "They shot you. You're bleeding."

Reggie released Ethan then shrugged and shook his head to indicate it was no big deal. He jabbed a thumb in the direction of the street.

Ethan glanced at the bright lights. "Monica." He grabbed Reggie's hand and shook it. "Thank you so much." He shook it some more. "You probably saved our lives. I'll call 911."

Reggie met Ethan's eyes evenly and shook his head once.

Ethan seemed to consider the bleeding shoulder, and then the safety of the well-lit street.

Reggie nodded in the direction the girl had run and released the young man.

Ethan took one more deep breath. "I like the hat." He ran off.

Reggie touched the brim of his flat cap. Plaid. He picked up the discarded gun from the concrete, hit the catch, and popped the clip which he tossed into a garbage can.

His shoulder hurt. Ah yes, he had been shot. He closed his eyes and pushed. A moment later, metal clinked on concrete. A moment after that, he opened his eyes and walked through the kitchen door into the bar itself.

A lot of shouting instantly cut off. Ten pairs of eyes stared.

The two thugs from the alley had bellied up to the bar, and eight men stood attentively around the room. Bernie, the bartender that night, looked over his shoulder. He jumped when he saw Reggie standing beside him, and he glanced at the open back door on the other side of the room.

"That's him." The thug who had shot Reggie pointed. "That's the guy. He broke Jerry's arm."

Bernie backed into the farthest corner, near the beer cooler. "Look, Muscle, I'll get fired if the place gets wrecked."

Without a word, Reggie held the gun up between two fingers as if it were tainted and dropped it onto the bar. How would Bernie react to that?

Bernie stared at the gun for a moment before bursting into

obviously fake outrage. "You assholes brought *guns* into my bar?"

That was no surprise. Bernie was as bad as the other men, if not worse.

Reggie moved slowly to avoid startling anyone. They all had their weapons put away, and he wanted to keep it that way. Bernie was a waste of human skin, but the bar's owner was a decent man, and Reggie did not want to get his place shot up.

The thugs took a few steps back as Reggie came around from behind the bar.

"Oh?" said the thug who had shot Reggie. "You going to teach us a lesson?" He looked at the other men, who rose as one with a profound sliding of chairs and slapping of pool cues on palms. The miscreant grinned. "You and what army?"

They seemed to want a fight, and Reggie was not one to disappoint. Besides which, he had not had a decent workout in some time. He cracked his neck one way and the other then cracked his knuckles. He allowed himself half a smile.

Opponents usually hated when he smiled.

Maestro snacked beside his favorite taco cart on East Sixth Street. How'd someone think to combine Korean barbecue with Mexican tacos? Inspired.

While sauce dribbled on his trench coat, Maestro kept one eye on the bar across the street. The Biker Bar was probably the most accurately, if least originally, named place in town after The Hole in the Wall.

The streets were nearly deserted since closing time had passed, but places like the Biker Bar tended to close late. Very late. The young fighter he'd been sent to observe worked there.

The guy, called Muscle for obvious reasons, was huge. While Maestro had ordered tacos, the young man had taken out the trash.

A gunshot had broken the night, but Maestro had sent his gaze down the alley and Muscle had seemed to handle himself all right. The bullet must've missed. So Maestro had enjoyed his taco.

A bit of action caught his attention through the bar's plate glass window. A couple of obvious lowlifes yelled at the bartender, and Muscle entered from the kitchen. What the hell? The place must have a back hallway he hadn't noticed.

After a moment, the other guys all stood up and a bar fight seemed inevitable. Yep. . . one man moved forward twirling a pool cue over his head. Like that would scare someone like Muscle.

The bouncer grabbed the spinning stick and pulled the man close. He popped the attacker once and dropped him. Nice. Nothing flashy or showy. Just take them down.

Maestro's taco was gone. Maybe he should order another. No. Greasy hands caused problems in a bar fight. He wadded up the wrapper, tossed it, and grabbed a couple of extra napkins.

The thugs weren't bad fighters. Once the showoff went down, the rest of them closed in without going for that stupid one-at-a-time nonsense in the movies. Four attacked at once, two with knives. More than that and they'd just get in each other's way. Hm. . . kid might need some help after all.

The guy in front of Muscle lunged.

Muscle grabbed his knife arm, yanked it, and used it to stab the guy who'd just jumped his back.

As the knife-wielder collided with Muscle's chest, the fighter snapped his neck with his free arm. He leaned just enough to kick another thug in the middle of his chest, and the thug, who had to weigh 300 pounds, flew through the plate glass window and landed in a heap on the sidewalk.

Okay. . . maybe the thugs needed some help.

Maestro dropped his trash in the bin and waved at the taco cart folks.

"No need to call 911," he told them. "I'm on it."

They smiled and waved.

He ran into the bar as someone chambered a gun.

"Put the man down," said the guy with the gun.

Muscle held someone over his head in the middle of the room. He probably only needed both hands for balance. Apparently, the ancient Japanese sensei who'd asked Maestro to hire the fighter had left out a few important pieces of information.

Muscle dropped the guy, whose neck distinctly cracked.

"What the fuck?" someone demanded.

"You should have said, 'Put the man down *gently*.'" Maestro's quip did its job, distracting the man long enough for Maestro to grab his gun arm and direct it straight up. The gun discharged harmlessly into the ceiling, and Maestro slammed an elbow into the guy's face.

Down he fell.

"I'm sure you could've handled these fellows on your own," Maestro told Muscle, "but I didn't get my morning exercise."

Muscle nodded, but had three more men to fight while the last two attacked Maestro. It wasn't pretty, and no one would get paid a lot of money to choreograph it in a movie. These guys were used to killing and killing fast, and Muscle was used to putting down rabid dogs, apparently.

So was Maestro. A very few moments later, he stood back to back with the young fighter.

Well, back to waist anyway.

The room fell still except for the moans and whimpers of the thugs who hadn't died or fallen unconscious.

"That was bracing." Maestro relaxed, and turned to face Muscle.

Oh, hells. Close up, Maestro recognized the young fighter. He'd seemed rather older at a distance. He hadn't met this young man the way he'd met the other two, but he'd seen the photos and videos often enough. All three in one day. Damn.

How old was he anyway? He seemed younger than he looked, especially when he dropped the fighter's stance. He radiated peace, as well, but a carefully constructed peace. Without even using his second sight, Maestro could tell this guy was fighting some demons.

Oh. Indeed. Well, *that* was interesting, too.

Maestro held out a hand, and the young fighter immediately took it, giving a short bow.

Yep. . . as soon as they touched, Maestro could tell demons were definitely involved. Intriguing. He'd need to have words with the old sensei.

To cover his brief silence, Maestro held out a card. "Have a minute?"

Muscle looked at the devastation then held up a broom that had appeared out of nowhere. He shrugged and gestured toward the bar, examining Maestro's card.

Maestro poured himself a scotch, neat. He watched Muscle in the mirror. The hat was an interesting choice. It must be a pretty snug fit to stay in place during a bar fight.

Maestro sipped his whiskey. It was cheap and harsh. Excellent. "I sometimes need a man with your skills," he explained. "It's not illegal." He started to sip again but stopped. "Well, not *really* illegal." He waved the glass over the nearest cooling body. "Well, not more illegal than occasionally killing some bastard who desperately needs killing."

Muscle shrugged. He seemed as intrigued about Maestro as Maestro was about him. His face told Maestro nothing was a problem.

Hm. No police sirens. Apparently, this was that kind of place, and the cops stayed away. Good.

"It pays better than bouncing." Maestro sipped his drink, very pointedly *not* looking at Muscle's hat. "And you wouldn't need to worry about your secret."

Muscle touched the brim of the cap and fear flashed across the young man's otherwise stoic features. He adjusted the hat, then gripped the broom tightly.

Maestro finished his drink and set the glass down. "I have a knack for spotting people with secrets." He held out a fist, flourished the fingers, and presented it palm up with a violet flame hovering an inch above his skin. "*Tation decore discere cum at.*" The flame changed to green and flared. "Call that *my* secret. One of them."

Muscle's eyes opened wide. The fire reflected in his pupils, and Maestro would've sworn it did a little dance that was not part of the reflection.

He snapped his fingers and the flame vanished. He clapped once and wiped his hands together quickly. "Interested?"

Muscle nodded like a little kid. How amusing to see that kind of enthusiasm on the face of a big fighter who had to be almost thirty years old. He seemed to realize his lack of decorum and squared his shoulders immediately with a more solemn nod. . . then he glanced at the broom and the surrounding mess. Anxiety wrote itself across his face.

He didn't want to walk out and leave a clutter? What a walking, talking contradiction. . . well, walking anyway.

Might as well leave him to it.

"Honorable. I understand." Maestro moved toward the door. The young fighter was not at all what he'd expected. On so many counts. "Go ahead and clean up your mess. I know how to contact you when I need you."

Reginald Sato pulled his bare feet together and executed a formal bow.

Maestro returned the gesture and left.

Someone moaned and pushed up to his feet.

Through the glass door, Maestro watched.

Without taking his eyes from Maestro's business card, the fighter popped the thug with the broom handle to knock him unconscious.

Maestro called the sensei who'd brought Muscle to his attention. "Greetings, honored one," Maestro said in Japanese. "I found him where you said he'd be."

"He is well?" The sensei's voice sounded old, but bright and alert.

"His interview was satisfactory. I've hired him."

"Excellent. I trust you will not tell him I arranged the interview?"

"Of course not. . . but you weren't wholly honest with me." Maestro stopped by the taco cart. Another? "You should have told me the truth about the boy."

The sensei chuckled. "Keeping that information from you was part of *your* interview."

Maestro considered the man's status and remained polite. "Okay. . . but no more surprises. I don't like them when I have a horde of *demons* on my ass." No response. Ah. He'd guessed correctly. "And I'm waving my fee. I think it's as good a deal for me as it is for you."

"That is most—"

Maestro cut the line. He didn't need to be *that* polite.

Across the street, Reginald Sato walked past the broken plate glass window. He carried four unconscious or dead thugs over one shoulder and methodically worked his broom across the floor with the other hand.

"Not much of a talker." Maestro couldn't tear his eyes away until the young fighter moved out of sight into the back room.

All three in one night. Drat. Maestro hated coincidences. He gave the girl at the cart his full attention, holding up two fingers and pulling out his wallet.

Maestro

Spook stood in the shower singing "The Girl from Impanema" while scrubbing the last of his makeup. Why did half of it bleed off with a little sweat when the rest required a Brillo pad?

Candles lit the room and the steam cleaned out Spook's pores, which was stellar since his pores didn't really do the job themselves anymore.

A glass of merlot rose from a glass table, lifted over the glass wall and drifted to Spook's waiting hand. He hummed while he sipped the wine. He scrubbed his chest with an oatmeal bar. When he reached his stomach, the bar of soap fell out of his hand. What the hell?

He looked down. Holy spit!

He threw himself back against the blue-tiled wall, arms spread in shock. Could he escape his own abdomen?

"What the hell?" He threw open the shower door and ran to the full length, steam-proof mirror on one wall. He stared at his reflection for a long, long time.

"Well," he said finally, "*that's* not something you see every day."

Maestro's card leaned against the wine bottle. Spook had found an address but not a phone number. Well, he'd all but dared Spook to find him. In all likelihood, this development was worth a visit.

Agent Turner exited the showering area and walked to her locker, grunting a goodbye to the Saurian with whom she'd been conversing.

The Saurian screeched back.

Turner passed a group of Caninities, who always smelled like wet dog no matter how much they bathed. They yipped at her as she passed, and she barked in response. For some reason, they'd taken a liking to her.

She averted her gaze as she passed the Ipsoliad in its glass encased acid bath. As open-minded as she was, the way they scrubbed their intestines and inner genitalia at the same time seemed a bit distasteful.

At her locker, she tapped her Doohickey to create a hologram of herself so she could see how she looked. The new humanoid shape was perfect, but she hated to just pick the first thing available.

How about a Rapsoloid? She found the genetic marker and shifted, so accustomed to the cracking of bone and stretching of skin she barely felt it anymore.

The hologram now showed her a seven foot, hairy biped with long arms and enormous legs. "No, this one makes my glutinous maximus appear engorged."

She shifted again, and the hologram showed her a reptilian Snarton. Thin, yes, but absolutely no ass whatsoever. No. . . no. . . not quite right.

For the heck of it, she shifted back into the humanoid. The new one. She still liked it.

She tried out a Distressi male, but she always tripped over the enormous reproductive organs of that species.

Back to the new outfit.

She still liked it best.

"I like that outfit on you," her partner said from nearby. "It suits you." On Earth he went by Peter Test. He stood at the nearby bench, a towel over his shoulder and one foot up in a pose he'd adopted since spending enough time on Earth to pick up the habits. He wore a brawny, red-headed outfit he'd found a few decades back. It looked good on him.

She turned her back to the hologram and regarded it over one shoulder. "You like it? It's new." Definitely a favorite. She'd keep it for now. She pressed her hand to her locker so her uniform would match her outfit, stepping briefly out of the way as a balloon-enhanced Spitava floated by.

"I heard pretty good things about your collar," Peter told her, a touch of pride in his voice.

Heat flushed her face. "One step closer to closing down the Consortium." His approval meant more to her than it should.

"The Council put a rush job on the trial. Faster than I've ever seen them move." He spoke slower than usual, which told Turner he was trying hard to sound nonchalant.

"Yes? How soon?" She could feign disinterest equally well.

He scooted closer to the bench as an eight-limbed Ghistorian scuttled past. Its erogenous zone extended three feet from its body, and no one wanted to get caught up in *that* mess. "Trial starts in two years."

Turner stopped with one sock on and one off. "That fast? That has to be a record."

No, no. Keep it cool. Her first collar, and for the Council to push it forward that fast? She might have just circumvented about five decades and eighty-five rungs on the career ladder.

"Congratulations." Peter's eyes twinkled. He would know she was jumping up and down inside and was kind enough to let it go

Instead of the happy dance she felt, she gave him a nod.

"One other thing." He radiated professionalism. She loved that about him. "They suspect there's a ship cloaked on the planet. . . near where you picked up your new outfit."

"Coincidence?"

"Doubt it."

All-seeing light! Wait. She should get used to human expressions. Damn it! That was the one. She collected her things and closed the locker. "I hate coincidences."

"I know that." Peter grinned. He looked positively human when he did so. It was kind of cute.

She threw the duffle over one shoulder. "I should go back and check it out. Is there a cruiser in orbit?"

Peter made a face. "The usual."

She rolled her eyes. "That thing is an antique. It should be in a museum, not orbiting the bloody Alpaca Homeworld."

He dropped his foot to the floor. "Well, you put those guys away and we won't even need to watch the lighted planet. We can deploy a drone to observe and go do something important." She knew he hated sentry duty on such a primitive world where there was nothing to learn.

Something about the place had started to grow on her, though. "It's a pretty planet."

He stepped over the bench and looked around to make sure no one was paying attention. "Are you getting sentimental on me, Stuff?"

She grimaced and glanced around as well. Her heart rate increased at his proximity.

"Speaking of sentimental," he whispered.

How could he bring up something like that *here*, where anyone could overhear them? "Not here. I haven't made up my mind yet."

He moved closer, and her outfit reacted to the pheromones his outfit radiated. Her thoughts grew a little fuzzy, so she took a step back.

Peter visibly reacted in a very human way as well. "Oh, you're just being mean," he teased. "This is our first contract renewal. Everyone renews at least once."

"Assuming makes an ass out of you and me." The words fell out of her mouth before she even knew she had said them.

Peter shook his head, and from his puzzled expression his translator microbes had had difficulty with that phrase. "That's a human saying, isn't it?" He'd never taken the time to learn Earth languages since he'd always assumed they wouldn't be there for more than four or five decades.

"Yes. . . I'm not entirely positive what it means, but the females do seem to say it a lot." Turner knew exactly what it meant, but didn't want to admit how much of an impact the culture had already had on her. Even Peter would start to worry. She wasn't compromised, though. She just wanted to assimilate their culture for the sake of her job. "Look, I need to get back there and check on that cloaked ship."

"You *are* something." He always loved it when she acted professional.

"You're sure this looks good on me?" She glanced at her outfit and turned this way and that to inspect it with clothes on.

"Wonderful."

She smiled. He did have his moments when he knew exactly what to say. No sense ruining it with unnecessary sentimentality. "Doohickey, teleport to Earth cruiser."

"Okay, Elizabeth."

"Thanks."

As the bridge of the Galactic Police cruiser in Earth orbit appeared around her, Turner cursed herself.

Chances were, Peter had chuckled at her for thanking the Doohickey. Growing up with a parent who programmed engineered lifeforms guaranteed that Turner never took a machine for granted. She never knew when it might be a person.

Alone on the bridge, she stepped up to the ring that circled the observation area and looked over the hologram of the planet beneath her. "Narrow scope to North America, USA. Texas, central." She dropped her bag. A blinking red dot signaled an unusual energy reading over a familiar residence. "Zoom in on energy disturbance."

The hologram showed a young, male human on the front porch of the house belonging to the man who'd just helped her make the arrest of her young life.

The readings surrounding the earthling were most bizarre.

Hm. Perhaps she should notify Maestro.

Maestro crossed the I-35 bridge heading south, toward home. The sun crested the skyline and threw orange and golden rays across the river. Spectacular. For some reason, sunrises still made him smile. As many days as Maestro had seen, he'd never quite given up the hope that today might be better than yesterday.

He made the simple turns into his neighborhood and pulled to the curb in front of his house.

He lost the smile.

Spook sat on his porch in a duster and boots, but at least he'd lost the Goth affectation for the day. Something had to be wrong.

Maestro strode to the front door with a purpose. Might as well play it surly and annoyed.

"I'm not stalking you," the young man said, jumping to his feet.

Maestro crossed his arms and settled in. "It looks like you're stalking me."

Spook shrugged. "You did tell me I should be able to find you without contact info."

Maestro suppressed a smile. "I didn't mean the same day."

Spook raised an eyebrow, testing the waters. "It was practically a challenge."

"Why are you here?"

He stepped closer. "There's something I really, really need to show you."

"That couldn't at least wait until—whoa!" Maestro covered his eyes.

Spook had grabbed the edges of his trench coat like a flasher.

"What are you doing?"

Spook whipped the coat open.

"No, no, no. . ."

"Don't be such a freakin' square, dude."

Maestro chanced a peek. Oh dear gods, how was that even possible? He took a step closer, unable to tear his eyes away. "That is one of the most incredible things I've ever seen."

Spook smirked. "I thought you'd feel that way."

Maestro crouched down and looked closer. "I mean, I've seen a lot in my day. . . but that?"

Spook chuckled. "And just think how much more impressed you'd be if I wasn't wearing pants."

Seriously? Well, he *was* stuck in the body of a teenager.

Violet smoke swirled in Spook's middle, with little sparks of lightning and tiny wisps of flame. It was an exact duplicate, although miniaturized, of the hellsmouth that had appeared over Spook's house. And it lived in his stomach now.

"A stable hellsmouth, portable and personally located." Maestro couldn't hide his amazement. "I doubt there's a witch alive who might have done this on purpose."

"I know, right?" Spook was glad he'd guessed correctly in assuming Maestro would want to see this right away. "Just think how much I could make if I could duplicate it. Eat all you want and have all the calories swept into one of the many layers of hell."

Maestro rose and shook off his insane curiosity. "Too bad it's a portal for creatures more evil than you can possibly imagine and will likely implode, taking you and three or four square blocks with it." He couldn't give Spook the satisfaction. He'd take it way too far.

Spook chuckled and shook his head. "See, I just knew you were a glass half-empty kind of guy."

Maestro glanced around. Was anyone out at that ungodly hour of the morning? "Okay, you've made your point. Close it up. How'd you get the coat to contain it anyway? It should get sucked in."

Spook closed the duster with an expression that shifted between smug and insecure, which meant Maestro probably didn't want to know how he had it.

Spook shrugged casually. "I got stuff."

Maestro's phone vibrated. "El-i-ot," it intoned in a low, scratchy voice. "El-i-ot. El-i-ot."

Maestro stepped away. "Sorry. . . I need to take this."

Spook pointed at his midsection. "Hellsmouth in my belly?"

"You have no idea." Maestro turned his back. "Hello, Turner. I told you you wouldn't have any trouble finding me."

"Considering the size of the file with your local Galactic Police, no. . . no trouble at all." The voice over the phone seemed to work hard to remain level.

Maestro glanced over a shoulder.

Spook contemplated his navel, which was far more understandable than usual.

Maestro grunted and gestured for him to close the coat.

Spook complied grumpily.

Afraid to take his eyes off the lad, Maestro maintained his blasé attitude with the conversation on the phone. "And only half of it is true and most of that exaggerated. Wait. . . we have *local* Galactic Police?" They had a local presence at this point in the timeline?

"I didn't call to chat," Turner insisted. "When I read your file, I noticed you seem to be a sort of local presence when it comes to... unexplainable phenomenon of a non-scientific or otherwise metaphysical nature."

"Magic?" Maestro asked.

Heh-heh. She must hate the idea.

"Whatever." Her discomfort with the topic radiated clearly, even over the phone. Technologically advanced species just didn't want to accept the possibility of anything supernatural. "There seems to be a localized phenomenon centered on your location."

Maestro was intrigued. "How do you know my location?"

"Cell phones have GPS."

"Not mine."

She paused. "Then I guess *we* still have a few secrets you don't know." Smugness bled from her tone.

Was she viewing him right then? He raised his middle finger to the sky just in case.

Her chuckle told him she had him on satellite imagery.

"Damn satellites." He lowered the arm. "Fine. And thanks for the head's up... seriously, but I have it under control."

Where had Spook gone? He sat on the tire swing that hung from the largest tree in Maestro's front yard. While Spook twirled back and forth, little flashes of magenta light escaped his trench coat and swirled away.

"I gotta go." Maestro crammed the phone into a pocket and hurried over to the swing, grabbing Spook by the coat and dragging him down. "We may be in Austin, but no one is so stoned they won't notice a godsforsaken hellsmouth lodged in your navel. How old are you?"

Spook pulled free and straightened his coat. "Over seventy. Age is all in the attitude."

Although he would never admit it, Spook's playful nature drew Maestro in. "I should let it consume you and be done with it." He shoved Spook toward the front door. He'd fix the problem and then send the stupid kid on his way.

Spook didn't really fight the push, though he did sort of turn and point at the tire swing. "Why do you have—?"

"It came with the house," Maestro lied. "This isn't a social call, and I would like to get some sleep today."

Spook let himself be directed into the house. "Oh, sorry, I forget people need to do that."

His visit was actually a good sign. It meant he wasn't so far gone to the dark magic he couldn't be saved.

Maestro wouldn't let Spook see that, though, couldn't let him see *anything* going on in his mind. This visit was a job like any other. Maestro would fix the problem and send Spook on his way. He couldn't risk the lad getting too close and finding out the truth.

They passed through the living room.

"Interesting décor choices," Spook pointed out.

Maestro shoved him through the dining room and kitchen.

Everything Maestro owned had been purchased at rummage sales and thrift stores to give his house that "homey, lived in" feel. He kept no actual mementos, just the cast-offs of other people's lives thrown together to fool visitors into thinking they saw a glimpse of Maestro's past.

They reached the basement entrance, which looked more like the door to a kitchen pantry.

"Whoa. . . you have a basement." Spook seemed to enjoy the trip far too much. "Nobody in Austin has a basement."

"You have a basement." Maestro nudged him through the door.

Spook hurried down the steps. "Most of the houses with basements get snatched up by magic users and serial killers." He shot Maestro a smirk. "Which are you?"

"Both." Maestro shouldered past him and into the empty space in the middle of the room reserved for spell casting.

He had to stay focused. However Spook had managed to lodge this hellsmouth in his abdomen, it was a bad thing. A very, very bad thing. . . and it just might be Maestro's fault.

He passed through the protection circle and approached his spell book, trying his best to ignore Spook's curious wandering.

"Get in the circle and give me the coat." As long as Maestro kept this visit all business, he just might save the kid.

Spook handed the coat over absently, checking out the jars of organs and herbs. He reached out to touch a three-foot stuffed salamander.

"Don't," Maestro barked, startling him. "Touch that and you release the tortured souls of a thousand Egyptian warriors."

Spook pulled back. "And this is something you have just laying around?"

Maestro focused on his spell book. "I don't get a lot of visitors." He had to avoid staring at the spiral tattoo on Spook's chest.

"I guess."

"Get. into. the. circle."

Spook looked up at Maestro's expressionless face, and something seemed to click. He finally seemed to realize that Maestro wouldn't be one of the warm fuzzy friends with whom he'd been chasing demons for decades. His face fell into something like despondency, and the look almost broke Maestro's heart but he wouldn't let it get to him.

He had a job to do. He had to save Spook and hurting his feelings was part of the job. He couldn't let anyone close.

Suddenly showing a professional side, Spook walked into the circle. "Thanks for helping. I'm not really sure what to do about it." He shrugged his bare, thin shoulders. "I'm not used to being the client. I'm usually the one on your side of the protection circle."

"I'm not sure either, to be honest. We have to close it without upsetting the balance." Maestro touched the page of an exorcism spell.

"Upsetting the balance is what you said earlier about me and a four block radius, right?"

Maestro ignored the question. The spells he had to cast would be dead giveaways to someone like Spook, who was a witch himself. What questions should he ask to hide what he already knew?

"What do I need to know about you that might explain how this happened? Anything out of the ordinary for a teen-ager about you?" Maestro looked up. "You've made jokes about your age. And something about being dead?"

Spook smiled in embarrassment and crossed his arms. "Well, the hellsmouth may have snagged on the magicks that keep me walking around. I have some pretty strong preservatives tucked away."

Maestro maintained his composure. "Preservatives? Like a Twinkie?"

Spook grinned and stared up at the ceiling, his arms falling to his sides. "Aw. . . I love Twinkies." He shook off the distraction. "No, I. . . died sixty years ago. I just never stopped moving around."

Maestro nodded and looked down at the spell book "You're a zombie? Self-directed or is someone else pulling the strings?"

"As far as I know, I'm self-directed." He shoved his hands into his pockets. "You seem pretty casual about that little revelation."

Oops. "I doubt you can shock me. And no jokes about your pants now or ever again." He stepped away from the spell book and closer to the circle. "Okay, I need to know a little something about the magic that keeps you moving around and ties your soul to this plane. Do I have your permission to examine you? You won't feel a thing."

"O-kay." Spook crossed his arms again. He definitely wasn't used to being the client.

Maestro centered himself. "*Ex pri dolor dolore.*" He passed inside the circle. His vision shot through with red sparks for a moment as he did so, but the circle held. He centered deeper. "*Ea doctus fuisset vix.*"

The hellsmouth had attached to the *gris-gris* that kept Spook animated. The connection glowed a bright green in Maestro's second sight. He stepped closer and lost himself to the magic. He hadn't been able to examine Spook since the kid had started walking around again sixty years earlier, and he wouldn't likely have another chance without explaining how he knew what kept the zombie alive in the first place. Which he wasn't likely to do.

"Okay. . . not really shy. . . but what are you doing?" Spook's voice was quiet. "And is this going out on YouTube?" He sounded so vulnerable.

Maestro focused on the magic coursing through the zombie's body. There were three different spells linked together to make the hellsmouth. . . and they were focused on . . . something.

An object.

"What did you find that made the original hellsmouth work?" Maestro asked.

Spook fidgeted.

"I will cut you open to find it," Maestro said.

The lad pulled a small idol out of his pocket. It glowed with ancient energy.

Maestro examined it. "Anubis?" It was a fetish of the Egyptian god. Almost five thousand years old. They'd been all the rage at the time. Waves of intense power radiated from it. "Did you know this was the real deal?"

Spook's face blanched. "*Real* real?"

Maestro closed a fist around the tiny statue. "You stupid, stupid child." He shifted his gaze to the normal spectrum. Whoa. His face was inches from Spook, and he had one hand pressed against the lad's bare chest. He stepped away. "Has anything tried to get out?"

Spook shrugged. "Yes, but so far, I've been able to keep them back. I'm not really sure how." His eyes took on the faraway look of a mage about to cast a spell. "I wonder. . ."

"*No!* Don't wonder!" Maestro grabbed his shoulders.

Spook's head snapped back, and he screamed.

Damn it. "When magic is working, you never *ever* wonder about it. You just let it work." He released Spook's shoulders. "*Ex delectus phaedrum suscipiantur vel, ad zril percipit efficiantur sit.*" He had to make it work.

The light from the hellsmouth in Spook's belly flickered, and an enormous scaly head poked through. A bald demon with a decidedly snake-like face flicked its forked tongue at the edges of the portal. It touched Spook's flesh, grinned, and licked its lips.

Spook pounded on the scaly head with both hands. "Go back, go back, go back!" His face showed a combination of fear and extraordinary pain.

"*Ex delectus phaedrum suscipiantur vel . . .*"

The demon slithered one scaly, grey arm through the portal and smacked Spook with it.

The kid staggered but managed to stay in the circle. If he fell out of it, an entirely worse situation would materialize. Literally.

Maestro raised his voice and threw all his power into the spell. "*Ad zril percipit efficiantur sit.*" It didn't appear to help.

Spook kept pounding on the demon's head, but the massive thing shoved another arm through to grab both of Spook's wrists. With a roar and a wriggle, the demon squeezed its massive shoulders through the portal for a better hold on Spook, who squeezed his eyes shut. The pain as the demon shoved its way through a hole that was, in fact, much smaller than the thing itself, had to be tremendous.

The lad screamed again and fell onto his back. He had enough presence of mind to keep his head from cracking on the concrete, but since the beast had a firm grasp on both of his arms now, there wasn't much else he could do.

Maestro stepped closer. "*Ex delectus phaedrum suscipiantur vel. . .*" Should he stop trying to close the portal and just attack the damn thing?

One massive arm released Spook and backhanded Maestro so hard he flew ten feet.

He passed through the protection circle with an audible "pop," and the magicks dropped.

Shit.

Maestro covered his head as he hit a pile of cardboard boxes. By the time he bounced to his feet, Spook lay unconscious and spread-eagle.

The demon stood over him, even spookier because it was lit from below by the purple glow of the hellsmouth in Spook's abdomen. It was about eight feet tall, reptilian with a snake head, long claws on hands and feet, and a tail that whipped around. Its tongue flicked out. From the wicked grin on the thing's face, it liked what it tasted in this dimension.

Most demons did.

Ignoring Maestro, it looked down at Spook and licked its lips again.

No way in any of the seven hells was Maestro going to let that thing eat Morri. Even if this entire situation *was* the damn kid's fault. If Maestro let him get eaten, he'd never be able to mock him for screwing up so badly.

"Get your paws off of him, you damn dirty ape!" Maestro launched himself at the eight-foot demon that could probably break him in half.

In the split second before Maestro impacted with the enormous beast, surprise lit the thing's eyes, as if it really couldn't believe such a tiny—and squishy —creature would attack it directly.

It also gathered energy.

A teleporter? Drat!

Maestro's shoulder hit the thing's stomach, arms closing around its waist. Red tendrils of energy enveloped them both. Maestro closed his eyes in case they ended up someplace especially abrasive to eyes.

And Spook lay sprawled out unconscious with an unstable hellsmouth in his gut.

Drat.

The heat hit Maestro first, but it was a natural heat and not the fires of hell. Then the demon stumbled, and the two of them rolled across sand.

Knocking the thing over had been pure luck.

Maestro rolled away from it before it could get a hold on him. He sprang to his feet. A desert. But which one? They all looked alike: sand and blasted hot.

The demon screamed.

Maestro dropped into a crouch. All his weapons were back in the basement.

Drat.

If he had a second, he could draw from his cache—

The demon lunged.

Maestro sidestepped. He jumped for the thing's back and wrapped an arm around its wide neck. He locked his arms and squeezed as hard as he could.

The demon grabbed Maestro by the shirt, tore him away, and flung him onto the sand at its feet. It chuckled, and, in a very human gesture, cracked its knuckles.

Maestro scrabbled backward. "This is gonna hurt. . . so much."

Teamwork

Reggie rented the garage of a very nice family he had found on Craigslist. Boxes and the sorts of things a family kept because you just never knew filled one half of the garage. The other half belonged to Reggie.

It held a small mattress where he slept, a small dresser where he kept his clothes, and a small speaker that sat in the exact center of the small dresser. Above the dresser a small mirror helped him check his grooming. On the wall above his mattress, a large map of the world outlined his journey thus far. Strings held in by pushpins crisscrossed the United States.

The string held in at Austin dangled, waiting for the next leg of the journey.

Austin was as much of a disappointment as the rest of his search.

Soft sitar music played while Muscle moved through a series of katas. The movements helped him center. Eyes unfocused in meditation, he cleared his mind and focused on the shift of weight from one bare foot to the other.

Austin had been so promising. All signs had pointed there. He had no idea where to try next. Alaska seemed as likely as Virginia.

He breathed deeply and closed his eyes, attending to the shifting air on his skin. He crouched and turned, bringing all his weight to one foot and lifting the other leg into a crane position. Balancing on one foot took more concentration.

Except that it did not. Not anymore. Reggie had moved through these exercises since he had taken his first steps in Sensei's dojo when he was a month old. Originally learned to help him center and find peace against the demon inside, the katas seemed too easy now to distract him from the monkey mind that leapt from thought to thought, chattering away like a gibbon.

Where the *heck* was his father?

Giving up on the kata, Reggie lowered his foot to the floor and stepped closer to the map. He hooked one thumb in the waistband of his briefs and raised the foot once again to the inside of his knee. He had traveled from one end of this bewildering country to the other and remained no closer to his goal than when he had left Japan a year ago.

Sensei had assured him this quest was a fool's errand. Perhaps he had been right, but Reggie hated to return in shame. Sensei might not *say*, "I told you so," but they would both know he had.

Time to move on. Reggie pulled the Austin pin from the map and dropped it into the little pin box at one corner. He pulled two or three more and dropped them in as well, pulling the string from the last and placing it in the string box beside the pin box. Order was important. Organization and structure helped maintain peace in a very disorderly world.

Reggie dropped his chin to his chest with a sigh. A very, very disorderly world. Every stop on his journey taught him a new lesson in just how much chaos existed.

Although. . .

A well-worn spot at the edge of the map called to Reggie.

This man he had met. Maestro. *He* seemed to know things. Perhaps he held information about Reggie's father. Perhaps his journey to Austin had, in fact, brought him to Maestro.

As he had a thousand times, Reggie slipped his fingers behind the map at the worn spot and pulled a strip of photos from its hiding place there. The photos were from a booth somewhere in the United States. The first showed a young Japanese man and a dark-haired, dark-skinned woman smiling wildly at the camera.

In the second photo, he kissed her cheek and she had flung her head back in joyous laughter. They also held hands.

In the third photo, the man loomed twice as large, so big he barely fit in the frame. He had foot-long, black horns, green, shiny skin, and black wings. His eyes glowed red as he held his clawed hands toward the woman in a threatening pose.

The woman recoiled from him in terror, but it was obvious that her fear was an act.

In the fourth image, they kissed, eyes closed and both of them relaxed, the man's shirt now in tatters.

With a sigh, Reggie glanced at the mirror. His horns were only two inches long so far, but they still proved that the man in the photo was his father. He owned a mirror so he could always be certain his hat was in place before he left his room. When he became angry, patches of his skin turned the same reptilian green as the man in the photo.

Avoiding anger balanced Reggie's life.

Demons in Japan existed in both good and evil varieties. Reggie wanted very much to believe his father had been of the good variety. If he could find him, meet him, then he could know for certain whether he, himself, was good or whether he was doomed to fall into evil.

In this country, apparently, all the demons were evil. Christian demons. And nobody seriously believed in them, except for some very outlandish people who spent so much time on the internet *discussing* demons that Reggie often wondered how they had ever found any demons in the real world to believe in.

So much he did not understand.

Tiny footsteps approached his door. By the time the little girl knocked, Reggie wore pants and a hat. He waited for her to knock before opening the door.

"Yes, Miss Gonzalez?" he asked quietly.

The little girl smiled at his use of the name. "*Hola*, Mr. Sato." She held her hands behind her back, obviously hiding something. She was about four years old and small for her age. "Are you dancing?"

Accustomed to her non sequiturs, Reggie looked back into the room where the sitar music played. "Yes, I was dancing." Her deduction was close enough to the truth.

She grinned and her deep, brown eyes lit up. "Can I dance with you some time?"

He nodded. "I would be delighted."

Wendy giggled and stared up at him as if she could do so forever.

He waited patiently for a moment before prompting her. "Is there anything I can do for you? Or did you just stop by to say hello?" Either would have been fine. He enjoyed chatting with her.

Children were so much less complicated than adults. With adults, Reggie always grew tongue-tied and worried about saying things that would make them suspicious. His apparent age afforded him a certain level of automatic respect. If others discovered his *actual* age. . .

While fluent in English and three other languages, he still did not always understand the complex meanings behind the things most adults said in this country. At the monastery, people usually meant exactly what they said.

Children in this country seemed much the same.

Wendy pulled a peanut butter jar from behind her back and presented it to him for inspection. "I want a peanut butter and banananana sandwich, and the peanut butter jar is stuck again."

Reggie feigned shock. "It is not!"

"Uh-huh."

He sat cross-legged in the middle of the floor. "You know, you may call me Reggie if you like. Most of my friends call me Muscle."

Wendy followed him, still holding the jar. "Nuh-uh! Daddy says I have to call you by your mister name 'cause you're so old. It's disdespectacle if I don't use the mister name with a dult, and you're definitely a dult."

Her logic was irrefutable.

"I would not want you to get in trouble." He gestured at the jar in her hands. "Why not give that mean old jar a try yourself?"

She twisted the lid.

"Come on. . . really try."

Her face scrunched up with her effort. "I'm trying."

He smiled. "I see that. Okay, other hand now."

She switched hands and tried again. "See?" She held the jar out to Reggie. "I'm not strong enough."

He took the jar from her. "But every time you try hard like that, you grow a little bit stronger."

He twisted the lid open, careful not to shatter the jar. It had taken some practice to open things like glass jars without crushing them.

"Look at that!" He presented the open jar to her. "You must have loosened it for me."

Wendy giggled and took the jar in both hands.

"Wendy?" Mr. Gonzalez's voice came to them from the kitchen. "Are you bothering Mr. Sato again?"

The girl looked up at Reggie.

He shook his head and smiled. She was never a bother.

"Mr. Sato says I'm not bothering him, Daddy." She called out much more loudly than needed.

"Oh, Mr. Sato *says* that, does he?" The man was nice enough, but he still intimidated Reggie. "Come on, sweetie. Time for breakfast."

Wendy pushed to her feet, working hard to keep her balance with the heavy jar. "I gotta go." She turned to leave but stopped in the open doorway. "Are you a daddy, Mr. Sato?"

"What? Me? That is years away." Of course, to her, he probably looked older than her own father. He pushed up to his feet as she dashed back and gave him a one-armed hug, her head pressed against the side of his hip.

"You'd be a great daddy." And she vanished.

Reggie stared after her.

He glanced at his reflection again.

At the hat that hid his horns.

No. No, he would not be a good daddy. Not at all.

His phone rang, pulling him out of a sudden funk. He checked the screen: Maestro?

"Hai?"

The distinct sound of inhuman screeching came from the other end. Most likely an Asmodeus demon from the sixth circle of the Christian Hell.

Maestro's voice cut through the noise. "If you want some extra beer money and have any. . ." His voice sounded strained and breathy as if he were fighting a difficult battle. ". . .way of finding me I would really. . . *really* appreciate it."

Reggie disconnected the line. If that *was* an Asmodeus demon, he had no time to waste. He closed his eyes and sought Maestro.

"Mr. Sato?" Wendy's voice called from the kitchen. "Daddy wants to know if you'd like to have breakfast with us."

He opened his eyes and regarded the open doorway.

He closed his eyes. He'd be gone before she reached the door.

Maestro had the demon in a headlock again, not that his efforts accomplished much more this time around. The thing backed into a giant rock. The air whuffed out of Maestro's lungs on the first impact. On the second impact, a couple of ribs cracked.

Why did that sort of thing always work in Star Trek? Jump on the alien's back. Choke it out. Ta-daa.

"Whoof." With the third impact, Maestro saw stars. Before he even realized it, he'd released the demon and slid to the sand. As the creature chuckled above him, Maestro could almost hear the soundtrack in the background. Lots of percussion. Star Trek had always used a lot of percussion.

He held up a hand and tried to focus enough for a spell. So far, he'd only been able to call up minor incantations and none of them had had any effect.

What he needed was time. Calling the bouncer had been a foolish waste of energy. How could Muscle possibly find him when he didn't even know where he was?

The demon glowered over Maestro, and the spell bounced harmlessly off its scaly hide.

Oh well, the damn thing couldn't kill him. Just how long would it take to pull all the pieces back together this time?

"Gaagh." A look of surprise broke over the demon's face. It rocketed backward and crashed into the rock where Maestro's blood had already dried in the heat.

In the demon's place, Reginald Sato held out a hand.

"Oh, thank the gods." Maestro waved the young man away and pointed. "Evil demon. Kill it, please."

Muscle turned calmly as the demon screamed and hurtled through the air at him. As if it were no effort at all, Muscle leaned out of the way and launched a fist directly into the side of the creature's head, abruptly cutting off the demon's cry and redirecting it into the sand, which blew up in a blinding cloud.

Eyes closed against the sand, Maestro leapt to his feet and muttered a major incantation. When he opened his eyes, his vision sparked bright blue.

Muscle grappled with the demon, who made even the substantial bulk of the bouncer seem rather small. Had it been a mistake to call him in? Was he strong enough?

Bone cracked and Maestro winced. Ouch.

But the evil demon cried out, not the bouncer.

Oh. All right then.

Maestro gathered energy for the spell. "*Nusquam minimum vivendum eu mel.*"

Muscle pressed the demon facedown in the sand, one arm pinned behind it while the other flailed uselessly to dislodge the man on his back. The demon's tail thrashed, but didn't seem to do anything more productive than display the demon's anger.

Muscle shifted his weight slowly forward, forcing the demon's arm farther up his back. The creature screamed louder and louder.

"*Ius cu falli delicatissimi. Cum an hinc exerci.*"

The bones in the demon's arm shattered under the inexorable pressure. The bone shot through the hide and black blood sprayed both the sand and Muscle's bare chest. He used the demon's moment of blind pain to shift across his back and grab the free arm, pinning it behind with its useless mate.

Muscle shook his head and blinked away the foul ichor from the demon's veins. That stuff was corrosive, but Muscle acted as if he didn't feel it, which gave Maestro the last piece of the puzzle concerning the strange young man a Japanese sensei had asked him to hire.

"Can you get it to its feet?" Maestro asked.

With a grunt, Muscle leaned backward, changed his footing and pushed up to his feet, dragging the demon with him.

The thing's leg had already mended, and its arm couldn't be far behind.

In that position, Muscle had much less leverage, but he'd followed Maestro's suggestion without hesitation or question. Good. He held the demon as steady as he could and simply stared over its shoulder at Maestro with absolutely no emotion in his eyes, waiting.

"*Delenit maluisset scripserit in eam, erant oblique.*"

Maestro held his hands up to provide a place for the ball of red energy he called into being. It grew quickly, spinning and swirling like a miniature sun gone mad. "*Usu ne, te legimus voluptua*!"

The demon's eyes opened wide and it went briefly still in Muscle's hold. The next instant, the thing went mad, struggling against Muscle's grasp with a ferocity that would overcome the young man's strength in a matter of seconds.

If it had had seconds.

Maestro thrust his hands forward, sending the blazing fireball directly into the middle of the demon's chest. It screamed once and exploded in a violent mess of blood and guts and bone that hurled Muscle over backward.

If Maestro was right about the bouncer, he'd be fine.

Maestro, however, didn't want to be bathed in demon blood.

"*Forensibus*," he called, building a shield before the acidic gore could hit him. When the last of the demonic tissue had plopped to the ground, he dropped the shield and brushed the sand from his hands. "Well, that was fun, eh, kid?"

But Muscle cowered nearby with his back to Maestro and his hands over his head.

Maestro took a step closer. "Kid?"

He didn't seem hurt.

"Muscle? You okay." He reached out.

The young man didn't speak, just pulled away and crouched with his arms over the back of his head, but there was no blood seeping from them. . .

Oh. His hat lay on the sand a few feet away where he couldn't see it.

Without a word, Maestro picked up the flat cap and bushed off sand and blood. He held it over Muscle's shoulder in his line of sight. Well, if he'd look. "Your hat."

Muscle looked up at the hat, grabbed it, and pulled it quickly over his head, but not so quickly that all of Maestro's suspicions weren't confirmed by the two inch horns that protruded from his dark hair.

The kid's breathing slowed down, but he stayed crouched where he was.

"Look at me," Maestro said as gently as possible.

Still panting, the big man rose to his feet and silently turned to face Maestro, but his eyes stayed glued to the sand beneath his feet.

"Look at me," Maestro repeated a little more firmly.

It took him a couple of tries, but Muscle eventually met Maestro's gaze. The fear and embarrassment in the man's face belonged on someone much, much younger. Every answer Maestro deduced simply created ten more questions. He had to feel sorry for the kid.

Maestro muttered a spell and gathered energy. "Pumpernickel." He waved at the cap and his eyes sparked. "Try to take the hat off."

Confusion and uncertainty clouded the dark face, but Muscle tried to comply. Surprise replaced confusion when he couldn't.

"It won't come off unless you say 'pumpernickel,'" Maestro explained.

Muscle's face showed more confusion, but a smile played at the corners of his mouth.

Maestro shrugged. "How likely are you to say 'pumpernickel' by accident?" How likely was he to say *anything* by accident, when it came down to it? Maestro could tell Muscle wanted to try it out, so he politely turned his back.

"Pumpernickel."

Maestro waited until the young man repeated the word. "I have no idea how you found me so quickly, but thank you. I owe you."

Muscle grinned with the most emotion on his face that Maestro had seen to date. Just like a little kid. He touched the brim of the hat and shook his head. Apparently, all debts were paid.

Allowing himself a smile of his own, Maestro extended a hand, which Muscle took firmly and shook with enthusiasm. Perhaps a little too much enthusiasm. Ow.

Muscle grabbed his hat. "Pumpernickel." He doffed it, bringing it to his chest while executing a deep and respectful bow. Just as quickly, he rose and replaced the hat. The grin seemed to have found a permanent home.

Maestro bowed in return. "You need a ride... somewhere?" Where the hell were they anyway?

Muscle shook his head and backed away a few steps before bowing quickly and simply walking around one of the massive boulders that dotted the landscape.

With the kid out of sight, Maestro allowed himself to rub his hand. "He needs to learn to relax the hand shake." He rubbed his broken ribs, inhaled, and pressed them back into place.

The satisfying pop as they reset was lost beneath Maestro's loud cursing from the excruciating pain. He breathed until the pain faded as the bones knit.

He looked around.

Sand. Boulders.

He turned a complete circle.

More sand. More boulders.

Drat. "Maybe I should have asked *him* for a ride." No matter. He pulled his Doohickey from a pocket. "Doohickey, call. . ." Although, he probably didn't want her to know about his Doohickey just yet. "Belay that, Doohickey."

Instead, he used his cell phone. "Hello. . . Turner? How would you like me to owe you a huge favor?"

"After your help with the Consortium, I hardly think you'll need to owe me just yet."

"Yeah?" He wished he could hold onto this one, but a stupid zombie lay unconscious with a hellsmouth in his chest in Maestro's basement. "Well, since I already know your gigantic galactic cruiser hiding in orbit has a great teleportation system. . ." He stared across the empty desert and wondered how Muscle had arrived so fast. "I need a lift home."

"As in initiating a transport on a protected planet?" The shock in her voice was obviously a put on.

"Yeah... yeah... I know how big. . ." Suddenly it was early

morning. . . and cooler. Much, much cooler. ". . .a favor I will owe you. Thanks."

Maestro stood in the middle of his front yard. Good. He slipped his phone into a pocket.

Anyone around? Oops. The little, old lady who lived next door stood on one side of a shrub with the world's largest hedge clippers held aloft and a look of absolute amazement on her face, staring directly at Maestro.

He automatically held his Doohickey up and pressed an app. The Doohickey flashed and Angie froze.

He stepped closer. "Maestro pulled up in his car and walked across the lawn." He put the device away. "That poor woman is going to end up with permanent brain damage the number of times I've had to do that." He touched her shoulder.

Angie blinked a few times before focusing. "Maestro?"

He carefully helped her lower the hedge clippers.

"I'm so glad to see you," she told him. "Have you seen Mr. Snuggles?" She dropped the hedge clippers to one side and pulled a carefully folded paper from her apron. It held a photo of the biggest, meanest feline Maestro had ever seen. "He's missing."

"No. . . but I will definitely keep an eye out for him."

Mr. Snuggles had only the left ear and the right eye, having lost the other of each in one of innumerable fights he'd enjoyed with a number of the neighborhood dogs. Other cats were too smart to go near him. The flyer pointed out that he was really just a sweet, old thing and listed Angie's contact information.

She smoothed the paper, folded it again, and stuffed it into her apron. "I know it makes me seem like a foolish old woman, but I just wish I knew if I did something. . . if he ran away for a *reason* or just got lost somewhere." Her face lit up with a sudden remembrance. "You solve mysteries, don't you?"

Hellsmouth in a zombie's chest in the basement!

"Drat." Maestro glanced over one shoulder before focusing completely on the little old lady who would probably suffer acute dementia at an early age because of all the times Maestro had wiped her memory. "I'm sorry, Angie, but I really need to go. If I find anything I will let you know!"

Without giving her time for another word, he ran to the house.

In the basement, Spook lay peacefully unconscious in the defunct protection circle. Apparently, nothing had crawled out and eaten the lad in Maestro's absence. None of his alarms screamed, either, so most likely nothing had escaped and gone wandering.

Maestro knelt down, taking advantage of Spook's unusual silence to regard him for a few moments. He hadn't seen the boy up close in sixty years, but he was completely unchanged since the day Maestro had tucked all his insides back inside. It was remarkable.

Maestro sighed. "What am I going to do with you, Morrison?" He brushed a few stray strands of hair off the lad's face.

Shit. No time for sentimentality. Maestro shook it off and pulled the statue of Anubis from a pocket. He placed it to one side and covered the tattoo on Spook's chest with one hand.

"*Corrumpit democritum te mea.*"

The tattoo glowed orange between Maestro's spread fingers. "*Nec deserunt contentiones ex.*" Maestro's vision sparked with gold and lost focus as he opened up to the second sight. His right hand found its way to Spook's forehead. "*Sed tritani salutatus ex.*"

Greenish, smoky light enveloped them and shimmered across the walls and clutter.

"*Corrumpit democritum te mea.*"

Wisps of a breeze moved the dust and began to loop the two men. The protection circle glowed golden. A similar image on the ceiling matched the protection circle's brightness.

"*Nec deserunt contentiones ex.*" Maestro switched hands, so his right was over Spook's unbeating heart. With his left, he retrieved the Anubis statue.

If this worked, life would be wonderful. If it didn't, life would suck, briefly and rabidly. Well, Maestro had long wondered what exactly it would take to kill him.

Thrusting the statue directly into the hellsmouth felt like shoving his arm into a vat of burning acid.

No! The voice echoed in Maestro's mind. Anubis sought to find his way into the material plane, to follow the statue's energy and make his way through the portal. Was it the real Anubis? The god himself?

If Maestro dropped the statue through, Anubis wouldn't be able find his way. It just might close the hellsmouth, too.

But he couldn't open his fingers. Damn.

He'd been prepared for the pain. He could block the pain.

He hadn't been prepared for the seduction.

Let it be. Let go and you will enjoy pleasures immeasurable by human understanding.

Maestro sucked in a quick breath as a tiny sample of those pleasures hit him in the loins. He closed his eyes and ignored the sensations.

You don't need to be alone anymore. Do you like being alone?

"Daddy?" a little boy said.

Maestro looked up. All five of his children stood nearby in a frightened cluster. For a moment, just one single moment, he almost bought it. He swallowed hard and closed his eyes. They weren't real. His children were gone forever.

He'd been promised more by better gods than this one.

It wasn't the real Anubis. He'd known the real Anubis and this seduction was too easy, not subtle enough. It was a shadow of him, a shard trapped in the space between this world and the next, held by the magic in a statue.

The concrete beneath Maestro's knees trembled and the walls shook. Dust rained down from the ceiling. Oh yeah, he was underground. That could be bad in an earthquake.

Sparks of lightning leapt from the hellsmouth and grounded on anything metal. It swirled faster and faster and sucked on Maestro's arm, drawing him in.

The rules seemed to change. The energies pulled on him now, as if the hellsmouth wanted to suck the statue out of his hand so it could spit it out again. The swirling energies opened larger by several inches, absorbing Spook's groin.

"Oh shit, not again." Maestro shoved his arm farther, so his face was nearly in Spook's armpit. Really? He shaved his pits? That was so beyond metro.

A violent tug forced Maestro to concentrate. "*Nec deserunt contentiones ex!*"

The ground shook more viciously and the lights flickered. A noticeable whirlwind circled them both. The portal edged a bit larger.

Drat. . . the dime-store imitation Anubis must be nearly at the portal's entrance.

A horrible electric shock coursed through Maestro.

His head jerked back and his jaw locked shut.

Bright bolts of lightning shot from his eyes and shattered against the ceiling, sending a shower of splinters and dust across the room. Spasms wracked his body and his eyeballs popped like overripe grapes, but he kept up his litany. "*Corrumpit democritum te mea.*"

He would not give up this one. Showing him his lost children had been a mistake, had only steeled his resolve.

Pull the hand out. Let it be. Do you want to lose the arm?

Maestro gritted his teeth and focused his energy on the idol. He poured everything he had into the little statue. He might not be able to overpower it. . . but he just might be able to over*power* it.

The basement shook. Tables rocked and broke. The excruciating pain of a thousand demon dimensions coursed through his body.

Damn the Anubis wannabe to the hottest pit of Asmodeus! He wouldn't win.

Maestro could grow the arm back. The eyes were already reforming.

He embraced his anger and focused it into the idol. He gave the little Egyptian statue everything he had. He had a lot. He poured it all into the statue. And when the spirit reached the edge of the hellsmouth, it raced directly into the idol avariciously, desperate for the power Maestro had shunted into the ancient statue.

The spirit suckled Maestro's life like a starving baby.

Let it.

"Suck all you want," Maestro muttered. "I'll make more."

The lightning flickered and grounded on the statue. The cyclone in the protection circle sped up as Maestro channeled its power into the little idol.

Like a greedy jackal, the spirit swallowed everything he threw it.

Until it was full.

Until it filled to overflowing.

Until it had to realize it couldn't stop the flow of life and energy.

What you did to my eyes? Maestro sent to it, *that's what I'm going to do to you!*

The spirit screamed.

Dozens of other demons and spirits raced into the idol as well, following the flow of power the Anubis spirit couldn't stop. It leaked out of the godling through cracks in his very soul.

I don't care if I lose the arm, Maestro sent. *When you bust like a balloon, you and every demon crowding inside that statue will be blown to the furthest reaches of the underworld for a thousand, thousand years.*

It was Maestro's turn to make promises. *You want to live? Shut it down.*

The idol pulsed and throbbed. The swirling angry thing in Spook's abdomen spun faster and faster.

Shut it down!! Everything. Maestro poured everything he had into the idol. He pulled the plug from the infinite well of his immortal life. It had to be enough.

The screams of a thousand demons filled the air.

You cannot have this vessel. You will not breach the gateway.

They screamed louder, and the tremors increased. Glass shattered. Smaller bits of garbage rose into the air and spun into the cyclone.

Die now forever or live to try again! Take it or leave it!

They took it.

Energy from the hellsmouth swarmed Maestro's arm, sucked violently into the statue. The floor rocked as everything in Spook's torso blasted the statue.

Maestro pushed the Anubis fetish so deeply into the portal his face pressed hard against Spook's shoulder and everything from the combined energy of so many different spells shot into it.

If it worked, it would be a miracle.

The energy of all those demons tore through Maestro's arm, sucked from the hellsmouth in Spook's gut and absorbed by the frightened spirit in the tiny statue in Maestro's hand.

In Maestro's mind, it lasted an eternity. . . but he'd already lived through a few of those.

As the last of the hellsmouth sucked into the statue, Maestro released it. *"Contentiones ex!"* He yanked his arm. Getting gene-spliced with Spook's stomach as the portal collapsed was not on the menu.

The idol exploded on the other side of the hellsmouth. The last thing Maestro heard was the insane cursing of a thousand spirits and the echo of Anubis as Maestro's life force blasted them out of existence.

"I lied," he muttered. "There's no way I'd take a chance one of you evil bastards would find your way back for revenge."

Then the hellsmouth sputtered and went out with a pathetic little "thwip."

Maestro blinked several times. His optic nerves had reattached themselves. The basement came into blurry sight. He'd wrecked it. Again.

"It worked." He'd never been certain.

Movement under his hand reminded him that he knelt beside Spook clutching the zombie's naked chest. Not something Spook should know. He pulled away and sat back on his heels.

"If I open my eyes," the lad asked, "am I going to regret it?"

Avoiding a settling sigh, Maestro worked to sound as casual as possible. "Well, you *will* have to see what I look like when I'm gloating because I've saved the day and you passed out like a little girl."

Spook groaned. "Maybe I'd be better off dead."

Since the lad's eyes were still closed, Maestro allowed himself a smile. "You're already dead."

"Oh, yeah." Spook opened his eyes. He seemed to notice that the basement had been through something unpleasant. He found Maestro. "Doesn't look like a battle to the death happened to you."

Maestro shrugged. "The demon who crawled out of your stomach teleported me somewhere on the other side of the planet."

Utter surprise painted itself across Spook's face. "But. . . then how. . . and you kicked his ass by yourself?"

Maestro maintained a respectful silence. He picked lint off his jacket, which was, truth be told, a trifle dustier than it had been. Let Spook draw his own conclusions.

Rising to his feet, Spook patted his belly which was now delightfully devoid of a frightening hellsmouth. He performed a happy dance right there in Maestro's basement.

Unwilling to join in the merriment, Maestro grabbed Spook's duster from the back of the chair where it reposed and held it out to the young man. "How shall I direct the bill?"

Spook froze. He glared at Maestro with all the petulance of youth. "Bill? Seriously?" He accepted the coat and slipped into it.

Maestro had to keep the transaction as businesslike as possible. "I am a professional."

The words completely bewildered Spook. "People pay you to save them?"

"Of course." Maestro maintained his haughty demeanor. "Why else would I do it?"

Astonishment contorted Spook's face. "Wow, all those years we were do-gooders, we should have been charging?" He pulled the coat closed over his chest. "I feel dumb." He held up a hand. "No comments from the peanut gallery are necessary or appreciated." He shook his head. "I. . . will come up with the money. Although right now, I'm afraid to ask how much you charge."

Maestro might as well cut him some slack. "How about this: you owe me a favor." After all, he didn't want the lonely spellcaster falling into the dark arts.

"A favor?" He obviously assumed Maestro would ask something far beyond his ability.

Maestro smiled. "I sometimes need consultants." With the crisis averted, he could afford to be snarky. "I give you this one for free and next time I need a whiny little girl to try and get herself killed I'll call you."

Spook stared at him, trying to decide if he was serious. "You're a grade-A asshole." He crossed his arms and stared at Maestro.

Maestro shrugged. "You're showing your age. It should be 'total douchebag, yo.'"

Anger filled the lad and boiled over. "How about stupid motherfucker? Is that hip enough for you?" He'd wanted Maestro to be all touchy-feely like his former team. Yeah. That wasn't going to happen. Better off he learned that right away.

The zombie stomped up the stairs.

Maestro smirked. He counted. He got to five before Spook reappeared.

"And I know 'hip' is old-fashioned." He stared at Maestro, daring him to interrupt. "I was being ironic"

And he left. His footsteps faded as he made his way to the front door. It creaked open and slammed shut.

Maestro heaved a huge sigh and let himself slump. His first official encounters with Spook had actually gone more smoothly than he'd hoped. If only all such encounters could go as well.

And then there were the other two.

So. . .

Maestro stepped over to a curtained alcove in a dark corner of the basement. He pulled the curtain aside and revealed a small area fully decorated for an episode of the *X-files.*

Paper clippings covered the walls, attached to each other by bits of string. Hundreds of them wallpapered the alcove like the decorating job of a serial killer. Photos of Spook. . . of Turner. . . of Muscle. Photos of them alone, in groups together. . . which should have been impossible since none of them had met. Articles about the three of them. . . and about Maestro.

The dates on the articles were all from the future.

Maestro placed his Doohickey on the desk. "Doohickey, visual interface, please."

A holographic screen appeared near the wall, showing his basic desktop and apps.

He sighed. "File Omega, please."

The screen flashed red. "Passcode, please." A red laser strobed over Maestro.

"Zanzibar234534 hetrncekehfn4r335." He lifted his right leg and turned in place. "345647373664 Rentrofecky." He lifted his thumb for fingerprint analysis and opened his right eye for retinal scan. "Barry58984743 litttlebarry4585739." He sang three notes from his favorite song and unzipped his pants, presenting his junk to the scanner. "Helotes 474728283."

"Password accepted."

He sat. "Doohickey, surreptitiously hijack the teleporter on the Galactic Police cruiser currently in orbit and find me a pitcher of martinis."

Only one place in Austin made decent martinis at ten o'clock in the morning. Maestro placed several bills on the desk so his favorite bartender would be well compensated for having to return to the bar for another round.

The bills disappeared and a pitcher appeared in their place with a cheap martini glass. "Thanks, Billy." The young man would likely curse him first then notice the pile of cash and shrug. A huge tip made up for almost anything with Billy.

The vodka hit Maestro's tongue cold, his throat hot. "Bossa nova, Doohickey."

The music started in the background while Maestro touched the photo of Spook with his brother Ross sitting on the lap of Santa Claus. "I finally break down and talk to Morrison." Damn. "And I end up meeting all three in one day." With a sigh, Maestro tugged the photo from the wall and placed it on the desk. "I hate coincidences."

Next was a photo of Muscle fighting an enormous balrog in a dark alley. The red stain oozing from behind a dumpster in the background had always raised questions.

After that, he removed a photo of Turner dancing with an attractive red-haired man. Maestro had known her in mulitple timelines, and he'd never seen or heard of a man like that. The way she smiled at him, he seemed to be important somehow.

It took an hour to pull down all the photos while he waxed nostalgic.

The holographic screen hovered in place near the wall the entire time, the image frozen, waiting. Static as it was, it could have been a page from any website. "TERRORISTS CAUGHT!" the headline blared. "SENTENCED TO DEATH!"

When the only remnants of the massive montage were the shadows and stains on the walls where some of the older articles had been mounted for years, the photos and strings filled a box on the desk. Several folders lay on top.

Maestro slugged back the last of the martini and stared at the frozen hologram. “Doohickey. Play file.”

The images beneath the headline jumped into motion and opened into three dimensions. Four grainy scenes, surveillance footage taken from an army base in San Antonio, Texas and rendered into 3D: Spook, Turner, Muscle, Maestro.

Another scene played out the devastating explosion that would burn all of Texas and Oklahoma—as well as much of Louisiana and New Mexico—less than one year from the day he’d met all three of the other culprits in a terrorist attack so horrific, history databases would mark it for over two hundred years.

Letters scrolled. “Death Toll: 45 million.”

Several panels offered eye witness accounts.

After a moment, the audio kicked in. “With a death toll approaching fifty million, the courts elected to throw out standard due process. . .”

An interactive display offered the executions from the points of view of A) the criminals, B) the executioner, or C) a disinterested third party perspective.

Maestro closed his eyes and dropped more money on the desk. “Doohickey, if you please?”

Billy would likely have a batch ready.

Without looking, Maestro picked up a new glass. Cranberry. Nice. He tossed it back while the Doohickey played the rest of the historical record. It was a file he’d discovered by accident while researching 21st century mysteries.

The file finished its playback and fell silent.

That was how Maestro found his clients. He researched his Doohickey’s historical records to discover those who’d needed the services of someone with his abilities, and then he’d go find them.

Although time could be ridiculously complicated. . .

“Doohickey, erase file.”

The screen derezzed as Maestro walked through it with the box under one arm.

If only the future were that easy to erase.

Minutes later, he stood in the rustic yard behind his house. The fire in the oil drum burned brightly as he dropped the photos and articles into it one at a time. When he held the last photo, that same picture of Spook and Ross and Santa, he slugged back the end of the second martini pitcher.

Now that all three were in his life, he could leave no record of what they would do in one year, in one timeline, in one dimension, in one way that Maestro might, or might not, find a way to prevent. Only idiots left information like that laying around for someone to discover.

Could he change the fate of millions?

Who knew, but it wasn't as if he'd never tried to do it before.

Of course the last time, he'd actually managed to blow up the entire planet.

Seventy-six times.

The sound of a throat delicately cleared behind him didn't startle Maestro in the least.

"I'll just leave it here on the picnic table, shall I?" Billy asked.

Maestro heard the sound of glass on wood and then liquid being poured. "Thanks, Billy."

"No worries, Maestro." His footsteps carried him away. "It seemed you were about due another round and my shift was over."

Maestro smiled.

Billy knew just how big a tip this delivery would gain him.

Spook and Ross seemed so happy together in the photo Maestro held.

He dropped it into the fire.

Episode Two: Snuggles

Splat

Austin, Texas.
Two weeks later.

The wee, dark hours of the night.

Not having to sleep afforded certain advantages. When surveilling a nest of griffons, Spook could always stay awake during his shift at watch. While trekking across the country after a recalcitrant incubus, he could drive all night while Ross slept curled up on the seat beside him, softly snoring.

No Ross? Nights just lasted a really long time, and Austin nights continued almost unto dawn.

What time was it anyway? Folks were still wandering around Sixth Street east of the highway where the fun people hung out. Spook headed to his favorite haunt, Bitter Sweets, where the freaks gathered.

But wait. . . what was that haunting melody?

Haunting, yes. Yearning, too. Really. . . yearning.

Okay. . . calling a place "Biker Bar" most likely told Spook all he needed to know, so he resumed his walk. . . but that song.

That voice.

What was a haunting woman's voice doing in *there*?

He sniffed. Roses? And he tasted chocolate.

Huh.

He glanced into the dive. Nearly empty.

The singer stood at the edge of the stage in a short, black skirt, ripped fishnets, and Victorian retro boots. In all likelihood, there was more to her than that, but the ripped fishnets already had Spook's attention.

A cute chick drummer with frizzy hair and a sports bra held the stage with the singer, as well as two guys. Whatever. The guys played guitars or bass or something.

While Spook bellied up to the bar, the singer danced over to the shirtless guitar player. She leaned in close, and he grinned.

The other dude started a really harsh bass lick. So that's what he played. Bass. And he wasn't thrilled about the attention Singer lavished on Guitar Guy. The flirting couple seemed oblivious.

A complete triangle, then. No point in caring.

Oh well. Spook was in a bar, and even if nothing but bikers lived there, all bars had alcohol. Lots and lots of alcohol. Since he had no blood running through his veins, Spook used a spell so the alcohol actually worked on him. And work it did to pass the time and forget the past.

"Who wants to dance?" Singer swayed at the edge of the stage now, beckoning to the five or six people in the room.

One couple wandered over to dance for the band, but it seemed more out of pity than any sincere desire to dance.

Singer hooted and applauded for the dancers, which just rendered the whole scene an even sadder shade of pathetic.

Spook bellied up to the bar. At one end lurked a guy who had to be the bouncer: huge, dark, and dressed in black tank top, slacks, and flip flops. Incongruously, he wore a forties-style flat cap. Plaid. Well, no accounting for taste.

The big man glanced Spook's way.

These are not the droids you are looking for, Spook projected for all he was worth.

The bouncer looked away. Perfect.

The bartender held an expression that told Spook he wasn't going to get what he wanted. Oh well, might as well try.

"Whatever's cheap on tap." Spook leaned casually on one elbow.

The bartender wiped absently at the same glass every bartender on the planet owned. "ID, kid?"

Spook flashed his latest driver's license. He made a new one every few years since he didn't age.

The bartender looked it over and his mouth did one of those

sideways smile things. "Sorry kid. I'm not buying this. You can't be more than seventeen. How 'bout a Coke?"

Spook hoped his smile didn't convey his true thoughts, which ran along the lines of, *How about you curl up and die?* "Gee, daddy-o, how about a ginger ale? Can a kid have one of those?"

The bartender kept cleaning the lousy glass. "I could just let Muscle kick your ass out of here." He nodded in the direction of the giant Black guy with maybe a trace of Asian about the eyes, who now stared at Spook. Blast. That kind of attention sucked.

"I'm actually quite fond of ginger ale," Spook muttered.

The bartender offered Spook a smile that made the zombie wish him dead again. "I thought you might be." He filled the glass he'd been wiping. Good thing Spook was already deceased.

The bartender slid the glass along the bar and Spook grabbed it. After his first quaff, he made a big show of a yummy face before dropping money on the bar and giving the band his full attention.

He a finger around the rim of his glass. "*Etiam partem te mel.*" The liquid swirled, sparkled, and turned darker.

Spook sipped. Mmmmm. Better.

His magic trick worked on ginger ale as well as it did on beer, but a part of his perpetually teen-aged brain knew that a beer was, well, beer. He glanced at the bouncer, who bopped along to the band and ignored Spook completely. Nice.

A cute blonde danced off to one side in a self-conscious way that said she'd like to dance more but inhibitions prevented her.

Spook zeroed in and set his glass at her table. "Would you like to dance?" He bowed low and offered his hand. It was corny, but it usually worked.

Yep. She smiled and took his hand. "What the hell."

He and Ross had spent a lot of time learning jitterbug back in the day for a case that'd involved a vampire jazz band. From the smile on the girl's face, all that training had paid off.

He dragged her into the free space between the pool tables.

They jumped. They spun. He threw her into the air. Being a member of the "life-challenged" made Spook stronger than he looked. They separated and he backed away, spun a couple of times and found himself smack dab in front of the bouncer. Oh well, might as well spread some goodwill.

Spook bopped and jived in front of the big man, who actually smiled and sort of bobbed his head with the music. Alrighty then. Spook encouraged the young man, who glanced around self-consciously before bopping awkwardly a little bit. Then he laughed, waved Spook away, and settled against the wall.

Score. Always make sure the bouncer likes you. Helps tremendously if you end up dancing naked on the pool tables. Things had changed since the Summer of Love, but Spook hadn't quite adjusted.

One mission accomplished, Spook turned back to his partner, spun her a few times and threw her into the air again. As he caught her, he backed directly into someone. Oops.

A biker. No surprise. Guy really knew how to work a frown.

"Sorry."

The much bigger man wore full leathers and lots of tats. Hopefully, he'd let it go. "This isn't a fag bar, asshole."

"That's okay. I'm not gay." Spook glanced in the mirror behind the bar. His eyeliner, velvet, and gel did rather contrast with the rest of the clientele. Well, Maestro had said not unless he was going out.

The biker laughed. "I didn't say you were gay. I said you were a fag."

What? Had someone changed the meanings of those words *again*?

Spook turned and quaffed his drink as if building strength. How should he play it? "*Vestibulum accumsan diam mauris.*" He kept his back to the biker.

The man's belt buckle glowed red for a moment before releasing. His jeans unzipped in an instant and his pants and boxers both plummeted to his ankles with Spook innocently turned away from the action.

The biker tripped with a heartfelt, "What the—?" and tumbled toward the girl with whom Spook had been dancing.

"Oh my God!" she screamed. "He made me touch it! Get off me!"

There could be little doubt what "it" meant.

Spook spun around with feigned surprise, far too late to be

responsible for the mayhem.

The biker fought to his feet, casually leaving his pants around his ankles. "Well, since you already touched it, shouldn't I buy you. . ."

The bouncer, Muscle, appeared between the girl and the biker.

She slipped farther behind the big man, who crossed his arms in what seemed to be a signature move.

The biker rolled his eyes and reached for his pants. "Why don't you mind your own business?" When he rose to his full height, he stared directly into Muscle's chest. He craned his neck to look up.

The bouncer wore a distinct frown.

"Ah, shit," the biker said.

Muscle grabbed him by the scruff of his jacket and the seat of his pants and threw him screaming across the bar and out the open door onto the street.

Spook leaned back a little to watch the biker roll head over heels and slide to a halt flat on his back with his pants once again around his ankles. . . right at the feet of a young couple out for a nightly stroll.

The taller of the two young men raised one eyebrow, held his cell over the man's unconscious form, and snapped a photo.

His date slipped an arm around his waist and chuckled. "Well, you know *that's* going on Tumblr."

Back inside the bar, the blonde dancing girl placed one hand on Muscle's chest, and the pheromones pumping out of her body filled the air.

The bouncer made a face. Hunh. Maybe he could smell them, too. He handed the girl a glass of water and his face turned red.

"Thank you, I'm fine," the girl told him, rubbing an index finger across his massive pectorals. "So are you." Her smile was about as subtle as a hockey mask and a chainsaw.

Oh well, Spook's flirtation couldn't have gone anywhere. He turned to the band as the bouncer quickly slid under the bartender's escape and popped up behind the bar. Playing hard to get? Really? Whatever.

Spook settled back to enjoy the show, but the song ended with a loud, earsplitting finale. Well, heck. Now what would he do with the night?

A bright flash of yellow filled the room.

Spook blinked.

A loud, squelchy "bang" sounded like fireworks detonating in a vat of pudding.

A wave of magic swept over Spook and hit him in the pit of his stomach the same moment something warm and wet splattered his face and hands.

All over him, actually. What the heck?

The tiny crowd shouted and screamed excitement over what had to be some kind of amazing pyrotechnics display. They picked at the reddish, bluish gunk that covered the room, laughing and whistling.

The band, however, stared wide-eyed and frozen at Singer's mic stand. Beside it a black scorch marked the floor and a wisp of smoke curled lazily to the ceiling.

Where was the singer?

Bad feeling about that.

Someone whimpered.

Spook turned to the noise.

The dancing blonde held something wet and hairy about the size of a soccer ball. She stared down at it with complete disgust and horror in her face.

Then she screamed, and not happy screaming. She managed a full-throated cry of terror that would have made Jamie Lee Curtis jealous.

She dropped the hairy soccer ball, which hit the floor with a far-too-familiar thunk and rolled just enough to face Spook.

Singer's eyes were wide and her mouth open in surprise. Well, who wouldn't have been surprised?

As the shouts of support turned into screams of horror, Spook drained his glass and set it down. At least he had something to do now.

The bar patrons wiped at the blood and gore covering them. Several threw up, which would only contaminate the scene, damn it. No one watching could be involved, though, unless they were consummate actors. The surprise and revulsion looked real.

Spook closed his eyes a moment and refocused.

The energy the bystanders radiated as they ran madly from the bar seemed genuine. They felt terrified.

The band members had yet to move. They all seemed astonished, yes, but what else was going on? The lines connecting them to the charred spot where the Singer had exploded were bright and white-hot. There was more to this group than met the third eye.

Spook shook his head to reset his vision for the usual spectrum as the last patron departed.

The bouncer stepped casually over little piles of guts to the bandstand. He looked the place over with a scowl, but it was a scowl that spoke to annoyance at having to clean up the mess. Perhaps there was more to him as well.

"It's supposed to be the drummer." The words, little more than a mumble from Drummer, echoed in a bar suddenly empty with only the drip of blood and the occasion splatter of flesh onto the floor breaking the silence.

"It's always the drummer." She spoke the phrase several more times as Spook joined her on the smallish bandstand.

He reached out. "It's okay, sweetie, this isn't *Spinal Tap*. Why don't you just come out from behind there?"

Apparently following his lead, Muscle stepped onto the platform as well.

Drummer looked up at Spook. "She blew up."

"Yes, yes, she did." Spook hoped to get her someplace away from metal drums and wooden drumsticks before the scary, frantic shock set in.

As casually as if he were a roadie, Muscle took the boys' instruments from them and set them aside. He glanced down at the scorch mark as if it offended him.

Drummer's eyes grew wide and went glassy as she pushed to her feet. "She. blew. up."

And there it was.

Spook rushed the last couple of feet and wrapped one arm around her shoulders, slipping the drumsticks away. "*Essent admodum has ne*," he whispered.

The spell flowed through him, but hiccoughed ever so slightly. He'd have to remember that. A blue spark lit her pupils briefly, then she fell into Spook's arms.

He picked her up. "A hand here?" He turned to—whoa!

Muscle had already appeared, taking the girl from his arms. The dude was like a Ninja, but saying so was probably racist. Spook kept his mouth shut.

"I gave her a sedative," Spook said to explain the faint. "Can you get her someplace comfortable?"

The big man hesitated for three seconds, holding Spook's gaze suspiciously.

This is all perfectly normal, Spook sent. *Not your droids.*

The dark eyes narrowed, but Muscle nodded and took the girl away.

The boys followed him to a room off to the side.

Hmmmm. . . interesting giant person.

Blood dripped onto Spook's shoulder. Ew. The mystery of the bouncer would have to wait.

Spook looked around and whistled. What a mess. He hadn't seen anyone explode for almost five years. How much did it suck he'd blinked and missed the actual money shot?

Closing his eyes again, Spook relaxed and centered. "*Nec et aliquid electram.*" He opened his eyes facing away from the stage to give himself a moment to adjust to the spectral energy.

Hmm. . . sparkles of gold filled the room. Someone had spelled the whole place? Or. . . no, it was all moving out towards the walls in gentle waves. The residue of the explosion perhaps, but for the magic to be that thick all the way to the walls. . .

He faced the stage—

Whatsa Jesus? Ow!

A white hot flare burned there.

"Shit!" He closed his eyes and turned away. Who the hell had the girl pissed off with *that* kind of power?

Ross had kept a database with all the usual suspects.

Spook had the data, now, but no clue how to use it. He'd never needed it, since he'd always had Ross. Well, Ross was gone into the real world. No help there.

Spook dialed back his sensitivity.

A small ball of light, for all the world like a miniature sun, hung in the air above the stage. It faded, finally, pretty, in its own way. But what a mess it had left behind.

Yeah. Spook didn't want to handle this one on his own. He knew someone who did this sort of thing. One of these kids' parents might even have enough money to make it worth his while.

He held up his cell. "Maestro."

Near the side room, Muscle punched buttons on his old-fashioned flip phone.

Maestro picked up. "If this isn't a matter of life and death I'm going to end you."

Sweet. He knew Spook's number or had him programmed. "I like how you're already used to avoiding 'I'm going to kill you' as a threat."

"Spook!" Maestro accepted that he'd need to cast his spell one-handed. He settled his weight evenly and turned his phone ear away from the noise of the blue-green, liquid beam of light pouring from his outstretched hand that intercepted the billowing flames of the medium-sized red dragon he was robbing.

"Okay, okay, Mr. Grumpy," Spook said over the phone. "I'm at this biker bar and a woman exploded. The spectral energy is off the chart." The lad did not know how to get to the point. "I think I need help on this one."

Oh. He was actually asking for help.

"Kinda busy." Maestro settled the muscles along his back so his spine would lengthen. Better conduit than all tensed up.

The dragon managed a step forward because of the distraction.

Maestro poured all of his energy into the spell. His vision blazed green and his jaw clenched.

The Doohickey beeped. A text. Drat. He hated multi-tasking. He pulled the device from his ear for a second and tapped the screen. The text appeared as a hologram.

"Put the call on speaker," he said.

"Are you at a party?" Spook asked. "Sounds like a bonfire or something."

The text read: *Muscle here. Grl exploded. Bsy?*

Drat and double drat!

"Yeah, Spook, it's all fruity drinks and paper umbrellas." Maestro frowned at the floating text. "Is there a really big guy in a hat there who doesn't seem like he's afraid enough?"

"Yeah," Spook told him. "He's the bouncer."

"*Drat.*" Those two could not meet. That would be one step closer to the future Maestro intended to avoid. "He's extremely dangerous, Spook. No matter what you do, do *not* engage him."

There was a pause. "O-kay."

Blast. Teenager.

The dragon must have noticed Maestro's distraction. It poured on the heat and drove forward. Maestro held his pose, but slid backwards until one foot hit the rock wall. No more room to give. "I mean it. Do *not* talk to him."

"Okay, okay. You're the boss, right? I will not talk to him." Was that sarcasm?

The dragon rose up onto its back legs with a ripple of sinewy muscles and pliable metallic scales. It sucked in a deep breath, and Maestro had never figured out how they did that while blowing fire. Its belly glowed a bright and frightening orange. . . and then an even scarier yellow. It raked its front claws in the air as if reaching for him.

Oh, hells.

"Okay-good-gotta-go. Will-be-there-as-quick-as-I-can." Maestro dropped the Doohickey, trusting its durable construction.

He brought both arms forward, forced all his energy into one massive burst that would hopefully distract the dragon for at least one second while he dove under its legs to blast it from behind.

Hopefully.

The strange young man extending an arm in Reggie's direction smelled like death.

"Hi there," the young man said with more enthusiasm than seemed strictly appropriate under the circumstances. "My name's Morrison James, but my friends call me Spook. I heard the barkeep call you Muscle." He smiled even more.

Politeness won every time, so Reggie took the offered hand and gave it a strong squeeze. Spook seemed far too calm about the situation. Could he be another investigator like that Maestro person? What were the odds?

Spook pulled away with a wince. "Might want to hold back a little on the handshake, there, yo."

Muscle cringed and nodded. His strength had gone through another rapid leap, and he was still adjusting. Hopefully, those jumps would stop soon. He did not want to grow any stronger.

"So you know a guy named Maestro?"

What? Another coincidence? Reggie nodded hesitantly.

"He's on his way." Spook moved away and explored the gory room.

It would take forever to clean up. And how long before the police showed up? Ugh. Police were so complicated. Always asking who killed whom. . .

Spook stepped around a leg. "Although I think he's at a party, so we may need to razz him when he gets here." He looked up at Reggie expectantly. "He told me not to talk to you, you know. Said you were dangerous."

What? Why would he say that? Had Reggie completely misunderstood the stranger? Had Maestro not liked him?

Spook smiled. He must have seen Reggie's concern. He stepped closer again and looked around as if Maestro might suddenly appear out of nowhere.

"Don't let it bother you," the little man said conspiratorially. "I think he was actually protecting you from me." What? How could *he* be dangerous? "I'm pretty badass." He wiggled his eyebrows.

Oh! He was teasing. Hard to say what the actual joke was, but Spook was being friendly. That was nice. Reggie had few friends in the US. In fact, little Wendy Gonzalez was the only one.

"Any idea what happened to the exploding woman?"

Reggie focused on him again. He had to stop letting his mind wander. Sensei said it was his greatest weakness. He took in a deep breath to center and shook his head. The remaining band members might know something, so Reggie jabbed a thumb in the direction of the side room where he had left them.

Spook glanced in that direction. "Yeah. . . let's see if Maestro gets here in the next minute or two." He glanced at a wristwatch. "Huh. No cops." He looked up at Reggie.

Reggie shrugged. The police rarely made an appearance and it would take a lot to convince them something criminal had actually happened. Well, something more criminal than usual.

Spook smiled. "You speak English?"

Reggie nodded.

Another smile. "Of course you do, otherwise you have been extremely lucky to nod and shake your head at just the right times. Sorry."

Reggie liked him. He smelled like death but was filled with more life than anyone Reggie had ever met. And he did not act like Reggie was weird. Everyone else seemed to pick up on it right away, that he was different. Spook seemed unconcerned. Maybe he was different, too. Maybe that's how he knew Maestro. Maybe Maestro collected people who were different.

Spook looked up suddenly and caught Reggie staring. Darn it. If he looked away, it would be even more embarrassing. So he held the little man's gaze.

How long would this staring contest last? Then something red and grey and squishy dropped from the ceiling to land on the edge of a table between them. It squelched a bit and slowly slid off the table to land with a plop on the floor.

"Is that a spleen?"

Cats

Japanese Tea Gardens. San Antonio, Texas.
Thursday. Dawn.

Turner stood outside the gardens on a driveway. The bleak, cloudless sky and a relentless yellow sun baked the air to an inferno. So much like home. Except back home both sun and sky had been holographic projections on a protective dome that kept the frozen vacuum of space at bay. For whatever reason, Mother liked the desert.

Here in Texas, on Earth, a stand of bamboo on one side of the Asian tourist attraction had been inexplicably cleared of undergrowth and trampled by many, many tiny padded feet. A number of bowls peppered the ground, filled to overflowing with food pellets and with water. Considering the heat, Turner found the untouched hydration most perplexing.

A few small domiciles stood empty and, apparently, abandoned. Strange contraptions dotted the grove as well, constructed of upright poles onto which small platforms had been attached at seemingly random points. Carpeting, normally reserved for human floors, covered the contrivances. Odd.

Turner raised her devise. "Doohickey? Analyze."

"Yes, Elizabeth." The device barely paused. "The structures are made to entertain members of the species *Felis catus*. Common name, household cat."

"Cats." What the light were the animals supposed to do with those contraptions?

Anthropomorphizing presapient creatures baffled Turner. Having worn many Terran species as outfits, she remained convinced that their mental faculties precluded the sort of homey, warm fuzzy feelings most humans attributed to them.

A red flag had gone up on the GP database when the sudden disappearance of hundreds of feral cats, inexplicably cared for by the locals, made the news. The strange event interested her even more considering the rumors of a cloaked ship somewhere in the city. Perhaps smugglers had decided to have a snack.

"Doohickey, scan for energy signatures, non-Terran metals... cats." She walked the area. If anyone saw her waving her Doohickey around, she'd explain that she had lojacked "Mr. Snuggles" and sought him on her app. "Keep scans to the onboard screen." No sense getting herself in trouble for exposing the locals to a holographic projection at least forty years too soon. Bother. The smartphone screen on her disguised Doohickey was too lighted small.

Something moved near a shallow, decorative pond.

She looked up. "What the shades?"

Mother stood on the path about twenty yards ahead, investigating the flowers of a shrub and wearing a Narcturan Ectozoid. She hadn't seen Turner yet, so she still had a chance to escape... yet... what the light was she doing there? And shaped like a giant purple Yeti?

Refusing to act on her instinctive desire to run screaming from the area, no doubt enhanced by all the endorphins her current outfit produced, Turner sucked in a deep breath and adjusted the Doohickey's scan.

Just as she thought. Aversion field. She raised her psychic shields and the image faded. Turner relaxed.

The field was fairly sophisticated, and no doubt set up around the aforementioned cloaked ship. Cloaks kept the locals from physically seeing the vessel, but an aversion field planted images in their minds that would convince them to avoid the area altogether without suspecting why.

Apparently, it wasn't *that* sophisticated. The image of Mother in a decidedly non-Terran outfit, albeit one of her favorites, had been a mistake. Yes, Turner was certain to turn tail and run from the incessant babbling and nagging, but Mother's extraterrestrial presence on a protected planet had given it away.

Movement ahead drew Turner's attention. A young couple walked a cross path, coiled around one another in a way that should have rendered their mobility nil. However, the smiles on their faces demonstrated that their movements couldn't be in the least hindered.

Hm. Peter would never display such ridiculous emotional intensity. . . not like her own parents, who were as flighty and emotional as Shifters could possibly be. No. . . Peter was solid, dependable. . . everything Turner's parents were not. She'd take that reliability over silly, gooey displays any day.

So why hadn't she already signed their contract renewal? They'd only been together for one twenty-year cycle, and everyone renewed their vows at least once. For a species that lived up to three eons, twenty years was one grain of sand on a beach, the shade of one tiny branch in a forest of shadows.

But Turner was only 124, and had so many—

Her Doohickey beeped.

There it was.

The ET vessel rested on the pond itself. Smart move. Less likely someone would stumble into it accidentally. The cloak seemed serviceable for a planet like Earth, but Turner was a Shifter with the Galactic Police and utilized the most sophisticated tech in the galaxy.

She glanced around before making her approach.

Uh-oh, the clingy couple argued on the far side of the pond. He pointed. She stood with her hands on her hips and a significantly less romantic expression on her face.

What did they see? The girl spun around and stalked away, her young beau following desperately.

Handy. Turner stepped to the water's edge. The Doohickey showed no humans in the area. "Privacy bubble, Doohickey. Extend across the pond."

"All right, Elizabeth." Now, not only were they cloaked, they were also soundproofed.

"Display badge, please," she requested, holding up her Doohickey.

A hologram disclosed her credentials.

"Ahoy cloaked vessel. You are on this planet in violation of the Primitive Planets Protection Pact." She squared her shoulders and held her most professional posture. "If you do not de-cloak immediately I will consider you hostile, and I am authorized by the Galactic Police to vaporize your vehicle and all occupants."

Nothing.

Bother.

"Doohickey—"

The air over the pond rippled and shifted.

Although the effort hurt her eyes, Turner studied the cloak in action.

A flash of light. A golden energy vortex. As the vortex cleared, the ship appeared inside it.

Hmph. Primitive. And showy.

"Good way to have your 'well-hidden' ship noticed by the locals," she muttered as a walkway extended toward her.

Ship? It was as aerodynamic as a brick. Shaped like one, as a matter of fact. A glass and steel brick. Obviously an observation lab, otherwise known as a "duck blind." More windows than walls, and she could see clear through it: lab tables, medical equipment and. . . and cats.

Lots and lots of cats.

Why would someone study cats?

The steel door slid open as the walkway reached Turner's feet, and two decidedly sheepish bipeds poked their heads out before moving to stand in the open doorway.

She glanced at the Doohickey readout as she neared them.

They'd come from a long way away. . . and quite far apart. The tall, emaciated male with eyes a little too large and dark to be human was from Estragon Prime. To blend into the local population, the blue pigment in his skin had been replaced and the skinny tail removed. His ears must have been clipped as well. Cosmetic surgery was common on research teams. Smugglers, too, when it came down to it.

The shorter, squat male was from Jonquil, so not so much surgery needed. As long as no one scanned him—or, on Earth, x-rayed him—no one would be the wiser. What were they doing so far from home?

The short Jonquillian spoke first. "We have our permits." He had to be in charge. His voice was firm. From Turner's studies, it also belonged somewhere in a fashionable neighborhood of London.

The nervous, taller Estragonite hovered half-in, half-out of the doorway. "We have every right to be here." He said it almost as a question, and *his* accent sounded as if he'd learned the language from American movies of Cockney chimney sweeps.

His compatriot shot him a dark glance. "We're anthropologists," the shorter man explained, "studying the primitive population of the planet."

Turner pushed between them into the lab. "Then this won't take more than a moment, will it?" The place was rank with the smell of cats. How did they stand the constant mewing? "So this is a sanctioned duck blind?"

"We have our permits," the leader said.

Turner displayed her most officious smile. "So you've said, and yet I haven't seen them."

The Jonquillian's smile was reptilian. He held out his Doohickey and a holographic screen appeared.

Turner held up her own device, which automatically copied the information. "Thank you."

"Indeed."

His name while on Earth was Phineas.

The Estragonite called himself Bogg.

"Everything seems to be in order." She scrolled through the information. Anthropological research.

How had they been here so long without the GP knowing about them? Unless they did, and she just didn't have clearance. She'd make some inquiries.

"Mew." Something small and furry rubbed her ankle.

She picked up a golden ball of fluff by the scruff of its neck. "Anthropological studies don't usually involve abducting the indigenous species."

She carried the kitten to a nearby trash barrel and glanced inside: bones and fur of a color quite similar to the cat she held, obviously disgorged after being devoured whole. "Or eating them. Unless you're doing a study on culinary habits?" She dropped the kitten onto a nearby counter.

Bogg's face lit up, but Phineas touched his arm before the tall man could speak. "They're all feral. . . a. . . a nuisance to the local monkeys," Phineas insisted.

Monkeys?

The Jonquillian exchanged a nervous glance with his partner. "Sorry, when you live among them for a while. . ." His voice trailed off then he jumped back in. "None of the cats had collars." He smiled as if that information should score a few points.

Turner pulled a folded piece of paper from her pocket, opened it with a dramatic flap, and held it up for both scientists to see a cat named Mr. Snuggles in all his feline glory.

"Did this one have a collar?" Although any connection to *this* cat's disappearance was a long shot, she'd found it online when searching for data.

Phineas took one look at the poster and glared at Bogg before he could stop himself, which he did abruptly and belatedly. He opened his mouth quickly, as if he were going to pretend he didn't recognize the one-eared one-eyed mongrel cat, but something in Turner's face must have stopped him.

If he even tried to lie, she'd haul them both in for questioning.

He closed his mouth and forced a tight smile. "Oh. . . well. . . there may have been the one."

She shook the poster. "In Austin? A hundred miles away?" She wandered around the lab, subtly scanning their equipment. Most likely, they'd never know she'd done so. "What were you doing there?"

Phineas took some time before answering, and he shot Bogg more than one pointed look.

The Estragonite presented a childish, disgruntled face to his partner and wrung his hands all the way to a far corner of the lab where he moved things around as if busy.

Phineas smiled again. "Well. . . you know what a misbegotten hellhole this planet is," he began in a conspiratorial tone. "We were bored out of our bloody minds and noticed a teleport into Austin. We decided to investigate. Maybe it would be someone worth visiting." He shrugged. "No such luck."

"Mm-hm. . ." She regarded the poster in her hands as if it were the most interesting item in the room. This person was good at lying, but she could still tell he lied, so. . . not *great* at it. "And where was this exactly? I may need to look into who teleported on a protected planet."

"Off Oltorf Drive, east of the river." He spoke at the exact same time Turner recognized the house with a tire swing in the background of the poster.

Maestro? Coincidences. She hated them almost as much as she hated magic. Hopefully, she covered her thoughts better than the two men here.

"And did you find anyone interesting?" How had they even detected her teleport? There was nothing in the duck blind to indicate they had the tech to detect a scrambled GP signal.

"Sadly, no. No people, just monk. . ." He stopped himself that time. "Locals. Just locals." Again with the smile.

Turner peered over Bogg's shoulder at the papers he shuffled around.

The skinny scientist did a double take when he noticed her. "It remains a mystery," he offered.

She held the poster in his face. "And while you were there, you grew a bit peckish, did you?"

Bogg's eyes darted back and forth from the poster to Phineas. "A wee bit."

"Bogg is always hungry," Phineas said with an expansive gesture.

Turner regarded the emaciated form. "It's his metabolism." Why not try conciliatory and see where it got her?

Bogg flashed a smile that was, perhaps, a trifle larger than the average human's. "Cat weren't wearing a collar when I et him." His childlike attempt at deception was almost charming. "He may have lost it chasing rodents." His grin grew. "Or ponies." He opened his mouth wide in a smile that was at once endearing and thoroughly frightening.

Phineas appeared on his other side. "Thank you, Bogg, that's quite helpful." He placed his hand over Bogg's in a manner both tender and possessive. "I do apologize for Mr. Snuggles." His face brightened. "If it would help, we could create a clone. Reproducing the missing ear and eye would be child's play."

Of course, it would.

"Do you have a growth accelerator?" she asked with false enthusiasm.

"Sadly, no." The smile grew a bit more strained. Knowing the scientist's species as she did, Turner had no doubt he was imagining her flayed over a pit of dractillian blastigons.

Something was very wrong, but Turner was blasted by light if she could figure it out. Diplomacy and patience were the key. "Okay, guys, I'm going to let you off with a warning this time." Give them time to hang themselves. "But you need to cut back." She stepped over a female suckling an entire litter in the middle of the floor. "And let some of these creatures out. The locals are noticing." She gave the scientists a pointed glare. "The purpose of the cloak is to avoid the locals noticing."

Phineas clasped his hands to his chest in a show of humble supplication. "Of course, officer, we appreciate your leniency. Thank you."

Turner turned to the door, where Bogg suddenly stood in her personal space, thrusting a tiny golden furball into her face with another inhuman grin. "Kitten? They're extra juicy."

Apparently, she'd won *him* over, at least.

She gave his shoulder a friendly pat. "Thank you, but I'm on duty."

He nodded knowingly and more than necessary. "Oh. . . right then, maybe another time, gov'ner."

As Turner crossed the walkway to shore, the men stood shoulder to shoulder in the doorway, smiling and waving. Stupid, yes, but definitely up to something illegal, and not so stupid they would make it easy for her to figure it out. She glanced down at the poster of Mr. Snuggles with Maestro's house in the background.

What the shades did he have to do with any of this?

Coincidences and magic.

And Maestro rolled around in both of them like a Blstriant in a wallow of ghsnsten.

Once the meddling cop moved out of sight, Phineas lost his fake smile and smacked Bogg upside the head. "Doohickey, re-engage primary cloak." How did he stand the rat's stupidity? He would be the death of them both.

"Well, *that* was close," Bogg declared.

"Precariously close." Phineas waved across a wall at the back of the lab. The secondary cloak faded, revealing another room beyond, darker, with steel walls, still fully cloaked in spite of the cop's "superior technology."

Damnable Shifters. They thought they were so much better than the rest of the galaxy. Well, it made it easy to fool them by playing dumb.

Tables filled the back room, each of them supporting a dead monkey.

"Doohickey, reactivate the doctor machine," Phineas said.

The beams from the doctor machine flickered to life over the corpses, keeping the naked bodies from rotting. Every time he entered the room, Phineas had to suppress a shudder. The corpses looked so much like his own people, and yet they were primitives, little more than beasts.

No, no better than beasts at all.

Petting his golden snack, Bogg followed. "I doubt she would've been so nice to us had she known we were chopping up the monkeys."

"Indeed not." Phineas set to work reactivating all their equipment. As soon as he'd noticed the Shifter at the feline stomping ground, he'd deactivated the entire room to keep her from spotting the energy signatures.

Bogg played with his food as usual. He held it high over his head, craned his neck and opened his jaw enough that he could simply drop it all the way down his gullet. He so enjoyed the sensation of his snack wiggling and squirming in his stomach while it digested.

Phineas sighed. In spite of his appearance, Bogg had the mind of a four-year-old. How could you not love a child like that?

Bogg giggled and rubbed his stomach.

So like the children Phineas had lost. . .

He almost stopped the screams before he heard them.

Almost.

"But she let me keep the kitten." Bogg's large, innocent eyes pulled Phineas out of the past.

"Indeed she did." He forced a smile.

Licking his lips, Bogg glanced around at the human corpses. "Although it hardly seems fair I 'as to give up the cats when I don't get to eat any of the monkeys." He regarded Phineas with a wistful longing.

That sentiment was easier to deal with. "Well, we did infect them with a fatal illness." Phineas grabbed one scrawny shoulder and directed Bogg out of the morgue. "You know what that does to your digestion."

The door slid shut behind them.

Bogg gave Phineas his biggest, wide-eyed pleading look, which was saying a lot for an Estragonite. "Just a small one, Phineas?" Somehow, he managed to widen his eyes even more. "Please?"

"I'm afraid not." Distraction. How to take Bogg's mind off the monkeys? Phineas led him over to the female feline still nursing an entire brood. "The last time I let you eat one of our subjects you were gassy all week."

"I don't mind." He truly was a simple child.

"I do. It's a small lab." Phineas produced a bottle of Texas hot sauce that he knew Bogg loved more than monkeys. He opened the bottle and poured it over the brood at his feet. They screeched and screamed as the spices hit their tender, little eyes.

Bogg clapped his hands and dropped to his hands and knees amongst the protesting throng. These, he'd savor with relish.

Bats

Back to Austin.
A tittle past dawn.

Reggie was patient. Sensei had drilled patience into his thick skull since he could talk. Patience controlled anger. Patience kept the demon half at bay. Patiently, Reggie leaned against the bar pretending to read a comic book.

The police had finally shown up, questioned the band members, and taken samples. None of San Antonio's finest seemed very patient at all. They wanted to solve a crime they had not the skills to explain. Reggie had seen the girl explode and had smelled the rancid odor of magic.

The police wanted to find some kind of explosive device. They would be disappointed.

Spook didn't seem patient either, but he did know how to handle the police. Very friendly. He distracted the police with a subtle wave of his hand and one of the strangest spells Reggie had ever heard: "These are not the droids you're looking for." It made no sense, but whenever Spook muttered it, the policemen wandered away and let him be. Remarkable.

Fast, heavy footsteps approached from the street. Maestro's. His right foot always struck harder than his left. Reggie's potential new boss ran into the bar full tilt and slid several feet to a halt. He wore the usual rumpled grey trench coat, but now sported a neatly trimmed beard and his coat smoked, little tendrils of grey rising from it casually.

As though his dramatic entrance were the most normal event in the world, Maestro looked around and shrugged the coat more comfortably on his shoulders.

Two police officers hurried to him, and Maestro dug out his wallet while he searched the room with quick eyes. He flashed some kind of ID, turned his face away from the officers, and his eyes briefly glowed golden.

He met Reggie's gaze as the light faded, and he winked. He gave Reggie a brief nod before turning his attention to the police.

The chief investigator, Ricardo Gomez, waved the men away and pulled Maestro aside. Maestro draped one arm across the man's shoulders in a friendly way but held a finger up at Spook, who had started toward him.

Spook slowed and wandered toward Reggie instead.

While the other two talked, Spook settled beside Reggie and angled his head, checking out Reggie's comic.

Reggie turned it for him.

Spook smiled, nodded, and favored Reggie with a thumbs up.

A few stray phrases from his boss's conversation stood out. Gomez said something about a man named Steven Spielberg and Maestro nodded. Who was this man and how might he relate to the unusual death?

Maestro turned suddenly and clapped his hands together before rubbing them enthusiastically. "What did I miss?" His coat still smoked.

Spook shrugged. "Not much." He wandered closer to the stage, glancing around at the police who were inexplicably packing up and leaving the bar. "Singer blew up. I'm getting conflicting residuals. . ." He jabbed a thumb over one shoulder at Reggie. ". . .and the big, scary man doesn't talk much."

Ha! Another friendly joke.

Maestro glanced at Reggie but made no sign of trying to keep the conversation a secret from him. "I asked you not to approach him."

Spook held up a finger. "In point of fact, you did not." He shoved his hands in his pockets and radiated petulance. "You didn't ask. You *commanded.* Had you asked, I'd likely have complied. Since you forbade, as though I have any reason to obey you. . ." He shrugged. "Well. . ." He glanced over at Reggie again. "Don't know why you bothered anyway. He seems harmless enough."

"Looks can be deceiving." Maestro smacked Spook's shoulder. "*How* old are you?"

"Seventy-four," Spook said with no hesitation.

What? Reggie had to work to pretend he was still reading the comic book.

"And yet you act like a petulant teenager," Maestro reprimanded.

"Function follows form."

The pair moved to the stage. Seventy-four? Reggie would have guessed seventeen, and yet they had not spoken as if it was a joke. It had been almost rhetorical, as though Maestro had known Spook's age and was making a point about his juvenile behavior. So then Maestro did collect. . . freaks. What else made Spook a freak? Could he really be as dead as he smelled?

Reggie focused. What would they do next?

"What do you see?" Maestro asked.

Spook shook himself all over and his posture relaxed.

Maestro glanced at Reggie, who pretended to give his complete attention to his comic. He had incredible peripheral vision.

His boss raised a hand behind Spook's back and his eyes flashed green. A miniscule line linked his head to Spook's. When the strange, young. . . well, young-*appearing* man looked from side to side, Maestro subtly matched his movements as if he could see what Spook now saw. Could he?

"Okay. . . big explosion." Spook's voice was quiet. "But we knew that already. Definitely a curse of some kind, freakishly powerful and splashy, no pun intended. This wasn't just to hurt, but to make a very public statement. When I look in the corners away from the explosion, I sense something more subtle." He sniffed the air and smacked his lips. "Tastes like chocolate. . . "

"Tastes?"

"I get tastes." Spook moved toward the door. "I noticed it before she went all scanners. It's why I came in." His voice grew even quieter, almost nostalgic. "I noticed something. It was kind of weird, just sort of pulled me in."

"An attraction spell of some kind?"

"Of some kind. Pretty good range on it for it to pull me off the street." Abruptly, he shook his head and made waggly noises.

The string connecting him to Maestro snapped.

He turned to Maestro quickly, as if he'd felt something.

Maestro opened his eyes and stared at Spook for a split second.

Spook's eyes narrowed, but Maestro spun away as if nothing unusual had happened. His coat continued to smoke.

Spook reached out as if to snuff out a grey tendril, but Maestro turned back to face him too quickly.

Spook turned the gesture into a brush at his own hair. "Good party?"

"Turned out to be a barbecue." He stared Spook down.

What a complex game they played. They both had to be witches.

Abruptly, Maestro turned to Reggie and stomped over.

Startled, Reggie lowered the comic book and regarded his boss with interest.

"Whatcha reading?" Maestro asked.

Reggie held it up.

"A comic book?" Maestro raised an eyebrow.

Spook hurried over. "Oh right, Mr. Too-mature-for-words, are you going to call him a little boy because he likes comics?"

Reggie's pulse raced. Had he given himself away?

Maestro reached for the comic, and Reggie handed it over.

Spook scowled.

Maestro scanned the comic and returned it. "Don't be dissing the Bat, man." He gave Spook a very blank face and held a fist out to Reggie. "And it's a graphic novel."

Maestro shook his fist.

Oh! It must be that American replacement for handshakes.

"Richie Rich and Archie are comics," Maestro said.

Hoping he had learned it right, Reggie bumped the offered fist then pulled his hand back, opened the fist and waggled his fingers.

"Already read it," Maestro said, still staring Spook down.

Hm. Graphic novel.

Maestro broke eye contact and walked back to the stage.

What complicated game was afoot? And what might Reggie's part in it be? He returned to the graphic novel and tried to ignore Spook's confused stare.

Spook made a little noise in his throat. "That is so unfair." He stalked after Maestro.

Reggie touched his hat with one hand, still magically attached to his head thanks to Maestro. Working with these two might be fun, especially if he ever figured out their game. Who knew what he might learn?

He dropped the graphic novel on the bar and followed them. Had Maestro really read it or was he just teasing Spook? Or maybe he had figured out Reggie's other secret and was covering for him.

Never a dull moment anyway.

An hour later, Maestro stood in the ratty green room of the Biker Bar with Spook too close on one side and Muscle rather more comfortably several feet away on the other. He'd released the three remaining musicians, telling them not to leave town and was waiting for Spook to say something annoying.

Three, two, one. . .

"Daddy-O, you sooooo need to teach me that spell!"

Right on time.

The trio faced three magical video screens, for lack of a better term. Maestro had chalked rough squares on the wall, intoned the proper spells and, abracadabra, frames of white smoke had enclosed all three and images obtained from a handy magical eye showed on the "screens."

"When I'm bored and desperate for entertainment," Maestro shot back. "You need the eye of Horus for it to work anyway."

"Where do I get one?"

"You don't." Maestro scribbled hieroglyphics on the wall and the images concentrated on the three separate interviews they'd conducted. "He only had the two and he owed me a favor."

"Wait. *The* Horus? The god?"

Maestro stood away from the wall and brought up the right time frames. "What? You've never met any gods?" There'd been odd similarities to the interviews, and he wanted to compare them side by side.

Spook scoffed. "What?" He made another scoffing sound as though he was about to dismiss the implied accusation. "Are you kidding?" Another sound and a rather profound pause. "No."

Maestro was vaguely surprised he'd admit it.

"I can never tell if you just say shit like that to make me feel bad," Spook muttered. "I was unconscious when the fake Anubis tried to crawl out of my gut."

Oh damn. He hadn't intended to make him feel bad, but a professional distance was necessary. . . especially with Spook.

"Or maybe it's just true," Maestro deflected. "There."

The three screens focused clearly, each on one of the remaining band members in the same chair in the green room. They all seemed very uncomfortable.

"I need to ask some questions," Maestro's voice asked each of them off-screen. "What do you play?"

The boy on the left wore a plain black shirt and sported a blond crew cut. "Guitar." Even with the one word, his British accent was obvious. Maestro narrowed it to East End, London.

The shirtless boy on the right sported a curly, black afro. "Bass." Also British, but more cultured. Kid was slumming.

The girl in the center had curly, brown hair that seemed to have a life of its own. She wore a white wife beater over her sports bra. "Drums." Which explained a lot. Local girl. "My name's—"

"Neh, neh, neh. . ." Maestro's voice interrupted. "You play drums, your name's Drums. How long have you wanted her dead?"

The girl sputtered in shock. "What? I didn't—"

"Want her dead." All three said.

"I love her. . ." Bass insisted. His face fell. "Loved her. . . oh, my gods. . ."

Hm. Interesting that he said "gods" and not "God."

Unless they were far more intelligent than Maestro suspected, they told the truth.

However . . .

Drums fidgeted a lot. "Well, not really *dead*. . . I mean, I mean I didn't *kill* her."

What a strange version of honesty.

Maestro pursued it. "But you aren't shedding a lot of tears."

She fidgeted more. "I'm in shock, okay?"

Over in his screen, Guitar leaned forward. "What do *you* think happened?"

Bass leaned forward in his screen, too, and chorused Guitar. "Was it some kind of suicide bomb thing?"

Drums asked the same question a second later.

Maestro's voice, comfortably off-screen, asked them whether they thought Singer could make a bomb.

The boys answered together. "A bomb? Yeah, prob'ly. She was *wicked* smart."

"And so beautiful," Guitar added.

Drums laughed. "She was dumb as a rock. She couldn't build Legos."

"Were you in love with her?" Maestro's voice asked.

Bass thrust out his jaw. "Of course I was in love with her. We were together over a year."

Drums laughed and laughed and laughed at the suggestion.

Guitar hung his head. "Yeah. . . yeah, I was. . . but I was, you know, cool with her and Melvin."

"Melvin?"

Guitar looked up. "Oh. . . I mean, Bass. They were together and he's my mate, you know? And there's the band, right?"

In his magical image, Bass nodded off-screen at a hypothetical Guitar. "Of course, he fancied her, too." He leaned closer. "But. . . I mean. . . just look at him. What girl's going to fancy him? He's too pretty."

Maestro paused all three screens. The rest was more of the same. He stomped over to the bar and grabbed a whiskey bottle then added a glass for propriety's sake and poured himself a shot. By the time he opened his eyes again, Muscle had already poured him another. "Thanks."

"This is more complicated than it looks, isn't it?" For once, Spook's proximity didn't bother Maestro, who leaned back against the bar.

Three interviews and a whole lot of nothing. Maestro drew out a spectral analyzer he'd picked up in his travels. He offered it to Spook. "Here. Scan around and see what you get. Use your own stuff, too."

Spook stared down at the device. "What is it?"

"It reads EM and other forms of energy."

Spook randomly hit a couple of tabs on the screen. "You have some kind of jiggety-whatsit that detects ghosts?"

Maestro was not about to tell him that it was technology from two hundred years in the future and that, yes, among other things, it could detect ghosts. "Hey, if it's good enough for *Supernatural*."

"I love that show." Spook stopped and looked off to one corner. "They're so silly." He shook his head and tapped the screen. "These gadgets don't work, inspector. Sorry to break it to you."

Yeah. Give it time. "Just aim and shoot."

Spook wandered around, waving the device and tapping the screen.

Impatient, Maestro reached over his shoulder and pressed the correct app.

Spook stopped abruptly. "Holy wow." He waved the device around, and it made its usual sounds, emitting the beeps and whistles of the trash Spook had mentioned so no one would realize its origins.

Spook held it closer and stared at Maestro. "Where'd you get this?"

Maestro, whiskey bottle lovingly in hand, stepped closer and pointed the "jiggetty-whatsit" in the direction of the stage, away from Muscle. "I get stuff. Around. How does it compare to what you see on your own?"

Spook examined the screen. "Similar, actually. Residuals on all three suspects read. . . something. Not much."

Glad to have redirected Spook from Muscle's vicinity, Maestro pursued that train of thought. "Enough to explain what happened here?"

Spook waved the device around more. "Not even close. They're all dabbling in something. Spells, potions. . . maybe even tarot or Ouija boards. Nothing like what I got from the explosion." He tapped all the apps closed and held the device out to Maestro.

Maestro waved it off. "Keep it. You can use it to back up your own insights."

Spook stood up straight. "Okay. . . thanks."

Drat. He'd make a big deal out of it. To prevent Spook getting any affectionate ideas, Maestro spun away and moved to Muscle's side. "Want to make a couple of bucks? We might need some heads banged together."

Muscle pointedly cracked his knuckles.

Behind Maestro, Spook would be stepping back and crossing his arms, his petulance obvious.

Maestro turned to him. Spot on. "You called me, remember? You want to try to get paid on this one, be my guest, but I don't smell any money here. I'm guessing this one is going to be pro bono."

"Too bad it's not 'pro-boner,' am I right?" Spook grinned and held up a sad fist for a bump. The poor lad was desperate to connect.

Maestro couldn't encourage such nonsense. He walked away.

Probably not sure what else to do, or not even sure what the joke had been, Muscle followed.

Spook stood alone as the magical video screens dissipated. "I miss Ross."

"Maestro!" Spook called after the obnoxious prick in a soot-covered trench coat. "There's something else we should try." He sniffed the air then smacked his lips.

Essence of terrified ghost permeated the room.

"Although it may not help," he admitted.

"Well?"

Spook moved closer to the spot where the girl had died and

carefully opened the door he normally held closed. "I'm a medium." He waited for the inevitable joke about looking more like a small. Nope. Fine. "She's still here. I can help you talk to her."

"Well, that would have been handy to mention before we spent an hour grilling the suspects," Maestro grumbled.

Fear trembled over Spook's skin. "I'll be worthless for a while afterward." His hands trembled. "She's stuck in a loop. I doubt you'll get much out of her."

"How long's the loop?" Maestro asked. He'd been there before. Good.

"About five seconds," Spook estimated, "which is usually too short to help. Think you can pull her out of it?"

Maestro's face fell back to his carefully practiced blank wall that told Spook how hard he had to work to maintain it. Jerk.

"Yeah," Spook said before Maestro could respond. "It's going to suck a lot no matter what." He turned to Muscle. "You ever see someone channeling a ghost?"

The dark eyes opened a tiny bit, and Muscle shook his head.

Most people hadn't. Not the real thing. "I'm going to call her spirit into my body to possess me so Maestro can talk to her."

Muscle nodded.

"The girl is trapped at the moment of her death. In shock." This was going to suck rabid bullets. "If Maestro can yank her out of the loop, we can talk to her. If not, I'll have to force her out of my body. If I can't do that, I'll need you to knock me out so she pops out on her own."

Muscle looked surprised.

"Not my favorite day at the office either, big guy," Spook admitted, "but I can get stuck."

Muscle nodded and moved closer, raising an eyebrow.

From all Spook could tell, he was asking permission. "Go ahead."

Muscle nodded, stepped behind Spook, and placed a hand on either side of his neck.

Friendly massage?

No?

"Why are you doing that?" Spook asked.

Maestro answered. "He knows how to knock you out without having to punch you." The annoying man grinned. "Which is kind of too bad." Okay, that was just trying too hard.

"Remember that that was the last thing you said to me," Spook snarked back.

He opened to the girl's spirit.

Boom!

White hot pain and light and more pain. Every nerve in her body splintered into fragments and filled with acid. It lasted forever, until the pain. . . abruptly ended.

She gasped but couldn't feel the air in her lungs. All around her people applauded madly and screamed in excitement.

What had happened? Why couldn't she feel her body?

A fan screamed in terror when a head dropped into her hands. A head? What?

Wait. She knew that face in spite of the blood and the look of shock. That was her *face.*

She looked down. Smoke rose from a black smudge. Wait. Where was her body?

More screams.

She tried to scream, too, but no sound came out.

No.

No, no, no, no, no! She had to go back. She had to find a way to stop it.

Boom!

White hot pain and light and more pain. . .

Maestro muttered a spell.

Spook, who fell unconscious into Muscle's arms, finally glowed a clean white. Good. She was gone.

"Put him on the couch."

Muscle nodded and took the lad into the next room.

And she hadn't been any help at all.

Maestro sucked in a deep breath. He'd never seen that effect so close. Well, not when it was Morri. He'd seen dozens of possessed mediums up close, and he'd seen Spook in action at a distance, but standing inches away while Spook screamed at the explosion again and again and again had unnerved Maestro.

The screeches had been identical to the first time Maestro had seen—

No. He had to get his head together before the boy regained consciousness. Hopefully Muscle hadn't noticed his worry. Concern for a teammate was one thing, but, although the lad didn't know it, Spook was much more than just a potential teammate.

Maestro leaned in the doorway in his most nonchalant manner.

Strange. Muscle took such care in arranging Spook's limbs and even placed a pillow under his head. For a huge man, he could be very delicate.

"That's how he got his name, you know," Maestro said.

Muscle looked over.

"Channeling spooks." Maestro smiled. The lad had so much untapped potential.

Muscle cocked his head.

Damn. "I googled his exploits after we first met," Maestro lied.

Brat

The sun passed noon and cast sharp shadows through the trees. Turner enjoyed the warmth of the Texas sun. Her homeworld was much warmer than Earth, but shadows held a special, comforting place for her entire species.

For the three-hundred and twelfth time, Turner glanced from the photo of Mr. Snuggles with the tire swing in the background to the actual tire swing with Maestro's house in the background. She sighed. Coincidences irritated her and almost always pointed to a deeper truth.

Waiting also irritated her.

The proximity warning on her Doohickey warned her that Maestro's archaic transport approached.

She shook out her black duster, which considerable research into detective wardrobe assured her was nicely inconspicuous. She shoved the flyer into a pocket and stepped across the street as Maestro's microbus turned into the driveway.

"Maestro?" As she reached the middle of the lawn, both front doors opened. The side door slid aside, producing the same strange human who'd been sitting on Maestro's doorstep the night she'd met the investigator. Another lighted coincidence.

"I'm sorry," she said. "I didn't realize you'd have company."

Maestro appeared around the front of the microbus. "Turner? What are you doing here?" He glanced her up and down. "Nice coat. You blend."

Aha. Success! But she shouldn't let it show.

"I was hoping to have a word with you?" She pointedly ignored his companions. The one she hadn't seen before loomed quite large. "Shouldn't take more than a couple of minutes."

The smaller man coughed, but his action seemed to have some implied meaning.

Maestro glanced at him, apparently understanding the strange communication. "Sorry, Turner." He waved at the young human with strange communication skills. "This is Morrison James AKA Spook." He waved at the large human. "And this is Reginald Sato AKA Muscle. Guys, this is Elizabeth Turner—"

"AKA Elizabeth Turner. FBI." Remembering etiquette on this part of the planet, she moved forward to shake hands with the two humans. "I promise not to take much of his time." She'd studied the indirect communication standards of the English language and hoped her first attempt at a "hint" would work.

Maestro's abrupt inhalation and nod indicated success. "Of course," he said. "Guys, can you wait on the porch for a minute?" Without waiting to see if they intended to comply, Maestro led Turner toward the street. "I'd let you go in," he said to the two men as he walked away. "But I put a barrier curse on the place that'll make all your hair fall out and your skin turn green."

Turner glanced over her shoulder to see whether Maestro's associates would comply. The one named Spook seemed extremely excited and sort of skip-hopped across the lawn, waving one hand madly at the other male. His goal appeared to be the tire swing.

Maestro stood with his back to the house when he came to a stop.

"You really have a protection curse on the house?" Turner asked, trying to ignore the distraction of Spook leaping onto the swing and spinning so fast it flung him to the ground.

"Well, yeah, but not with the green skin and hair loss." He smiled. "Way too conspicuous. I just don't want the little girl nosing around my stuff."

"Girl?" Turner paid more attention to the smaller human. "The little one is female?"

"No. . . he just acts like it most of the time." Maestro scowled. "What is this really about?"

Right. Business. Ignoring the antics of the other two proved difficult as the big one pushed the little one on the swing.

"I'm investigating a couple of loons from the other side of the galaxy in a duck blind in San Antonio eating way too many cats." She dug the poster of Mr. Snuggles out of a pocket and held it up. Since the GP had such a prodigious file on Maestro, Turner likely didn't need to belabor the conversation with explanations.

"When I scanned the region, I found a lot of cats reported missing in your neighborhood, too. It seemed like too much of a coincidence." She handed the poster to Maestro. "When I showed the loons this poster, they admitted eating the represented feline. They claim they came to investigate a teleport they'd noticed."

Maestro glanced up from the poster. "Last week? When you dropped me off?"

Behind him, Muscle had grabbed Spook by the seat of his pants and twirled him around and around on the swing while Spook held onto the tire and grinned like a simpleton.

Turner nodded. "Exactly. But I don't accept that. That teleport was scrambled. From what I saw in the duck blind, they don't have the tech to detect it. I'm trying to deduce their true objective in your neighborhood."

Maestro shook his head and passed the flyer back. "I hate coincidences."

Good. Thank the shadows she wasn't the only one who didn't buy it. "Me, too. I imagine you keep a pretty close eye on the neighborhood and on your property. Any chance you noticed anything?"

Muscle pushed Spook on the swing again. Higher and higher the young human sailed. The big man had to jump now, to catch him. When his feet hit the ground, Muscle threw the swing so hard it soared completely over the branch and wrapped around it several times.

Spook and the tire swing ended up tied around the branch.

Muscle jumped impotently at the foolish figure high above.

"Not myself, no." Maestro started to turn back to the house. "But we can check my surveillance equipment. Come on in."

"I didn't detect any equipment." How could he possibly have equipment she couldn't detect?

Maestro gave her a very self-satisfied grin. "That's because it's magic, not tech."

Turner closed her eyes and let herself droop. "I hate magic."

Magic was irritating. It didn't follow rational laws. It didn't need to accept cause and effect. Nearly every advanced civilization in the galaxy had tossed it aside. Only Aeschtvich had ever managed to integrate magic and technology. . . but they were an isolationist planet, so no one else had to deal with their strange beliefs.

Turner opened her eyes. Maestro had already walked halfway across the lawn.

Spook and Muscle stood nonchalantly beside the door.

Turner glanced at the tree where Spook had so recently been entwined. The swing hung innocently without motion. Light it. Magic had to explain that as well. She plodded to the front door. Maybe this contact hadn't been such a good idea after all. "Stupid lighted magic."

Maestro's living room had been furnished from Goodwill. A low, rectangular 1970s couch with scratchy brownish upholstery rested beneath the one long window. Across from it, a matching love seat separated the open space from the dining room. Tall, dried bamboo poked up from behind it in a brick planter. A rather large painting of a bridge in gold-tones covered one wall.

An alcove on one side of the room held a wall of the same brick as the outside of the house. Three large whiteboards hung there and two separate partner desks dominated the space, each of which sported two rather current laptops. On the old-fashioned wooden desks, the computers immediately drew attention.

"Why don't you two grab computers and start googling the band?" Maestro waved at the two computer screens that faced each other in the middle. Best to get them working before Spook could start asking questions. Not a concern when it came to Reggie.

"Why do you have so many computers in here anyway?" Spook asked, hurrying to take his place at one desk. His eyes absorbed every detail, trying to find meaning in everything he saw. Apparently, he'd been too distracted by the hellsmouth in his gut to pay much attention on his last visit.

"Leftovers from a team I had." Maestro hoped to keep it as simple as possible. "I need to show Turner some surveillance footage." He moved into position between the two desks and centered for the spell casting. "And don't worry, Turner, they've both seen magic before."

She stopped at his shoulder, her sullen mood obvious when he opened himself.

"*An nec tamquam equidem*," Maestro intoned. "*Alia assum ad vim*."

Tiny spots of smoke swirled in the center of each white board. As Maestro continued the spell, they stretched to the edges of the boards, revealing surveillance screens courtesy of the Eye of Horus. Little crackles of purple lightning highlighted the clouds framing video footage of the yard.

Spook watched in rapt attention.

Turner rolled her eyes and cocked one hip in a very human display of annoyance.

Reggie worked on his assigned computer.

Maestro turned to Turner. "Time frame?"

"When did the cat go missing?" She didn't look at him, but was she just a wee bit impressed that magic could emulate technology so well?

Maestro suppressed a grin. "Two weeks ago, then." He closed his eyes. "*Vis populo nominati ei decore dissentiet*." The images blurred and swirled. When they cleared again, a sickly green colored the screens from the night vision filters. "Normal time or accelerated?"

Turner squinted in a way that told Maestro her optic lens was trying to analyze the scene. "Can you scan forward fast until a foreign object enters the image?"

Maestro nodded. "*Integre adipiscing dissentiunt*."

The leaves on the trees shook rapidly.

A distinct throat clearing drew everyone's attention to Reggie, who pointed at the computer screen in front of him.

"What did you find?" Maestro hunkered down beside the big man, and Spook rolled over.

Turner remained where she was, staring up at the video screens.

Reggie's search had uncovered thousands of photos of the band, a huge number of which displayed the two young men cavorting in nothing but their underwear, nearly always uninteresting tighty-whiteys. Shots of them on stage, on playground equipment, in and out of swimming pools, at fast-food restaurants, and none of them, to Maestro's way of thinking, in the least sexual. Just two boys playing around. Interesting. Bands usually went for sexy in their gratuitous self-promotion.

A definite scoff from Turner drew the attention of all three men. She stared down at the computer screen. "Why do supposedly adult males get such delight in cavorting around in their underwear? Is there a cultural reference I'm missing?"

Seriously? Most intelligent species in the galaxy? Neither of their companions was vacuous enough to miss her verbal slip.

"She's from Canada," Maestro said. Would that explain why she'd miss a "cultural reference" without any sort of foreign accent?

Reggie and Spook exchanged a knowing nod and a barely aspirated, "Ohhhhhh." Good. Canada would apparently explain her occasional odd mannerism.

Before Maestro could give her his take on the psychology of young men, Spook snapped his fingers a few times. His head cocked to one side as he closed his eyes.

"It lets them feel. . . like little kids again." He spoke in a quiet, rhythmic voice. "There's something innocent and child-like about it. Especially like this. . . nothing sex-u-al. Just uncomplicated and playful. Naked. . . is always seen as sexual, but a dude in his undershorts? Fruit-of-the-Loom?" He shook his head. "Nothing really sex-u-al about that."

He snapped the fingers again.

Wait. . . wasn't that a thing from the Beat era?

Reggie and Turner stared at Spook, perhaps a little dumbfounded by his insight.

"What?" Spook shrugged, probably annoyed at everyone's surprise that he could have insight. "I was a Beat poet."

Turner's eyes unfocussed for a moment. She was likely searching for Beat poetry in her data lens. She scoffed. "When? In the womb?"

Spook turned back to the computer screen. "Early 60's." He

reached over Reggie's shoulder and scrolled the images. "I hung out with Kerouac and Ginsberg." He looked into Reggie's face. "Hanged? Hanged out? Hung out."

Reggie nodded at "hung out."

Where exactly would this go? With the possible future created by the four of them meeting. . . would they get along? Would they hate each other? Could Maestro change things?

Turner laughed a bit, startling Maestro back to the present, but her humor faded when no one else laughed with her. She examined the three men. "Why am I the only one laughing?"

"I'm older than I look," Spook explained innocently.

Without thinking, Turner whipped out her Doohickey and scanned him. "You're a corpse."

Spook shrugged. "Zombie." He seemed accustomed to this part of the getting to know you cycle. "Although I hate that word. I prefer 'life-challenged American.'" He pointed at the device in her hand. "What's that?"

Maestro was about to field the question, but Turner covered for herself. "My iPhone has an infrared app. FBI, remember?" She regarded the screen, and thank the gods she had enough sense to keep the holographic interface turned off. "You're a zombie?" She pointed the device at Reggie.

Hopefully, it wouldn't be able to detect his irregularities.

"What are you?"

"Muscle's a badass!" Spook exclaimed and held a fist out to Reggie, who obliged him with a gentle bump.

In his current form, Reggie likely registered fairly normal to a cursory scan, and the spell on the hat should hide his horns. Time to divert her attention, though.

"Um. . . Turner? Is this what you were looking for?" Maestro gestured at the video screens.

Two of them showed the same spot in the backyard from different angles. A tall, thin man with huge eyes entered the shot and picked up a cat.

"Possibly." Turner raised an eyebrow and sniffed in surprise. "That's one of my loons. Bogg. He really likes cats."

The man rose and stroked the animal.

"Aww, that's sweet." Spook shrugged. "*I* like cats."

"Not as much as Bogg likes them," Turner said flatly.

Ah, that should prove interesting then. Would it would be a first step to joining the *ET* to the *Poltergeist* factions of this. . . team? Was he trying to create one of those? The word held unpleasant ramifications.

Maestro muttered a spell and a screen zoomed in. "Well, that's Mr. Snuggles anyway."

Turner opened her mouth, but then so did Bogg.

He tilted his head back and the lower half of his jaw unhinged and opened up grotesquely wide, stretching the skin as far as it likely could go.

"Whoa. . ." Spook said. "Didn't see that coming." But his surprise was on par with watching a somewhat unexpected play in a football game.

Reggie barely reacted.

Bogg lifted the cat over his mouth and dropped it in like a frat boy swallowing a goldfish.

Squish, crunch, squish.

So. . . the guys probably weren't supposed to see that.

Turner held up her Doohickey, and Maestro knew an immanent mind-wipe when he saw one, but Spook's enthusiastic shout almost made her drop the device.

"Oh, wow, daddy-o. You have to replay that!" He waved at the screen. "That was off the hook."

Turner glanced from Maestro to the other two men. "You're all rather blasé about the man who just swallowed a cat whole."

Spook scoffed. "Lady, I'm a zombie. He's a witch, and Muscle's a badass. I've spent almost sixty years fighting shit that would make *that*. . ." He waved at the screen. "Look like a Disney cartoon." He bounced up and down in his chair like a teenager. "Play it again. Come on. I wanna see him eat Mr. Snuffles again."

Turner crossed her arms incredulously.

Maestro shrugged and leaned really close. "Not a lot of difference between the supernatural and the extraterrestrial when it comes right down to it."

Then. . . it happened.

Bogg pulled out a Doohickey, made a big gesture and tapped the screen. A golden shower enveloped him and he evaporated.

Oops. Well, that right there demonstrated the difference between magic and technology.

Spook jumped forward, and even Reggie stiffened in his chair.

"What the seven hells was *that*?" Spook demanded. "He used a. . . a *thing*. He teleported with a. . . a *thing*?"

And there it was. While, technically, using an iPhone as the trigger for a spell wasn't out of the question, magic played havoc with most forms of technology, so if a device teleported the man, it had to be the machine itself.

And no one on Earth had that kind of device.

Might as well get it over with.

"Actually," Maestro said quietly, "it isn't a Thing, it's a Doohickey. Brand name."

Spook turned from his stare at the screen. "He wasn't a cat-eating demon was he?"

"If it's not a Doohickey, it's just shit," Maestro quoted from an ad, glad that this was really Turner's problem. He was protected from any repercussions by his status as a quantum jumper and Earth native. "It's like a galactic iPhone, but with much better apps."

"Replay that." Spook grabbed Maestro's arm and dragged him closer. "Did ET just phone home?"

Reggie joined their impromptu huddle, and Maestro waved a hand, rewinding the image.

"Awww. . . you boys are so cute like that." Turner's exclamation drew everyone's attention. "Group photo!"

Bother. Maestro closed his eyes and secured his memory with a quick spell. His mind would eventually recall anything mind-wiped, but why waste the time?

The flash from her Doohickey flared so bright it almost seared his eyes right through his eyelids. He opened them to discover the other men blinking a lot and sort of frozen in place. Would the Men in Black memory wipe work on them?

"Well, that solves that." Turner pocketed her Doohickey. "What you just saw—"

"What did you do that for?" Spook wiped his face and shook his head. "Ow." Then he opened his eyes wide and stared at her. "Oh my God, you just tried to mind-wipe us." He clapped his hands. "That is *sooo* cool." He patted Maestro's shoulder and pointed. "She's Men in Black."

He slipped past Maestro and reached for her device, apparently oblivious to any concept of personal space.

She waved him off. "Why. . . why didn't that work? It works on every known species in the galaxy." She back-peddled into the middle of the room.

Reggie finally came out of his freeze, but his sidelong glance at Maestro implied he'd been faking. Hm. Something to file away.

"It worked on him." Spook pointed at Reggie and reached up to pat his shoulder as well, but had to settle for patting his bicep. "Don't worry big guy, we'll catch you up."

Reggie glanced from one face to another as if confused, but, yeah, he was faking it.

Maestro raised an eyebrow at the big man, who blushed as much as possible for someone with such dark skin.

"I'm a corpse." Spook made another grab at Turner's coat. "My brain's a cauliflower."

Reggie's look of surprise at that comment seemed quite genuine.

"Not literally." Spook snatched at Turner again, and she slapped his hand away. "Can I get that app for my phone?" He rubbed his hand.

"Okay, Spook. . . please back off." As much as Maestro enjoyed the ET's discomfort, he'd had enough fun at her expense. "Turner has real work to do." He turned to the officer. "Sorry, Turner. He's a little overenthusiastic."

"They're not allowed to know *any* of this" Her horrified expression was very unusual for a Shifter. Uh-oh. "I'm going to get fired." She glanced from one face to another as if trying to divine some possible way to cover her tracks. "Oh, light it all to a star." She flapped her arms in submission and glared at Maestro. "I knew it was a mistake enlisting your help. I should have believed everything they said in your file. And you know what? No one's going to believe him anyway." She pointed at Spook. "He's exactly the kind that would report cow mutilations or. . . or an abduction."

Ouch. ETs had a real hang-up about abductions.

She stormed out the front door. It slammed loudly.

"Sorry I chased your friend away." Spook shrugged and made a huge apology face.

Maestro closed his eyes and followed her with his second sight.

She hurried to the side of the house.

"You have a file with the Men in Black?" Of course, Spook would be impressed. "That's cool."

Maestro held up a hand to silence the chatterbox.

Outside, Turner checked the area for cameras. "Lighted human body. Too many hormones." She paced a bit. "Giant frontal lobe with too many lighted chemicals and emotions." She stretched her neck to one side and it cracked loudly as it elongated far further than should've been possible.

Maestro opened his eyes to allow her some privacy while she shifted.

Huh. Spook simply waited. Patience hadn't seemed a possibility. "So," he asked, "Men in Black?"

Reggie saved Maestro the explanation with a gentle nudge. He pointed at the middle videoscreen. Ah. *That* was likely what Turner actually sought.

The man in the video Doohickeyed a window open and climbed in, slipping far too easily past Maestro's barrier spells. Hm. Was an ET actually using magic? It seemed unlikely.

"What happened to green skin and no hair?" Spook asked.

Maestro drew closer to the screen and rewound the image. "I lied, but I do have some pretty potent protection spells in place." When the image replayed, all he saw was the Doohickey used. No evidence of a barrier crossing spell. Blast. Nothing in a Doohickey should be able to circumvent a magical barrier.

Another screen showed the man striding purposefully through the house and into the basement, where another screen followed him into the curtained off portion of the room. Whoops.

"*No vix,*" Maestro muttered.

The images held position outside the partition. No reason to let the boys see what was behind curtain number one. Had the ET's visit been before or after he'd removed his investigation paraphernalia? As old as Maestro was, he had difficulty tracking increments of time less than a decade or so.

"You have surveillance there?" Spook asked.

"No, I don't need it," Maestro lied.

"Oh?" Spook raised one eyebrow. "Curiouser and curiouser."

"Dial it down, Hello Kitty. This is serious." Maestro waved the screens blank and moved into the middle of the room.

"What's with the Hello Kitty?" Spook complained. "You said no catch phrases."

"It's not a catch phrase," Maestro countered. "It's a nickname."

He could play it ten different ways. He couldn't tell these people what the ETs might have discovered, but he might need help after all. Normally, he made decisions in nanoseconds, but with so much at stake. . .and with Spook abruptly a part of it all. . .

The lad opened his mouth.

Maestro stopped him with a gesture.

Spook closed his mouth. At least he'd learned that much from Percy.

Damn. Well, one decision was easy enough.

"Muscle? I have a huge and possibly inappropriate favor to ask." He met the big man's eyes. "You have every right to say no since it doesn't involve hitting anyone or killing anything."

Muscle seemed to consider how much he trusted Maestro then nodded and stood a formal at ease, his hands behind his back, chin up.

Maestro pointed across the room.

Two pairs of eyes followed.

"That. . . is a bar," Maestro said with all the seriousness he could muster. "It contains Vodka, lime, cranberry juice, and, if we are very, *very* fortunate, ice. And stemware." He met Muscle's gaze. "Are you willing to make cocktails?"

Muscle considered the question with all due severity. He nodded.

"Thank you." Maestro pulled out his phone. With one decision made, the next fell into place.

"Did. . . you. . . just. . . crack a joke?" Spook stared at Maestro dumbfounded.

Maestro scoffed. "I never joke about cocktails."

Spook shook his head and hurried after Muscle, who was already pulling ice out of the mini-fridge

"Check and see if he has any little umbrellas," Spook said, further proving his reality as a little girl.

Maestro hit Turner's number.

"Who are you calling?" Spook sucked on an olive.

"I want to see if I can get Turner back here." He turned away from the others. "She needs to see this."

"I'd guess she's long gone by now." Spook's muffled voice told Maestro he'd stuffed a large number of olives in his mouth.

"I doubt it," Maestro said absently. "If I have her pegged, I'd guess she's still slithering around the neighborhood somewhere."

"Heh, heh. Slithering."

A loud choking sound erupted behind Maestro. He refused to look. The damn kid was already dead. How could he forget that he didn't actually need to breathe?

Apparently, Turner refused to change into something with an opposable thumb and pick up her phone.

"Look." Maestro only turned around after the choking subsided.

Spook stood there with a handful of green yuck.

Maestro sighed. "After you wash your hands, save everything you have on both computers. Leave it in a desktop folder on one of the computers. We'll pick it up in the morning after we talk to the dead girl's parents."

Muscle held out a wastebasket and a handi-wipe.

Spook dumped the olives. "Thanks." He took the wipe. "All four of these kids love themselves more than Justin Bieber. There is so much there." He wandered over to the computers, then turned back to Maestro. "Where you going?"

Maestro pocketed his phone. "She's not picking up. I'm going to see if I can find her outside." He left without a backward glance to convince them he trusted them but stopped just outside and cast his vision inside again.

Spook waved Muscle to his side. "Let me show you a trick."

Muscle moved to his side rattling the martini shaker.

Spook muttered a spell and touched the computer screen. The screen glowed and when he lifted his hand away, an exact copy of the screen followed it.

Wow. Kind of impressive. It looked like a two-dimensional hologram. The zombie rolled over to the other computer and pressed his hand to the screen. The images merged, and when Spook pulled away, a folder named "spooky stuff" appeared on the desktop.

"Ta-daa!" He performed a bow.

Damn, that was a trick Maestro actually wanted to learn. Leave it to the geeks. Maybe he had a chance to merge witchcraft and tech after all.

Muscle nodded his appreciation and smacked Spook on the back, surprising the much smaller man and knocking him forward. The chair slid out from under him, and he fell all the way to the floor onto his face.

So much for impressive.

Maestro opened his eyes and headed around the corner.

Spook was in seventh heaven. Well, not literally, but he was pretty stoked. Muscle made awesome martinis, and, for a man who had to be almost thirty, he acted almost like a kid. He'd even agreed to teach Spook a roundhouse kick.

So Spook stood in his stocking feet in the middle of Maestro's living room beside the giant, who was barefoot and demonstrated the kick, but really small and low.

Okay, Spook could do that. He tried it and sort of stumbled. "How do you keep your feet together when you spin?"

Muscle nodded. He demonstrated the first part of the kick and paused before the turn.

Okay, Spook did that much.

Muscle crouched down and grabbed Spook's feet. He held one close to the other, looked up and nodded with eyebrows raised.

"Okay, yeah. Feet together."

Muscle tapped a foot and pointed at it, apparently indicating that Spook should keep them that way, then he grabbed Spook's hips with both hands and spun him in place.

"Whoa."

Muscle held Spook's ankle and lifted his leg in the kick he'd been demonstrating.

Oh. That made more sense. Spin first and *then* kick.

Muscle nodded, seeming to understand that Spook got it. The ginormous badass rose and demonstrated the kick again.

Okay. Uber cool. Spook set, spun, lifted his leg. . . and. . . his foot connected with one of Maestro's ugly lamps.

The lamp flew across the floor and shattered.

Muscle cringed.

Spook patted his arm. "No, no. I got this." He pointed his index fingers at the fractured remains of the lamp. "*Prompta perfecto.*"

The shards of ceramic glowed and rose into the air.

Spook drew his fingers together and the lamp reassembled as it settled into place on the table. Spook picked up the ugly lampshade and placed it over the bulb. "He will never. ever. know."

Muscle grinned. He punched Spook's shoulder gently.

Spook repressed a moment of nostalgia. That moment was so him and Ross. But fifty years ago. Heck, sixty.

He sobered and went for the martini. No matter how much fun this new partner might be, Muscle was human. He'd grow old, too.

He'd die.

Spook swallowed the vodka and cranberry juice he'd spelled behind Muscle's back. No sense in divulging all his secrets.

Maestro tromped through the trees in his backyard until he found the pile of clothes he'd expected. Apparently, she hadn't even bothered to disrobe before shifting. Odd.

Human emotions always took some getting used to. Maestro could usually tell where Turner was on the timeline by how well she handled them. He muttered a spell and turned his back to the pile of clothes.

Wispy tendrils of smoke swirled about his feet before reaching out into the brush. A dozen coils slipped through the trees, branching and re-branching as they sought her out, calling her silently.

After a moment, the grass rustled a few feet away and an enormous rattlesnake slid between Maestro's feet to Turner's discarded clothing. She reared up like a cobra, growing in size as she did so.

Maestro politely kept his back to her transformation. In general, Shifters considered it impolite to shift forms in public, much the way 21st century humans felt the need for privacy when changing clothes.

A series of uncomfortable squelchy noises reached him, followed by the distinct cracking of bones as her skeleton reordered itself. Muscles stretched and pulled with a sound like angry rubber bands at their limits.

"Did you spell me?" Turner demanded.

Maestro turned to face her. "I called you. I let you know I wanted to talk. There was no coercion at all."

Turner frowned, wiping the leaves from her naked skin. "And the rest of them?"

Lizards and snakes covered the nearby shrubs, staring at Maestro expectantly. Well, she did have a reason to be suspicious. "They just think I have lots of bugs for them to eat." A simple gesture dispelled the spell and the animals slithered, crawled, and hopped away.

"How could you possibly know I would be a reptile?" Turner cocked a hip and crossed her arms.

Maestro tapped his forehead. "No frontal lobe. All the emotions and chemicals in the human brain take Shifters a while to get used to. The easiest way to balance it is to go reptilian for a while." He gestured at the pile of clothes at her feet.

Turner stared at his hand. "What?"

"You should probably dress," he told her. "I'd like to avoid the neighbors calling in the local constabulary."

"Archaic." Turner rolled her eyes but crouched down and retrieved her clothing.

"You'll get used to it," Maestro assured her. He'd learned to keep up with local niceties after the first hundred years or so, but he did often miss ancient Rome.

"Why did you call me?" Turner asked as she hooked her bra and slipped it into place.

"You were right about my place being compromised," Maestro admitted. "After you left, I found images of the ET breaking into my house. Not sure how he did that, since most of the protections are magic and tech shouldn't be able to touch them."

"Did he take anything?" She slipped into her shoes.

"No." He'd checked the time stamp and convinced himself the ET's visit had occurred after he'd already emptied the research alcove.

He led her to a blank wall at the back of the house. The land sloped sharply down, which exposed the basement. He waved a hand and the plain, dirty cinder blocks faded away to reveal sliding glass doors.

Turner Doohickeyed the spot and clicked her tongue. "I hate magic."

Once inside, he slid the door closed and it faded from view as dirty cinder block replaced it there, too. He shoved aside a few boxes, opening the same spell-casting area where he'd handled the hellsmouth in Spook's stomach.

He led Turner to the curtained partition in one corner.

"My visitor went for a very specific area of my house as if he knew what he was looking for." Maestro drew aside the curtain.

"He took everything?" She scanned the walls covered with marks where old photos had been.

"Nope," Maestro said. With the timestamp, he understood exactly what the ET had wanted and was truly grateful it hadn't been his research project. "A bit of luck there. I'd just done some spring cleaning and trashed everything on the walls and burned all the files. Everything here is brand new. . . and my new toys likely drew his attention."

Turner scanned the empty space again. "If this is yet another sophomoric joke. . ."

How would she react? Oh well, nothing for it. He clapped twice.

"I'd step back," he warned.

The walls flipped open and the best equipment money could buy off-world emerged. The floor panel slid aside and Maestro's glass table rose to waist height. The computer inside the table powered on and a hologram showing the GP cruiser in orbit popped up. His medical equipment dropped out of the ceiling and sort of waved a few arms around, just for show.

Turner's mouth hung open. Wow. A speechless Shifter was a rare sight indeed.

"How the light did you get your hands on this stuff?" she demanded at last.

"Space monkey from two hundred years in future." He touched a panel so the medical equipment would stop moving around. "Ook." He shrugged. "I sold a portrait Da Vinci painted for me and contacted a few people I know on Septimus Beta. Decided it was time to upgrade my operations."

"You realize. . ." She ran her Doohickey across the space and red flags appeared over every square inch of the alcove. "You realize I'm a cop, right? This violates. . . every single statute of the Primitive Planet Protection Pact."

"Nope." Maestro accepted the martini the doctor machine offered him. "None of that applies to me, remember? I'm a time traveler so I'm exempt from the prohibition on ET tech since nothing in the galaxy today is as advanced as what I had in my own era. I'm a local, so I'm also exempt from the quarantine, which means I get to come and go as I please. I get to live here and I get to keep my toys."

Turner whistled and put away her Doohickey. "You must have a really, really good lawyer in the future."

"Saundra Delacroix. She'll be the best in a few decades." Time travel complicated life. "Retroactive exemption will be, I believe, the crowning achievement of her career." Maestro held up the empty glass and the doctor machine retrieved it.

"So why show me all this," Turner asked, "other than to gloat over my impotence?"

"My guess is that the loons you're investigating in San Antonio are investigating you as well," Maestro said. "Even you didn't scan this stuff. They did. I have no idea how they got past the magical barriers, but they came in and checked it out. They left it intact, which means it's no big deal to them." He waved a hand and the equipment retracted into the various cubbies and sliding panels. "If they detected my equipment *and* the teleport two weeks ago then chances are they have the tech to know it was you who teleported me."

"Me?"

"The Galactic Police anyway."

Hands shoved into her pockets, Turner wandered into the now empty space.

"They have to be part of the Alpaca Consortium," Maestro said. Hopefully, she'd learned to listen to his suggestions.

She nodded. "After the collar we made, there's been an uptick in Consortium activity." She turned to Maestro. "Most likely trying to make up for their losses and proving a point."

She didn't need to elaborate. Like all *mafiosos*, the leaders of the Consortium would want to make sure everyone in the galaxy knew they were still up and running in spite of the impending trial. Which brought up an interesting point.

"Why are you still on Earth?" Maestro asked. "I'd think you'd be in deep cover somewhere. Without your eyewitness testimony, the case could fall."

In spite of his own involvement, the testimony of a local, even scientifically achieved testimony from the psychic link they'd used, wouldn't be enough without Turner's corroboration.

She smiled. "What's the last place in the galaxy anyone would think to look for me?"

Well, she had a point there, but it was still a ballsy move.

"In the same outfit, though?" he asked. "Wouldn't it make more sense to wear someone else?" Shifters were the only race advanced enough to recognize one of their own once they changed shape.

Turner frowned then held her arms out, glancing at them appreciatively. "I like this outfit. It suits me."

Hm. A Shifter attached to a specific shape. And he'd met her in it in every time line. Hm. Maestro let it go. He gestured towards the outside door, and it reappeared.

A series of thumps from upstairs sounded like elephants playing hopscotch.

Damn. Maestro pointed at the ceiling. "Look. I'm sorry I set you up to reveal the existence of ETs to those two."

She crossed her arms and held her silence, one eyebrow raised.

Okay, with her he could be honest. . . to a point.

"I knew you wouldn't go along with it," he said, "but the thing is it's been a while since the Galactic Police maintained an ongoing presence on this planet. Me, and a few people like me, have been the last line of defense for the entire world. I like knowing I can call in the big guns if I hear that something's going down, so I'm hoping you and I can work together once in a while. But the thing is, I do the supernatural thing, too, and I'm also tired of doing that on my own."

Something crashed upstairs.

Maestro shook his head. "If I want those guys to trust me at all, I can't lie to them about every aspect of my life. Technically, I'm protected by the Pact. Since I'm a local, it's no different from someone getting abducted and telling his friends about it over a beer."

"Abductions are an urban legend." But she almost smiled.

"Point taken." Had he won her over? "The thing is, if I'm going to play both sides of the fence, they need to know that ETs exist. We can keep telling them you're FBI. They don't need to know you're ET. The whole Men in Black thing should keep them entertained enough they don't dig."

Turner sighed. "I apologize for the emotional outburst." Her hands wandered to her pockets. "And I could use some assistance on the duck blind situation. To be honest, as much as it horrifies the anal retentive Shifter in me, it's kind of handy having a local who's exempt from the Pact."

Was bringing these three together a good idea or a bad one? Maybe if he could keep an eye on them, knowing what he knew, he could change things.

"It did come in handy two weeks ago," Maestro said. He slid the door open. "Look, I want you to see the supernatural part of it. I know you hate magic, but it could help to have a devil's advocate. We're meeting the parents of a victim tomorrow morning. I'll send you the info. You could meet us there."

She stepped outside, turned to him briefly, and nodded.

As he slid the door shut, he heard the distinctive noise of a skeleton rearranging itself. . . so at least she'd be more settled the next day. Too much time in any one form was bad for Shifters.

Chat

Reggie loved mornings. Back home, mornings had meant training sessions with his friends then breakfast and meditation. Perhaps he would swim a few miles or soak in the hot springs with Ōkami and Sarutahiko. He had had structure and companionship before breaking into the work of the day.

Since his arrival in the States, he had kept the structure with exercise and meditation, substituting the swimming with running because people had noticed his unusual endurance and speed in the local pools.

But he missed the companionship. He missed his brothers and sisters at the monastery. He missed Sensei.

With a deep sigh, he closed his inner eyelids and looked up at the sun. What time was it? So many people outside the monastery had casual relationships with time. He'd spent his entire life with a fastidious attention to his schedule and tardiness seemed a bizarre ritual of rebellion.

He adjusted his posture and prepared to meditate. No one inside the dead girl's house had noticed him sitting on the bottom steps of the wide front porch, so he might as well perform some centering exercises while he waited.

Footsteps approached from opposite directions on the sidewalk. From the sound of them, Maestro approached from the south and Agent Turner from the north. They were both exactly on time.

The gate creaked open and Turner offered a thank you that meant Maestro must have opened the gate for her. They approached Reggie's position side by side.

A third set of footsteps, softer because they wore some kind of rubber-soled shoe but moving at nearly a sprint, raced from the north.

They stopped for a moment then landed hard on the walk leading up to the porch, so Spook must have jumped the fence rather than opening it.

A screech startled Reggie into opening his eyes in time to see Spook slide to a halt and drop an arm around Maestro's shoulders. Smoke rose from the ground beneath Spook's feet.

Maestro scowled, and Spook removed the arm.

"How did you make that sound?" Turner demanded.

Spook waggled his eyebrows mysteriously.

Reggie grinned but hid the expression behind a hand and covered it with a cough. Did Maestro sincerely loath Spook's childish antics or did he secretly approve? The man was harder to read than anyone Reggie had ever met. From what he could tell, though, his boss liked Reggie well enough, and that was all that really mattered.

"Muscle." Maestro nodded and extended a hand.

Reggie rose and took it, shaking it carefully with a small bow.

Maestro's wink told him he had "toned it down" enough.

Maestro faced the group. "Okay, Mr. and Mrs. Singer are grieving. Let's all be—"

"Wait," Spook interrupted lightly, "her name really was Singer? What a gas."

Maestro scowled. "Amy Singer. And let's be respectful, people."

Spook nodded an exaggerated, fakey agreement.

Maestro passed Reggie to mount the stairs. A yellow piece of paper with the words "kick me" fluttered from a piece of tape on Maestro's shoulder.

Turner snatched the note and frowned at Spook.

"But he's so mean," Spook whispered.

Turner glared at him and followed Maestro.

Reggie smiled. He couldn't stop himself.

Spook nudged Reggie's arm. The strange young man pasted an exaggerated serious expression onto his face and stopped just behind Maestro with his hands folded, so Reggie matched his pose, if not his expression, behind Turner.

Maestro rang the doorbell, and everyone settled in to wait.

Reggie hadn't enjoyed a morning this much since he'd left Japan.

A long, slow whine broke the silence, like a balloon losing air, or—

No. It couldn't be. . . then the smell hit Reggie's very sensitive nose, and he involuntarily stepped back.

Spook matched his move, lifting a hand to cover his face. He stifled a laugh as well.

Maestro exhaled a scoff. "Erm. . . outside. . . *Canada*. . . we try not to do that in public."

Turner scowled at him. "What? It's a perfectly natural—"

"I know, I know. . ." Maestro stared directly ahead. "And I know that in. . . Canada. . . one has to adjust to abrupt changes in. . . mass and air pressure. . . but here in the U.S.—"

The door opened. A middle-aged woman with red eyes and her hair in a bun smelled of grief and exhaustion. The fact that she seemed unsurprised at their arrival spoke to the number of strange people who must have rung her doorbell recently.

Maestro held out his card. "We're so sorry for your loss."

She read the card with a sigh so soft that Reggie was likely the only one who heard both the recognition and the resignation in it. The bereaved mother stood aside. The front room smelled like wilting flowers and far too many perfumes and colognes.

The silence of grief filled it from wall to wall.

"I don't know what you hope to accomplish that the police can't," Mrs. Singer said. "I really don't believe in anything supernatural, other than my faith in the Lord Jesus Christ."

Maestro froze. His sweat started up, sharp and nonplussed.

Turner stepped forward. Her face held a perfect expression of compassion and concern. She took the grieving mother's hand.

"Your daughter exploded, Mrs. Singer." The agent's voice held a warmth and love totally at odds with her words. "While I hate all their Disney Princess hooey balooey magic nonsense more than anyone on the planet, there was no incendiary device, no trace of explosives of any kind." She squeezed the hand and pressed her lips together. "Even I have to think there might be something more than completely natural at work."

She patted Mrs. Singer's hand and stepped away, passing the torch back to Maestro with a subtle nod.

"And where is Mr. Singer?" Maestro asked, pointedly ignoring Turner's words.

"I'm afraid he isn't speaking to anyone." Mrs. Singer sat in a high-backed chair, holding her posture ram-rod straight. Her face was stony with all the obvious signs that she only maintained her composure with great effort.

"I understand what a difficult time this must be—"

"You *don't* understand." Mrs. Singer glanced to one side. A hallway. Mr. Singer's bedroom? "He's not speaking period. The doctor says he's in shock. He hasn't said a word since. . ." She sighed. "He just lays there and mutters to himself."

Reggie faced the hall and closed his eyes. In spite of the overpowering cologne, he could smell the faintest hint of some kind of magic. He had to let someone know. From Spook's lack of reaction, Reggie could only guess that the other scents in the room masked it from him. But how could he. . . would anyone listen?

Darn it. He had to do something. While Maestro spoke words of consolation, Reggie touched Turner's arm.

She turned to him, startled. Well, it *was* the first time Reggie had touched her. She raised an eyebrow.

Reggie nodded in the direction of Mr. Singer's room and silently mouthed the word "magic."

The agent held his eyes with absolutely no expression then they flicked back and forth as if she saw something Reggie couldn't.

"Where is your bathroom?" she asked the bereaved mother.

Maestro cast her a dark look.

"You said." Nothing in her face, tone, or smell gave away her true purpose. Impressive.

Maestro rolled his eyes then smiled at Mrs. Singer. "Ma'am?"

"Down the hall on the right." She pointed down the same hallway Reggie had indicated. How did Turner know the house layout?

Silently, she left the room.

Maestro dropped to one knee beside the mother's chair. "I apologize for her, Mrs. Singer. She's Canadian."

Understanding lit Mrs. Singer's face, and she sighed with an elaborate series of nods and an affirmative noise.

Turner escaped down the hall, glad to be away from the grieving woman. Her night as a snake had left her cool and collected, and all the emotions in Mrs. Singer were annoying. So were Spook's childish antics and Maestro's equally childish need to constantly rebuff the young man. . . or zombie, life-challenged. . . whatever.

Ugh. Magic. And how had the bodyguard sensed it? Was there more to him than met the multiband scanner? Her data lens had tracked down the house blueprints, but that was about all she could get from it.

She pulled out her Doohickey and played it up and down the hall. Nothing. She fiddled with the settings, opening it wide to all energy sources and dialed it to discard everything but the absolute faintest traces.

Wait. She had a blip. She adjusted the device further and narrowed it down. Something coming out of the open door on the left. The Doohickey couldn't isolate the energy signature, but at least she could detect it.

Hm. So that's what magic looked like? Light it, maybe she needed to find a contact who knew more about Aeschtvick.

Soft muttering from the open door reminded Turner that she had her Doohickey with an open holographic screen on a protected planet. Chameleon app or no, she had to make sure she never forgot her responsibility to avoid contamination. Even if Maestro made that almost impossible.

Poking her head into the bedroom, she slid the device into a pocket.

Mr. Singer lay on the bed, muttering and shifting awkwardly. He seemed paler than the photos she'd found online and had dark, sunken eyes.

"I'm so sorry," he muttered. "It's all my fault. . ."

Hm? Why would he possibly think his daughter's death was his fault? What part might he have played?

She scanned him quickly. As suspected, so much medication coursed through his veins that she could likely fly him on a tour of the solar system without him thinking anything of it.

Perhaps that presented an opportunity. She slipped into the room and gently closed the door.

She'd accessed Maestro's genetic material from the dead girl. She sampled DNA of almost every lifeform she encountered. Cultural habit. You just never knew when you'd need that perfect outfit.

She closed her eyes, cracked her neck, and brought up an image of the girl in her mind, sifting through the hundreds of samples in her memory. Since Singer had been fairly close to the size and shape of the outfit Turner already wore, the shift was nearly painless and silent.

Okay, now she had to sell it. She bent at the waist and let her hair hang loose while she dried and stiffened it.

When she pulled up to her full height, her hair surrounded her in a billowing cloud. Two seconds with her Doohickey mapped a hologram to her face rendering it a death mask, with black around her eyes and sunken cheeks. She added eldritch lighting and wafting smoke to complete the supernatural effect.

"Dad-dy?" she moaned. "Dad-dy, are you awake?"

"Baby?" Mr. Singer opened his eyes. When he spotted Turner in the guise of the ghost of his daughter, he pushed himself to sit up. "Baby? Is that really you? I. . . I thought you were dead."

Really? The ghost make-up and eldritch lighting effect weren't a dead giveaway?

"I. . . I am, Daddy," she moaned, glad for once that Peter had forced her to watch all those horrible Earth movies so she knew how humans expected this sort of confrontation to go. She moaned loudly and waved her arms around, letting the smoke effect sell it.

"I'm so sorry, baby," Mr. Singer called out. "I didn't mean for this to happen."

A-ha. Would it work? "Why do you blame yourself, Daddy?" she asked. "How could it be your fault?"

"If I hadn't shown you my damned book of shadows." He

reached toward her, tears streaming down his face. "If I'd never shown you magic. . . none of this would've happened. I should burn it."

"Now, now. . ." Turner reassured quickly. "Let's not be hasty. . . uh. . . Daddy. You couldn't have known what would happen." What the hell did people do with books of magic? Safe deposit box? "I'm sure you've hidden it so no one else can find it. . ." Think, think, think! ". . .in the usual spot?"

He flailed at a painting of flowers. "It's back in the safe where it should have stayed." He hunched over, weeping and covering his face. "I'm so sorry. . ."

Mission accomplished. Turner pointed the Doohickey at Singer and hit her knockout app. No need to wipe his mind. With all those drugs in his system, no one would believe a thing he said. The man fell onto his back, sound asleep.

Turner scanned the painting, pulled it away from the wall on its hinge, and unlocked the safe. The "book of shadows" was enormous. It had to weigh forty pounds. Well, there was more than one way to skin a cat.

Wait. Where had she picked up that grotesque expression? Bogg?

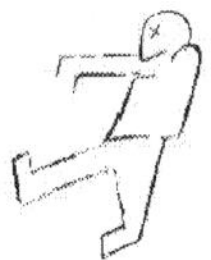

Why the hell was Turner taking so long to fart? Maestro glanced at the empty wrist where he'd worn a watch for over a hundred years.

Mr. Singer's voice reached the living room, and his wife sat up straighter. With such a stiff stick already up her back, how did she manage that?

"Something's wrong." She hurried to the same side hallway Turner had used.

Muscle examined a large Chinese vase there, and his considerable bulk completely blocked the hall.

Mrs. Singer cleared her throat politely, and Muscle turned to her, startled.

Well, *apparently* startled. The way he faced her managed to appear accidental, but he still blocked the doorway.

"Excuse me, please," she said.

Muscle glanced over one shoulder in the direction of the voices down the hall. He turned to one side. . . but still obstructed the hall.

She shifted to go around him, and he jumped to one side to move out of her way at the exact same second so he once again barred her passage. His ability to skip out of her way while still blocking the hall while they danced back and forth was impressive.

But why would he bother?

Mrs. Singer finally managed to slide past the huge man, who focused on Maestro with silent intensity.

Maestro opened his third eye.

"Blast it." He dashed after Mrs. Singer. There was magic back there.

At his shoulder, Spook sniffed the air, then sneezed. "Polo isn't strong enough you have to take a damn bath in it?"

The bathroom stood open, dark, and odorless.

"I'm sure there's a perfectly logical explanation." Maestro called. What could Turner *possibly* be doing with the bereaved father? No, he shouldn't try to imagine it. Every horrifying, logical, ridiculous possibility frightened him more than the last.

Mrs. Singer opened the door. "What do you think—"

The poor woman stopped so abruptly Maestro had to brace himself against the door jamb to avoid running into her.

Of course, Spook crashed into his back.

Thank all the gods Muscle had coordination enough to keep the scene from blowing right past Abbott and Costello into the Three Stooges.

After shoving Spook away, Maestro focused on Mrs. Singer, who stared wide-eyed into the room. Dear God, what. . .

Turner sat on the bed beside the deeply unconscious form of Mr. Singer, her back to the door.

"He hasn't slept a wink since it happened," Mrs. Singer whispered.

Turner turned. Tears covered her face. Her makeup ran freely down both cheeks. The sorrow on her face was so sincere, Maestro had a hard time reconciling this with the woman who'd pretended to have a dead identical twin sister two weeks earlier.

"He was muttering," Turner said quietly, her eyes locked with Mrs. Singer's. "So sad, restless. I had to tell him how sorry I was. I lost a child. A son." She turned to Mr. Singer. "Then he fell asleep."

"You wonderful angel." Mrs. Singer clasped her hands over her mouth and rushed to Turner's side.

The agent reached out to the woman, drawing her to sit on the bed.

Maestro wanted to applaud.

A few minutes later, Maestro led the team down the walk while Mrs. Singer waved at them from the porch. He hadn't wanted to push his luck with a complete search of the house so soon after Turner had won the woman's trust. They could always return later that day or the next to find out what had generated the faint magical aura in the bedroom.

"Why are you touching me?" Turner said curtly.

Maestro stopped. Now what?

"I'm so sorry." Spook's hand rested on her shoulder. "What you said in there. We didn't know." He squeezed the shoulder.

"Know what?" Turner shook her head with annoyance on her perfectly made up face. Then the light bulb went on. "Oh, that. I lied. I don't have any children." She scoffed. "Don't be such a little girl about everything, and why are you still touching me?"

Spook jumped away. "No touch rule. Got it."

She faced Maestro. "I made a copy of his 'book of shadows'." She said it with finger quotes and everything. "It sounded. . . 'witchy'."

Nice—Wait. What?

"What book of shadows?" Maestro demanded. "How'd you get his. . . What?"

Turner held up her disguised Doohickey.

"You copied an entire book of shadows with that?" Spook made a grab for it. "You were in there one minute."

"Men in Black, remember?" She held the Doohickey out of his reach, although he did jump once or twice to try. "Keep up, zombie lad."

She turned and stalked away, but Maestro managed to match her stride. Her walk had all the strength and fluid movement of a dragon. Impressive.

"Liking the snake?" he said too quietly for anyone else to hear.

"I fucking love snakes," she replied.

But how had she known to look in the bedroom in the first place? She couldn't have noticed the magic there or even thought to look for it on her own.

Wait. Muscle had blocked Mrs. Singer. To give Turner a few more seconds? Had he known? If so, he must have been the one to set Turner on the scent.

Of course! The kid smelled magic. He made faces he made from time to time. Maestro had to remember not to underestimate Muscle just because he kept so quiet.

And Turner hadn't allowed her prejudice against magic to interfere with the investigation.

Was all that cooperation good news or bad?

Drat

Reggie's new companions thoroughly confused him.

Maestro held Agent Turner's cell phone and swiped the screen, paging through the shadow book she had copied in the dead girl's house.

The images from the screen appeared magically in the air through some spell Maestro had cast, although the "spell" carried no magical scent. Also, no matter how good her apps, no iPhone could copy through a closed book, yet Maestro pretended her Men in Black excuse made sense.

"It's all hedge witch magic," Reggie's boss said.

Turner crossed her arms and scowled, which seemed a nearly permanent posture. "Hedge witch?"

She smelled wrong. Not dead like Spook, but like nothing Reggie had ever encountered. She smelled human enough. . . but at the same time. . . not quite.

Maestro spoke to her without taking his eyes off the projection. "Sorry. . . nature magic. Healing spells, prophylactic spells, one spell to make sure puppies all come out brown." He frowned. "For whatever reason."

Spook stared at them, one then the other, as if he knew they shared some secret. "You copied the entire book in one minute?" He must consider the story a lie, as well. Would he call them out on it? No?

Therein lay Reggie's confusion. They all had secrets one from the other, and they all told lies. So why did they want to work together?

"There!" Turner pointed at the floating image. "That torn edge. A page is missing."

"I wonder what that was." Maestro peered closer. "There's nothing in the book that comes close to the power needed for what happened."

"Let's see what I can figure out." Turner reached toward the image as if she could touch it then pulled back abruptly. "Doo—" She glanced at Spook. "Do, do, doo. . ." she sang.

She yanked the iPhone away from Maestro who regarded her with a raised eyebrow. "What I can *do,*" she said, "with my *phone*, because that's where all the apps are, of course."

Because that wasn't ridiculously suspicious.

The image shifted into negative.

"Open three dimensional data package," she said in a sing-song voice, tapping the screen randomly. "Create representation in 2D." Her voice normalized. "A page actually has depth; we just don't usually think of it that way." Back to sing-song. "Select all ink on page. Select all depth generated by selected ink. Remove both."

Why would she pretend to tap the commands? Her movements were obviously random. Obvious to Reggie anyway. Why pretend her phone didn't just have good vocal recognition? Canadian didn't explain her bizarre relationship to technology.

"What is she doing?" Spook asked.

Maestro scowled at him. So much scowling.

"Highlight remaining impacts," Turner continued.

On the screen, faint ridges and troughs appeared on the page then letters popped into view.

Oh. Her objective made sense. She was—

"The writing from the missing page left an imprint on the next page," she said. "I simply erase the existing writing and. . ."

Text appeared on the screen.

Spook laughed. "She's doing the Men in Black version of scribbling on the next page of a memo pad."

Turner glared at him. "What's he gibbering on about?"

With a sigh, Maestro grabbed a note pad, wrote on it in ink, ripped the page off and tossed it. He scribbled on the next page with a pencil and the writing appeared in negative. He handed the memo pad to Turner.

She glanced it, then glared at Spook. "What I did is much more sophisticated than—"

Spook tsked. "It's not a contest."

As far as Reggie could tell, with these three, *everything* was a contest. But what was the prize?

"An attraction spell," Maestro said loudly, drawing everyone's attention. "It's nothing more than a love hex. Shouldn't have blown anyone up."

Spook moved closer to the floating image. "It uses chocolate and roses, and that's what I tasted. This could be a side spell, the background energy. I'd guess she was trying to draw in a larger crowd."

"Drat." Maestro waved the image away. "Dead end. First of all, thank you, Turner. I couldn't have eliminated this so fast. We would've wandered down a blind alley for days. Secondly, shit." He shrugged. "This isn't the final answer." He grabbed his trench coat. "Okay, time to talk to the boys in the band." He slipped into the coat and pointed at Reggie and Spook. "Can you two handle that while I help Turner with something?"

Spook perked up. "What? Is it Men in Black stuff? Pussy eater?" He grimaced. "Okay. Sorry. That wasn't meant to be as graphic as it came out."

"Just go interview the boys," Maestro said.

Spook raised an eyebrow.

"Again. . . you called me in on this one," Maestro remarked coldly. "You want my help, do what I tell you; otherwise, have fun on your own. I'm not going to waste my time with pretty please with sugar on it every time I need you to do something."

Goodness. Reggie knew how to take orders, but Maestro's recrimination seemed harsh for a new recruit.

"Dick." Spook turned on his heal and slammed out the door.

While such direct insult shocked Reggie, he could not entirely disagree with the sentiment.

"Rather harsh for a reason?" Turner asked, apparently also surprised at Maestro's tone.

"Yes." The boss raised an eyebrow at Reggie.

Oh! He should go. As he passed through the door, Reggie heard a snatch of conversation.

"We'll need to drive if we're going to check out the duck blind," said Maestro. "They detected the teleport last time."

Teleport?

Bam! Reggie bumped into Spook, who was already reentering the house. The small man apologized, then brushed past into the living room.

"All right, you unmitigated douchebag," he said, "I am not. . ."

Reggie peeked over his shoulder.

The room stood empty.

"Maestro?" Spook scanned the room. "Dick."

But the others had gone.

Spook seemed so upset by Maestro's dismissive comments, Reggie grabbed him around the neck and ruffled his hair. That had always helped Reggie feel better, back when Sensei had actually stood taller than him a couple of years ago.

Wait. What was that? Reggie sniffed. Teleport? Smelled like it, but like no teleport he'd scented before.

What confusing new friends.

The Oriental Gardens in San Antonio were one of the most beautiful spots in the city. Soft waters dotted with peaceful coy and rippled by a soft breeze held the bustle and noise of the city at bay.

Well, except for the police siren. And the screaming baby.

Maestro glanced at Turner as she tapped the screen of her Doohickey. The city sounds faded to nothing. As far as anyone nearby was concerned he and his companion had done the same.

"Doohickey," she said. "Please show us the ship parked directly in front of me."

"Yes, Elizabeth."

She glanced furtively at Maestro as the 2D screen rezzed into position. Heh. She had her Doohickey programmed for pleasantries like please and thank you. How human.

Viewed through the screen, the duck blind appeared just as Turner had described it: a glass brick. The tall, skinny ET named Bogg, who'd swallowed a kitten whole, worked inside. If Maestro had it right, he was brewing tea in a glass beaker.

"It does look harmless enough." Maestro checked the readings at the edges of the screen which displayed the basic composition of the duck blind. Nothing interesting.

"But their tech is far beyond what it should be for an operation like this." Turner adjusted the screen and a second window opened with a close up of the ET.

Yep. Tea. According to the Doohickey, Bogg was a long way from home. An Estragonite. He brought his beaker of tea to a blank stretch of wall that slid out of the way as he approached. A largish room appeared beyond.

"See?" Turner exclaimed. "I don't even register that chamber." She fiddled with the screen. "Wait."

Three more rooms appeared on the screen. Also basic bricks, but comprised of metal. What was in there?

"Well, I'll be," Maestro muttered.

After a moment, Turner turned to him. "You'll be what?"

"Colloquialism." He fiddled with the screen. Could Turner's Doohickey could see through metal? Nope. Drat.

"You'll be a colloquialism?" Her brow had furrowed.

"What's the plan," Maestro redirected, barely able to suppress an eye roll. "The boys'll be checking in soon."

"That should be interesting." She gave her attention to the screen as the skinny cat lover wandered into the main room. "Does the big one talk at all?"

Maestro chuckled. "Not so much."

Bogg drank his tea and watched the surveillance screens.

"We need to get in there," Turner said. "Without him."

Bogg waved a hand and one of the surveillance screens switched to a YouTube video of a kitten playing with a ball of string. The ET wiped his mouth.

"He really does like cats," Maestro pointed out, raising an eyebrow. Would she get the hint?

Turner rolled her eyes. "Fine. I'll lead him off."

Okay, enough fun. "Let me give it a try," Maestro said.

He closed his eyes and opened up to the surrounding bamboo forest. A dozen cats raised their ears. "*Id mollis delectus.*"

The spell projected the sound of a can opener.

The cats hurried over.

The ET inside glanced from one surveillance screen to another as they filled with cats. In one screen, a tiny white ball of fluff sat down and stared directly into the camera.

It mewed.

Its eyes opened just a wee bit wider than should have been physically possible.

Turner favored Maestro with a withered glance.

"Hey, if it works, right?"

Bogg wiped his mouth and set down the tea. "Phineas said no."

The kitten lifted a paw and proceeded to lick itself seductively, still staring directly at the screen.

"Phineas said not many." The ET headed to the airlock.

"You have no shame," Turner muttered, but she smiled.

"I lived through the most decadent phase of the Roman empire," Maestro said blandly. "Shame doesn't enter into it."

Bogg hurried from the duck blind as the bridge extended to the edge of the pond.

Maestro waggled the fingers of one hand, and the cats all hurried off, but not so fast as to dispirit their pursuer.

"Oh, bother." Bogg rushed in pursuit.

Maestro chuckled. "He even left the door open for us."

"Bless his heart." Turner derezzed her screen and pulled up a standard scan app.

"Hey for the appropriate cultural reference." Maestro followed her into the duck blind.

Inside, the main—easily visible—room seemed lab standard, but in the previously invisible side room—

Twenty human corpses lay on exam tables.

Maestro whistled. "Looks like they had more than Mr. Snuggles on the menu." He let Turner move ahead then pulled out his own Doohickey behind her back.

"It has to be more than that." She examined the data on a couple of corpses. "This many kills can't go unnoticed. This is a huge risk."

"As far as I know," Maestro said, fiddling with his own Doohickey, "there hasn't been a rash of missing persons." The cause of death appeared. "Oh."

"Oh," Turner said.

Maestro hurriedly pocketed his Doohickey.

"'Oh' what?" they asked simultaneously.

Maestro pressed two fingers to his temple in the standard pose of a psychic doing his thing. "What did you get? Magic is usually fuzzy on this sort of information."

Turner nodded and fiddled with her screen. "I doubt they wanted these corpses for food. Diseases like HIV tend to make the meat taste all hinkey." She showed the screen to Maestro.

He feigned surprise. "AIDS victims? What do they want with those?" These corpses couldn't have been easy to acquire without someone noticing. "Whatever. We don't have a lot of time. Copy the data and let's get out of here."

"Get out of here?" a stocky man said from the airlock. "But the hosts have only now arrived at the party."

Turner took point with the newcomer. "Phineas. Bogg." She gestured at the corpses. "You realize your permit doesn't allow collecting a sentient species."

As if they had expected it to do so. Maestro muttered a spell and brought a hand behind his back. It wouldn't do to let them see it glow.

The new ET, Phineas, hemmed and hawed. "Yeah. . . About that—" He yanked a weapon from behind his back and fired.

"*Electram tractatos.*" Maestro swung his hand forward, creating a shield.

The laser hit it and sprayed harmlessly.

Turner and Maestro dove for cover in the morgue.

Lasers split the air through the doorway.

"You realize that firing on a member of the Galactic Police," Turner shouted as she slipped a hand around the doorway and fired blindly, "is a serious offence and will definitely compromise your ability to gain future permits."

Maestro lost concentration and his lightning bolt fizzled. "Seriously?"

"I have to follow protocol." She fired through the door a few more times during a brief lapse in deadly laser blasts.

"Tell you what," Phineas called out. "Come on out and we can discuss it."

"Over kittens," Bogg added, "and tea."

Turner crouched with her back to the wall and caught Maestro's attention. She tapped her chest a few times, acted out a moment of intense pain, then shrugged as if it was no big deal.

Oh, yeah. Maestro was immortal, and she couldn't be killed by a laser. It would hurt, but wouldn't actually kill either of them.

"Okay," she called out. "We're coming out to talk. Cease fire."

The lasers of horrible death stopped.

Bogg actually chuckled. Phineas shushed him.

Maestro sighed. Why were these two in charge of anything?

He and Turner rose and stepped into the doorway as one.

Twin flashes of green death struck them each in the middle of the chest

Drat. It really hurt.

Really, *really* hurt.

Turner fired her doohickey.

Maestro threw a bolt of lightning. "*Lorem ipsum fuck you.*"

The ETs hit the floor simultaneously.

"Oh. That was just a stun thing, right?" Turner asked a bit too late.

"Yep."

"Fuck you is a magic spell?" She wandered closer to the unconscious forms.

"The words aren't always so important." Maestro stood over the shorter, squat ET. A Jonquillian? With an Estragonite? Huh.

The floor vibrated.

"Oh drat." Turner spread her feet and braced.

What—?

The duck blind and both unconscious bodies suddenly ceased to exist.

Air rushed in to fill the void with a loud pop.

Maestro dropped a few feet into knee deep water.

Turner waved her Doohickey, fingers flashing on the 2D screen. "Drat."

Should he use his own Doohickey to follow the teleport? No, he wanted to hold that card out of play a little longer. She was a big girl.

"Someone teleported them," she said.

"Obviously." He tromped his way out of the pond. "How many civilizations have the tech to teleport the entire blind and the Bobsy twins while leaving us behind?" On the path, he shook out his pants legs. "*Consequuntur.*" The water evaporated.

"Very few," she said in all seriousness, obviously assuming Maestro wouldn't already know the answer. There was that Shifter arrogance again. She looked at his face, which he had tried hard to turn into a mask of incredulity. "Oh." Apparently, the face had worked.

Other than the Shifters themselves, the only folks advanced enough to accomplish something like that, without dragging the Galactic cop along, were the Alpaca Consortium.

Drat.

Maestro's Eye of Horus spell found Spook and Muscle in separate rooms of a decidedly middle class home in south Austin

Spook stared at Guitar, who sat on a couch in the living room.

Muscle shoved Bass into the garage where amps, guitars, a love seat, and a drum set filled the space. Posters of pop and punk bands covered the walls. The huge man folded his arms across his chest, looming over the skinny, dark-skinned kid with an afro.

"I don't know why you're talking to me," Bass told Muscle in his cultured British accent. "I don't even know how to spell dynamite, let alone make it. Or C4."

Muscle's enormous shoulders strained against the thin fabric of his black tank top.

"Well, maybe I could spell C4," Bass admitted "but not make it." He dropped onto a stool by the drum set. "I didn't do anything."

Guitar ran a hand over his short blond hair and slouched back into the plaid sofa. He glared at Spook. "And Mrs. Singer told me you're some kind of Ghostbusters or something?" He crossed his arms over his bare skinny chest. "What does this have to do with ghosts? All that supernatural crap is. . . well, it's just crap." His East End accent stood out even more than it had before.

Spook stared at him evenly. "What spell did you cast on her?"

"Pft," Guitar scoffed. "It wasn't a spell. It was a potion."

Spook smiled.

"Bloody hell!" Guitar managed to slouch further into the sofa.

Bass reached into an instrument case and handed Muscle a small glass bottle. "It was just a love potion, and it didn't even work."

Spook read the label on the bottle Guitar handed him. "Love Potion #9." Scrolly lettering and little pink hearts. Spook grunted disgust. "And this is why no one respects us."

"It was just a love spell," Guitar insisted. "I wanted her to notice me. Bass is my mate and all, but he didn't give her enough attention. He didn't really love her."

"And you did?" Spook pocketed the little bottle.

"I still do." Guitar sat forward on the edge of the couch, glaring petulantly as only a teenage musician in a garage band could.

"I don't expect you to understand," Bass told Muscle. He slouched dejectedly. "Guitar was making moves on her, so I needed to make sure I didn't lose her. He just wanted her because I had her."

"He only wanted to keep her because he knew I wanted her," Guitar told Spook at almost the exact same moment.

"Why not just share her?" Spook asked rather matter-of-factly.

"What?" Guitar's shock filled the one word.

"Sorry." Spook sighed. "I miss the seventies."

Bass tried to snatch the bottle back from Muscle, who held him off with a dark glare.

"The damn thing didn't work anyway," Bass insisted. "Not enough. . . so. . . so I tried an amflipication. . . amplification." He patted a nearby speaker. "Like an amp spell. To turn up the volume." He shrugged. "But you saw them at the gig. It's not like it worked at all. I was losing her."

"It was just a stupid love potion," both boys said at once. They each looked up at their respective interrogator with huge puppy dog eyes. . . almost as big as the fluffy kitten's had grown in the surveillance video at the duck blind.

"I didn't kill her, did I?" they both asked in desperation.

Spook's stare softened a bit. "No. I don't see how you could have killed her."

Muscle's expression remained as inscrutable as ever, but he shook his head once.

"Did you make this yourself?" Spook demanded.

"No!" Guitar bounced on the edge of the couch. "I got it from Drums. She knows how to do all kinds of shit."

Bass gasped. "Oh my gods, you don't think she had anything to do with it?"

After a moment, Muscle shrugged.

Spook rubbed his chin. "We won't know anything until we talk to her." He dragged Guitar into the garage.

Muscle looked over as Spook and Guitar entered.

Spook raised an eyebrow.

Muscle shrugged.

Spook shook his head and shoved Guitar onto the love seat.

Muscle pointed at the empty spot and glared at Bass, who gave his bandmate an angry look but followed Muscle's obvious directive.

Spook took position beside Muscle and held up Guitar's bottle.

The big man held Bass's flask up to the first.

Identical.

"For now," Spook said, "you two should stay here together in case someone comes after you, too. You probably have a lot to talk about anyway."

The boys on the love seat glanced at each other then looked away. Bass scooted as far from Guitar as he could on the tiny piece of furniture.

The other boys turned their backs to the musicians. Spook held up Bass's vial and shook it. "*Id mollis delectus posidonium.*" The liquid in the vial sparkled. "This one's just herbs in water," Spook declared. "Minor, minor magic. I wonder what the amplification spell latched onto?"

The boys on the couch whimpered.

"Your guy get it from Drums?" Spook asked Muscle.

He nodded.

"Mine, too."

The boys on the couch fell into each other's arms, sobbing.

"All signs point to the drummer." Spook dropped both vials into a pocket.

Muscle nodded.

They turned to the boys on the couch, who had stopped weeping and pulled apart a little, uttering snuffly noises.

"I hope they'll be all right," Spook said. "At least they still have each other."

The boys latched onto each other and started making out like a pair of rabid weasels.

Spook startled. "Not what I meant, really, but oh well."

The boys fell onto the floor together and knocked over the drummer's stool.

Spook chuckled and headed for the door. "I so do not miss being a teenager. They're all insane." He left the garage with Muscle a step or two behind. "And their music? It's just noise."

Muscle paused in the doorway. He touched the poster for Jem-n-I, a Korean band.

A loud crash of cymbals and the rattle of a snare didn't seem to penetrate his silent musing.

The snare drum rolled into Muscle's foot and drew his attention. The boys had vanished behind the couch, but Muscle's gaze surveyed the room, taking in all the normal detritus of teenage boys as if he stood in some kind of shrine.

What could that be about?

Maestro ended the Eye of Horus spell as Muscle exited the garage.

Beside him on the noisy street, Turner stared with one eyebrow raised and a Korean taco half-eaten.

"Sorry," Maestro said. "I'm back. The boys' interrogation points to Drums." He bit into his own snack.

"Any idea where we'll find her?" Turner asked.

"I have an idea."

Phat

Reggie could barely breathe. Under strobing lasers and obscured by fog machines an assortment of demons, angels, krickfaloos, and just about every variation in the Unknown supernatural world danced together with humans, as if it were perfectly normal! Most of the humans dressed as if they wished they were part of the Unknown. Some even wore horns! Openly!

Reggie swallowed hard. The club was so much like his home in Japan where mingling with humans was considered the norm. He had seen nothing like it on his journey through the States.

There, on a platform above the stage, a young Korean couple danced and sang. Her little white dress hugged her body, sliding around her curves as she undulated like a serpent. The boy's movements were just as fluid under a metallic mesh shirt reminiscent of a dragon's hide.

Oh. Wait.

Reggie slid his inner eyelids into place. Tremendous golden and red dragons glowed around them, slithering and sliding in the space, dancing together even more sensuously than the human forms in the visible spectrum. Their true forms almost blinded him.

They were the couple from the poster in the band's garage. Jem-n-I. Were they not brother and sister? But then. . . Reggie looked away. Those dragons seemed awfully friendly for siblings.

Spook's dancing caught Reggie's eye. In jeans and white tank top, he seemed tremendously understated for the crowd on the dance floor. He edged closer to a pair of abnormally thin girls and smiled at them, but they just turned their backs to him. "Boring," the girls intoned.

Spook smiled and shook his head.

If only Reggie could be that suave. He would die of embarrassment at such a callous brush off. Reggie's new friend made his way to their actual target, the girl they called Drums.

She stood by herself, scowling at the crowd.

Spook kept his back to her, and she did not seem to notice his presence or recognize him. Tendrils of magic grew around him, reaching out and caressing her aura, which, truth to tell, glowed a fairly dark grey but mostly in a way logically explained by her recent loss.

Yet something else showed through. Something bad.

Had Reggie been close enough to smell her, he would have discovered the cause, but a room full of intoxicating aromas and sandalwood-scented fog nearly blinded his olfactory senses.

"I love this song," Maestro said. "I must have a hundred versions of 'The Boy from Ipanema' on my playlist."

The music hit an exciting dubstep bridge.

"Interesting remix," Maestro added.

Turner tucked her iPhone into a pocket. "I get nothing on the drummer. But I don't have an app for magic."

Maestro's eyes narrowed and glowed bright yellow. Reggie opened his inner eyelids. The glow didn't show in the Known spectrum.

"She reads witch," Maestro said, "but nothing special. Spook gets more detail than I do, and he gets nothing, either. Muscle, any thoughts?"

Oh! His boss wanted his opinion. But how to explain why he had no clear sense? Ashamed at disappointing Maestro, Muscle shook his head.

"Too much ambient odor?" Maestro asked.

Reggie nodded. His boss knew about Reggie's acute sense of smell? Hm. When had he figured that out?

Maestro patted his arm. "Sorry I've never asked before."

What else had Maestro figured out?

A young man in an outlandish outfit stopped at the table with a tray in one hand. He sported straight black hair with sharp-cropped bangs and lots of make-up, especially dark around the eyes but pale everywhere else. His full length black velvet coat had a collar that rose up behind his head in an elaborate fan. And a top hat. Was the enormous mole on one cheek real?

"Martinis!" Spook skated past the waiter into the booth, patting the interesting man's side with one hand and shoving a wad of cash into his pants pocket. That was a lot of money!

Reggie scooted around closer to Turner to make room.

The waiter settled more drinks on the table than there were people in the half circle booth. He kissed the top of Spook's head.

Spook handed the waiter a martini and held up one of his own. "A toast!"

Reggie hesitated then raised the glass in front of him. Appearing almost thirty years old had its advantages.

"Exploding chicks and missing cats," Spook said with all seriousness.

The others repeated his words, including the waiter, who sipped his drink, tucked his tray under one arm and sort of dissolved into the fog and crowd.

Spook wiggled his fingers over his drink and muttered a few words. The drink sparkled.

"What's that?" Turner asked.

"Oh, I found a great spell to make liquor work on me," Spook explained. "Since I don't have a working heart or blood, booze has no effect on me." He sipped.

Turner drained her glass. "I don't understand the appeal of alcohol. I'm still thirsty."

With a suspiciously innocent smile, Spook slid another glass to her.

She slugged it like a shot. "Why are the glasses so small?"

Maestro watched the sullen girl across the floor, pointedly ignoring the action around the table.

What would Spook's spell do to Reggie? He nudged his glass a bit closer to Spook, who raised an eyebrow.

Muscle nodded with certainty.

Spook smiled and waggled his fingers over Reggie's glass. It sparkled.

Muscle sniffed the drink. The spell was subtle. He sipped.

Whoa. A nice sense of warmth crept up Muscle's spine, like sliding into a hot spring until the water closed over his head.

Spook smiled. "Nice."

"Aren't you afraid someone will notice all that?" Turner asked.

Spook made a funny noise in his throat. "This place is so *out there* it's not even *here*." He raised a fist to his mouth, whispered into it then raised it in the air. "Hard to tell the spooks from the freaks."

As he opened his fingers in a tossing motion, Reggie closed his inner eyelids. A soft white ball of light spun and darted across the floor, deftly avoiding the dancers.

"I have no idea what you just said," Turner complained.

"Here in Austin, Texas," Spook explained, leaning across the table and giving her his full attention, "especially at Bitter Sweets, the normals are weird enough that the paranormals can move through the city without comment.

The spinning ball of light hit the waiter's ear. He jumped a bit but then smiled, leaned over the bar, and spoke to the bartender, who also smiled. What was Spook doing?

"This place is a hangout for the Unknown," Spook explained. "With a capital letter. The Unknown are folks like me, friendly gremlins, vamps, wolves. . . whatever Maestro is. Whoever can pass as human will hit this club and, in general, only those who don't treat humans like cattle. The bar serves food and has a strict no eating the clientele policy."

The waiter arrived with more drinks.

Spook subtly shoved a large tumbler of water and ice in front of Turner. It was nice of him to—

Yikes. As the glass passed Reggie, the sharp smell of hard liquor hit his nose. Vodka? That much?

Oh. That was tonight's game. Spook wanted to get Turner drunk. Heh. Heh. That could be funny.

Maestro dropped a large stack of bills, carefully folded in half, onto the tray. How did they have so much money? Would working for Maestro solve Reggie's financial issues?

The waiter executed a little bow. "I'll be right back with your change."

Maestro shook his head. "Keep it."

Spook made an approving face. Was this part of the contest?

Reggie might never understand adults.

The waiter bowed again and melted into the crowd.

"So your heart doesn't work," Turner said more loudly than necessary, "but you still eat and drink?" She finished off her vodka.

"Everything else works," Spook said. "My digestive system does what it needs to do. I can eat and drink, with the necessary byproducts." He spelled his and Reggie's drinks. "I don't need to, but I can. My lungs work, too, so I don't seem weird. I don't need to breathe but the body just keeps doing it on its own. Tear ducts work."

"Well, goody for that," Maestro muttered, his attention still across the floor.

Spook scowled. "I am a real boy in just about every way, except for my heart. Never did figure out why."

Reggie reached for his glass. No. He needed to slow down.

"The zombie lad with a broken heart." Maestro turned his head abruptly and glared at Spook. "Ah, gods, you wrote a punk song about that in the 70s didn't you?"

"You know it?" Spook brightened.

Maestro turned away. "Damn. I loved that song."

"Yeah?" Spook's need for approval shone like a beacon, even without Reggie's inner eyelids.

Maestro scowled then glanced at the drink in his hand. He favored Spook with an unusually friendly glance. "Yeah. . . yeah, I like it." He turned back to the dance floor. "Start singing it and I will end you." But his tone didn't really hold any menace.

Spook deflated. "Ah, see. . ." His disappointment had to mean he didn't realize their boss was just teasing now.

"Do you need to make a deal about everything?" Maestro asked.

"Why are we here?" Turner's voice definitely projected a bit too loudly now. "Shouldn't we interrogate the drummer in private?" Her eyes seemed unfocussed.

"I wanted to see her in the real world." Didn't Maestro see how drunk Turner had become? He smiled. Ah. He likely enjoyed this game as much as Spook. "You can tell a lot about someone," Maestro continued, "by seeing her in her natural element that you don't get in an interview. This one perplexes me. No one involved should have the power to pull off a spell that big."

"We're in a duck blind!" Turner pounded the table, rattling the glasses.

"What?" Spook asked.

"Duck blind." She waved vaguely. "When hunters are doing their hunting thing, they hide in a hut that's camouflaged to blend in with the environment so they can watch the ducks without being seen. Anthropo-o-ologists use the same thing when they want to observe primitive planets. . . peoples. Primitive *people*."

Wait. Planets?

Spook nudged Reggie. He waggled his eyebrows. He must have noticed the slip as well.

"Why ducks?" Spook radiated innocence but he smelled deceptive.

"How do I know?" Turner shrugged. "It's your language."

"Our language?" Spook led.

"American," she said far too quickly. "I'm Canadian. I speak Canadian. Why are my glasses empty?"

Spook raised an eyebrow to Reggie, touching the base of his full martini glass.

Reggie nodded, and Spook slid the glass over to Turner.

Maestro seemed to ignore the entire spectacle.

"We're inves—tigating a duck blind in San Antonio, Maestro and I are. . . doing." Turner sucked down yet another martini. "In San Antonio, Extraterres-s-terress-s-strials. . . ETs. In a duck blind, investigating Earth." She lifted a finger to her lips and shushed them for rather a long time. "No one can know. It's top secret. . . for the Men in Black." She giggled then laughed out loud, leaning into Reggie's shoulder for a moment. "Martinini's are fun."

"What did you find?" Spook asked.

Maestro gave the group his full attention. "To be honest, it's kind of a poser. These ETs have twenty bodies of AIDS victims."

Spook looked surprised. "Random much?"

"Can't be." Was Maestro intentionally divulging such information?

"The data goes back to 1925." Turner ran a finger around the edge of her martini glass.

"Which is impossible." Maestro leaned forward on his elbows, all business now. "I don't think the virus came out of the jungles that early."

Turner handed him her iPhone and lifted the glass, trying to let one more drop fall onto her tongue.

Maestro tapped the screen a few times. "Nope. That makes no sense. How could they study it before it even existed?"

"Why are they hiding in a duck blind?" Spook asked. "Why the secrecy?"

"Well, you know, Bob." Turner set her glass down so hard, it could have shattered. "It's the Primitive Planet Protection Pact. ETs aren't allowed to touch down or interfere with your, whatsit, natural progression thingy." Her tone assured them that the information should have been apparent. "It keeps backward planets like yours from being abused."

"Backward?" Spook asked, obviously leading her again.

Maestro leaned back with a wry grin. Had he set up this entire conversation?

"Oh, come on." Turner's lips made a long, drunken sputtering noise. "You haven't even left the planet yet. I mean, your satellite doesn't really count, am I right?"

"Satellite?" Spook raised an eyebrow.

"The moon," Maestro explained.

"Which doesn't even count on any scale I have ever seen." She nudged Maestro. "Am I right?" She took a martini from in front of Maestro and drank it. "Stupid name for a satellite, too. Might as well call the planet Dirt." She snickered. "Oh wait. . ." She giggled.

"And how long have you been on this planet?" Spook's tone remained decidedly matter of fact.

"Few weeks," she said.

Whoa. She was extraterrestrial? Wait. This entire conversation had been orchestrated to accomplish that revelation, hadn't it?

"Shadows," Turner slurred. She looked around, as if hoping she would find some way to recover from her slip.

No. No real chance of that.

She grabbed her iPhone from Maestro and pointed it at Reggie and Spook. "Snug up, you two," she slurred. "You're cute together!"

Reggie covered his eyes with one hand as the bright flash hit so he would not have to pretend it had worked this time.

Turner dropped her head on her hands on the table. "Dratted martininininis."

"Uh-oh." Maestro stared across the bar.

Reggie followed his gaze.

The tall, skinny man who'd eaten a kitten whole in Maestro's backyard stood at the door with a smaller, stockier man. Were they both ETs?

The taller man held a small kitten, but the interesting waiter blocked him with an outstretched arm. He pointed at a sign. "No outside food. No eating the clientele. The management assures you that our kitchen can provide for a wide range of culinary requirements."

The waiter took the kitten and held out a menu.

"As fun as this is, I need you coherent." Maestro grabbed the iPhone from Turner.

"My doohickyickyicky," she muttered into her arm.

Doohickey? Maestro had mentioned that word earlier.

Maestro tapped the screen and Turner sat up abruptly, scowling at him. "You set me up again."

What had happened to her drunken stupor?

"Yes, I did." Maestro handed the device back to her. What was it really? "But I assure you I did it purely to be manipulative and have a laugh at your expense. We have company." He nodded in the direction of the pair following the waiter toward their table.

"Drat," Turner said, "if they see us, we'll have a battle right here."

"You need to shift," Maestro said.

Her eyes opened in shock. "What? Here? In front of all these natives? Don't be repulsive."

Spook nudged Reggie who shrugged. Apparently, they were both in the dark.

"This place is too crowded to get out without them noticing," Maestro insisted.

"You must know what you're asking." She raised her chin and clenched her jaw.

"Yes, and I also know what's at stake." They stared at one another. Maestro focused on Spook. "Close the curtain. Now."

Uncharacteristically, Spook complied without comment. Apparently, he knew how to obey direct commands when it really mattered. He rose and reached for the curtain pulls, leaving his back to the rest of the table.

Maestro looked Reggie dead in the eyes then covered his own with one hand.

Reggie knew how to follow orders, too. Strange squelching sounds drifted across the table, but Reggie refused to peek.

"I know you've seen a lot of crap in your day, Spook," Maestro said. "I need you not to make a spectacle of yourself. You've both seen shapeshifters before."

"Huh," Spook said.

Reggie uncovered his eyes as Spook turned to face the table again.

"She's a shifter?" Spook asked.

In Turner's place sat a young red-headed man in good physical condition.

In Maestro's place sat an old man. "Capital S," Maestro said. "Her people are called Shifters. She works for an organization called the Galactic Police, which should be self-explanatory. The word alien is offensive. Call her an extraterrestrial or ET. And please open the curtains again."

"And her initials are E.T.?" Spook asked. He opened the curtains.

Maestro grinned as Spook resumed his place beside Reggie. "Happens more often than you'd think."

Everyone turned to Spook, who made a big show of not reacting.

"Not even my first ET," he said.

Reggie smelled his deception.

"How did you change?" Turner asked Maestro.

"Magic." The old man waggled his eyebrows and his eyes sparked green. "It's called a glamour."

Turner furrowed his eyebrows. "Glamor? But you're not fancy."

And then time slowed down as the two aliens, er, ETs walked past, following the waiter. The tall one looked down then away in complete disinterest. The stocky one sniffed once or twice but moved on without comment.

Time resumed.

Reggie waited.

Another second passed.

"Okay, you *are* my first ET." Spook leaned across Reggie to poke Turner's shoulder. "That is so cool. Do you have a space ship? Can I see it?" He spoke very fast. "Do you have a penis now?"

Maestro scoffed. "I knew that was too good to be true. This is serious."

"I'm perfectly serious." Spook glared at Maestro. "I wanna see a spaceship."

The man who still smelled like Turner grunted. "Why is he even here?"

The extraordinary waiter appeared and cleared the table. "Thought you'd like to know your two friends seem to be throwing a party."

Across the room, a group of very large men joined the two ETs at their table. Everything about the new men screamed violent hooligan. Were they even human?

Spook shoved more bills into the waiter's vest. "Thanks, Billy."

The man stopped him with a wink. "Just trying to keep the place from getting wrecked." He patted Spook's head. "You can go out the back if you want." He slipped Turner's many glasses onto his tray and smiled at her. . . er, him. "Did you like the martinis?"

Turner did a complete double take. "Yes. Thank you."

The waiter, Billy, smiled and left.

Turner watched him depart. "How did he know it was me?"

Spook snorted. "Not even close to the weirdest thing he's seen in here."

Maestro led the way out of the booth and across the room.

But. . . Well, Reggie's new job was to handle fights and things. He could take those men. Assuming they were men. If not, Reggie might need to reveal his true nature to defeat them.

Would that be acceptable in this place?

Maestro's hand dropped onto his shoulder. "I'm sure you could take them, but it would be rude to wreck the place after Billy gave us warning."

Oh. Well, that made sense. The waiter had been very helpful.

Maestro led the way through the club toward the kitchen.

Just in case, Reggie glanced over a shoulder.

The stout ET yanked back the curtain on the booth next to the one where Reggie and his new friends had sat.

Two enormous armor-plated fleas looked down at him in what Reggie had to assume was surprise. "What?" Reggie heard with his very sensitive hearing.

The stout ET twitched the curtain back into place and smacked the tall alien upside the head. He'd had to jump a little to reach.

Really? Giant fleas. That was a new one even for Reggie. Wait. Were they ETs, too? Was there any way to tell the difference between ETs and the Unknown?

His friends, er, coworkers. . . the others had crossed the room without him.

He ran to catch up.

They hurried through the busy kitchen where so many odors mingled, Reggie only barely noticed the kitten beside the pot on the stove. With a quick glance around, he scooped up the kitten and tucked it into the crook of his arm before it could mew.

Outside, he looked it square in the eye and sent it directions to the box where *Bakeneko* lived. The kitten meeped, jumped to the pavement, and set off to meet her new brother.

Maestro stared at him, back in his usual form.

Reggie would have blushed had his skin not been so dark, but Maestro nodded and patted his shoulder. Oh, good. He did not consider Reggie a sentimental fool.

"Fancy meeting you here," Maestro said, apropos of nothing, until he turned and drew Reggie's attention to the girl in the shadows of the alley.

Combat

If Spook had rescued a fluffy kitty, Maestro would have mocked him. Unfair. He'd even patted the big guy's shoulder. Fine. Spook would not get jealous and prove Maestro's accusation that he was a little girl.

Drums stepped forward into the light. "Are you freaks following me?" Her tone managed to convey both petulance and ennui.

"We're running away from someone, actually," Turner said, her voice back to usual. "Meeting you is a complete coincidence."

Wha-tcha? When had she found time to change back to a woman?

Drums nodded with her chin. "Who's the lady?"

"An associate," Maestro said.

Spook leaned over. "Why'd you change?"

The ET (Whoa! ET!) leaned down to him. "She saw me wearing this outfit in the pub."

"Club," Spook corrected automatically.

"What?" she asked.

Spook stood on tiptoes. "Outside of *Canada* the only place to call a club a pub is England."

Her brow furrowed. "But they speak the same language."

"Only peripherally."

Maestro smacked his shoulder. "How long have you been using magic?" he asked the girl while scowling at Spook.

Really? E.T. had started it.

Heh. Heh. Elizabeth Turner the extraterrestrial. E.T. Heh.

"About three years." Drums settled into one hip and crossed her arms. "How long have you been trying to throw people off their game with random questions?"

"I learned it from Plato," Maestro countered without missing a beat. "You don't seem strong enough for what happened to your friend, and that might mean someone else is out there with a grudge. You could be in danger."

The girl scoffed. "I can take care of myself."

"Oh, I seriously doubt that." Maestro's raised eyebrow seemed to affect the girl not at all.

"Better than you." She pointed up the alley.

Well, Spook knew who just had to be back there.

Yep, ginormous gang of bad guys (well, about ten) in the alley entrance, headed by the two ETs. Phineas and Bogg, right? Hadn't he seen those names when stealing a look over E.T.'s shoulder?

And the alley was a dead end. Of course.

"Drat." Maestro reached toward Drums. His eyes sparked white and a matching glow enveloped the girl.

She squeaked and froze in place.

He waved his hands as if shoving her to one side, and she slid sideways like a conveyer belt, screaming loud enough to wake the dead. She slid through the wall into the building, her scream cut short as she vanished.

"Whoa cool spell," Spook muttered. "She okay in there?"

"Better than we are," Maestro muttered back. "Billy has her in hand." He tossed a bit of sound fluff at Spook's ear. Huh, he knew that spell, too?

"I just... I came through the wall!" Drum's voice said into Spook's ear.

"Mm-hm, sweetie," Billy replied. "This tray goes to the big table in the corner. You pass intangibly through the wall into my kitchen, you can expect to carry at least one tray onto the floor, thank you very much."

Nice.

"Now pay attention," Maestro said. "This is grownup work."

The bad guys squared up in formation behind their leaders, an ersatz Abbot and Costello if Spook had ever seen one, and he'd seen several over the years. From the lack of obvious bulges, the thugs couldn't be packing more than smallish hand guns.

Nice. Spook readied a compact force bubble to stop low caliber bullets.

"Slumming, officer?" Phineas asked with a British accent that seemed odd for an ET. "I'd hardly think a respectable member of the Galactic Police would spend a night carousing with the monkeys."

"Monkeys?" Spook asked, looking around. Monkeys were the cat's meow.

"He means us," Maestro explained with a characteristic glare.

Oh.

"And it's an insult."

Double oh.

E.T. stepped forward. "I thought we had an amiable understanding, Phineas. Your permits were in order."

"Then why did you sneak back into our lab whilst Bogg had his back turned?" Phineas inquired.

"Well, you did have a number of human corpses on slabs," E.T. retorted. "You're hardly in a position to toss pebbles."

"Oh." The ET shrugged. "That."

Maestro stepped to E.T.'s side. "Why are you studying AIDS, and where did you get the data going back to 1925."

E.T. gave him a look. "You're as bad as zombie lad."

Zombie lad again? What about 'Spook'? He already had a cool handle.

Phineas chuckled darkly. "You really haven't worked it out, yet?"

The other one, Bogg, clapped. "Oh good, then we can eat them and no one will be the wiser."

"Oh yes," Phineas agreed, "these monkeys you definitely get to eat."

Bogg's smiled grew. . . and grew. . . and grew.

Wow. Well, he had eaten Mr. Snuggles whole.

"I still want an answer to my question," Maestro insisted.

"You're missing the obvious because you don't want to believe it." Phineas seemed far too pleased with himself.

Of course, Spook had already sussed it. "How long did the Wright Brothers study wings before they invented an airplane?"

Everyone looked at him in surprise. Right. Because he was just a kid. Man!

"The data goes back before the disease was discovered," Spook explained, "because they used the research to create it."

Everyone looked at Phineas and Bogg, the latter of whom took a few steps after a kitten that had leapt out from under his coat.

Muscle growled. The sound actually rattled Spook's teeth.

The thin ET rose and opened his eyes wide, looking for all the world like a guilty, naughty boy.

"Not them specifically," Spook admitted. "You know what I mean."

"I do," E.T. said, "and it's not as stupid as everything else you've said."

Of course, the only compliment would be back-handed.

"But why?" Maestro demanded. "And on a protected planet? There are any number of unprotected worlds that are still isolated. Why take the extra risk?"

Did he really expect the bad guys to just lay out their entire plan to him? Only idiots on TV shows did that.

"Money." Phineas smiled smugly.

O-kay. Never mind.

"When you started shooting calculators out of the solar system," Phineas continued, "the Galactic Center discussed making limited contact, possibly removing your protected status. Then AIDS hit, and everything changed."

"What?" Spook asked. "Were they afraid of the disease spreading?"

"Don't be stupid." Phineas scoffed. "The disease wasn't a threat, but the way the planet reacted was. Had the US government responded quickly, it could have wiped the disease out before it went pandemic, but since a fringe minority was affected first. . . they tried to pretend it didn't even exist. If you reacted that way to a subset of your own species. . . how would you treat extraterrestrials? Removing the Protected status was universally rejected after that."

"Okay, I get the history lesson," Spook said. "We suck as a species. Where's the money?"

"There's a huge black market for goods from Protected planets," E.T. interjected. "Rare and illegal, anything from a Protected world is worth a fortune. These guys must work for a family—the Consortium—at the center of trade from Earth."

"Figuring that out was easy," Bogg pouted, as if upset about losing his kitten and trying to score a point, "but you'd have to be a Shifter to have the tech to copy our data and prove any of it."

"Oh yeah?" Spook shot back. "Just so happens she *is* a Shifter."

"Bogg!" Phineas barked.

"Spook!" E.T. shouted at the same time.

Phineas raised an eyebrow. "You're a Shifter? That changes things. I guess we get to have fun after all."

Maestro glared.

Oops. How was a corpse to know?

Muscle cracked his knuckles wow loudly and stripped off his jacket. He slipped out of his shoes as well but left the plaid flat cap. Hm. He had a serious boner for that hat.

Phineas smiled, then raised one hand, index finger to the sky.

He snapped his fingers.

All ten hoods moved closer and reached into their jackets.

Spook started to ready his—*holy second mother of Satan*!

The gargantuan weapons they pulled out made rocket launchers squeak and hide in shame. Where the hell had those been hiding? And Holy Star Trek, Batman! They screamed "we are horrible lasers of death!"

Even Muscle's eyes widened, and he cast a hopeful glance Maestro's way.

Maestro shook his head with a pinched face.

Muscle frowned. Must've wanted one.

"Now, gentlemen," E.T. said. "I don't see the need for violence."

"Oh, I do, my dear," Phineas insisted. "I do."

ET tapped her Doohickey. "I just laid down a stasis field." She sighed. "No energy weapons or teleports."

The thugs pulled the triggers of their weapons, with a whole lot of no result.

Even Muscle shot her an angry look. What was that about?

Well, in any case, magic would save the day!

Spook waved his arms in a grandstandy spellcasting shtick. "*Graeco dicunt.*" He thrust both hands forward, wrists together, hands spread vertically in the standard "kill them all" gesture while he lunged forward on one foot.

The goons cringed.

Ha! But the horrible fireball of death Spook had planned grew to the size of a pea and generated the heat of a matchstick before dripping to the ground with the grinding sound of a dying Model A.

What the heck?

"Doohickey, take a note," E.T. said, "magic is considered an energy weapon as far as stasis fields are considered."

Well, shit.

While the bad guys chuckled and elbowed each other, Muscle leapt forward, snatched an enormous gun from the nearest of them and swung it like a baseball bat.

The man he hit grabbed at least five feet of air before crashing into a second guy ten feet away.

"Oi!" Spook exclaimed. "Bitchsmacked with your own gun, yo."

Two other men dashed forward toward Muscle.

"Yo?" Maestro asked, rolling up his sleeves.

"Hey, yo, I'm street." Spook dropped into a defensive crouch and extended a hand to give the traditional "come get me" finger wave.

"Sesame Street," Maestro muttered, leaping to Muscle's side.

"Man, why's he always have to be so mean?" Spook muttered.

"Perilously close to a catch phrase!" Maestro called out.

E.T. dashed forward into the overwhelming odds.

But Spook had to pay attention to the enormous wall of flesh lumbering his way. He dropped into his best impression of a defensive pose, took one step forward, and waggled his arms over his head.

"Wooga! Wooga! Wooga!"

The bad guy paused to figure out what the hell he was up to.

So Spook kicked him as hard as he could, square in the nuts.

Hopefully, ETs had nuts.

And kept them in the usual spot.

The guy's eyes closed and his face pinched tight as his hands cupped the white hot fountain of pain in his crotch.

Score.

Work smart, not hard.

Another guy aimed a roundhouse kick Spook's way, so he dropped back and rolled away, tumbling to one side and popping to his feet.

Muscle grabbed Spook's attacker by the collar and simply tossed him into the brick wall ten feet away.

Nice. Everyone seemed to be having fun beating on the bad guys, who seemed equally entertained.

Hm. Spook backed away and held up one hand. A fireball popped up easily. He had to be outside the sphere of E.T.'s stasis field.

Okay.

He closed his eyes and opened his center. "*Electram tractatos.*" He held his arms over his head and focused on drawing what he needed.

Twin scimitars appeared, and he twirled them in a hokey display he'd learned on a gig when he'd met Ali Baba.

"Muscle!" he shouted, launching the blades. "Heads up!"

Muscle snatched them out of the air and immediately crossed them in front, neatly decapitating the man there. His arms swung wide, providing a similar service for two more bad guys, one on either side.

E.T. glanced Spook's way, and he made a cutting motion across his neck with one thumb then pointed at Maestro with two fingers. It was a gesture he'd used a hundred times with Ross. Would she get it?

She nodded and glanced around. Seeming satisfied, she leaned to one side to kick Bogg in the face while reaching into her pocket.

Swell. Spook cupped his fingers over his mouth, whispering, "Poppies will put them to sleep." He tossed the words to Maestro, drawing his other hand to his mouth. "Get to Maestro." That message went to Muscle.

Maestro didn't even react. He just dealt with his opponent and raised an arm. A very cool, gnarled staff appeared. He twirled it, like, a hundred times then rammed it into the concrete. "*Per ea movet dolorum.*"

At the same moment, Muscle somehow appeared, flying through the air in a backward, somersaulting-back-tuck-gymnastic-godliness-maneuver that ended with him landing peacefully with his back exactly against Maestro's.

Wow. Spook *had* to learn Muscle's mad skills!

A familiar wave of white smoke spewed from the staff and flashed outward much faster than the last time Spook had seen it.

It reached E.T. and slipped around her feet as if repelled by some kind of force field.

Wait, she had a force field? Cool!

Every thug it touched dropped to the ground unconscious, just as the bystanders had done the first night Spook had met Maestro. . . only lots faster and probably more painfully.

Spook also had to learn *that* spell.

Phineas dropped like a sack of flour on top of an already unconscious Bogg.

Maestro and Muscle circled, their backs together, as if making sure all the bad guys were down.

E.T. raised her Doohickey and a little screen popped open above it like the spell Maestro had used earlier. She waved the device over the bad guys, and her whole posture relaxed. Wait. Was that a hologram?

Muscle stepped over to the ringleaders, dug into Bogg's coat and extracted a calico kitten. He set it on one massive shoulder where it mewed happily. He wiped the blood from the scimitars onto Bogg's jacket.

"Wow," Spook said. "That was almost like teamwork."

"Good work everyone." Maestro twirled the staff and it vanished, most likely back to his repository. "Especially you, Spook. Good thinking."

"I may look like a kid," Spook said, trying for cool, "but this is *not* my first ride on the merry-go-round." He would not go overboard at Maestro's compliment.

Well, not until he was alone.

Muscle held out the swords.

"Like 'em?" Spook really liked the big guy.

Muscle twirled them with more authentic prowess than Spook had seen in a number of years. He tucked one under each arm and nodded appreciatively.

"Keep 'em," Spook said. "I have a bunch."

Muscle grinned and examined the blades more carefully.

"Well," E.T. said, "when you can magic them out of thin air."

"I *wish* I could do that," Spook admitted. "No, I have a stash hidden away. Stuff with a standing retrieval spell I can call up when I need it." He shrugged. "I got tired of never having the right toys for the playground."

Maestro wore a wry grin.

"You have one, too, I bet," Spook said.

Maestro held up a hand. "*Vide graeco dicunt.*" A diamond encrusted tiara appeared in his hand. He held it out to E.T..

She took it, waved her Doohickey over it, and then stared at Maestro with wide, wide eyes. Well, it was a diamond encrusted tiara, after all. Wasn't it?

"Is that thing real?" Spook asked. "It looks like something a princess would wear."

"Queen, actually." Maestro patted Muscle's kitten.

E.T. slipped it onto her head and held up the Doohickey. The hologram above the device switched to a perfect copy of her with the tiara on her head.

Holy Hell! What kind of tech did she have?

She turned this way and that with a smile, then jumped a bit, as if realizing she had just let all three men see her act like a frivolous girl with a new bauble.

Yeah, Spook wouldn't forget that moment. . . ever.

"Queen?" he asked.

"Mm-hm. Gwen." Maestro's voice held that infuriating lack of emotion again.

Wait. Gwen? Guinevere?

"You say shit like that just to see if I'll squeal like a little girl," Spook growled.

Maestro smiled. "Mm-hm. I guess I need to try harder."

E.T. ripped the tiara from her head. She did, however, keep it rather than handing it back to Maestro.

"Thank you gentlemen," she said calmly, "that was quite impressive."

"That's what she said," Spook said without even thinking. Ross would have expected it.

E.T. shot him a dirty look.

"What?" he snapped to cover a sad moment. "I can't play completely against type. You'd get bored." Spook missed Ross.

E.T. rolled her eyes, which also seemed pretty human for an alien, extraterrestrial, whatever. "I can wrap these guys up from here." She puffed up her chest. "I can't tell you how much this bust means to the galaxy."

Oh, well, if she was going to leave herself wide open—but Muscle jabbed him and scowled.

What? Spoilsport.

Well, damn. The big guy had a kitten on one shoulder. How could Spook scowl at a guy with a kitten on his shoulder? He patted the kitten. How did he get it to sit there?

Maestro sighed. "Hopefully, we can get a teenage girl to spill as easily as we did the intergalactic smugglers."

E.T. glanced at the tiara in her hand. "You know. . . I have an idea. You helped me. . ."

The boys sat on the couch in Maestro's living room, sipping blood red martinis and watching a magic screen on the wall. Maestro made a point of having Reggie sit between Spook and himself. Give the zombie an inch, he'd take a mile.

The screen showed Drum's bedroom, which, against all possible assumptions, exploded with frills and lace and girly pink décor. She muttered under her breath in her sleep. "The drummer's supposed to explode."

Poor thing. . . unless she'd *meant* to blow up her rival. In which case, Maestro would have to put her down like a rabid dog.

Turner appeared at the foot of the girl's bed, the spitting image of the dead singer in full-on ghost makeup with lights and winds and the whole nine yards. She inhaled, obviously about to go for the ghostly moan, but she stopped, looked puzzled, seemed to almost have it, and looked puzzled again.

"Drat," she whispered and tapped her Doohickey.

Maestro's phone vibrated, and he tapped it over. "Yes?"

"What's her name?" Turner asked.

"Drums," Maestro said teasingly.

"No, her real name," Turner asked, completely missing the tease.

Muscle grinned.

"Emily." Maestro exchanged a smirk with the young man.

But he still wouldn't give Spook the satisfaction.

"Oh." Turner dropped the Doohickey into a pocket and sucked in a deep breath. "Emily. . ." She added a ghostly moan. Huh. Must've watched a few movies.

The girl under the pink frilly canopy didn't move.

Turner tried again, a bit louder.

Still no response.

"Under sedation?" Spook asked.

Even Maestro had to smile.

"Emily!" Turner barked, and the girl finally sat up.

All three boys chuckled and clinked glasses.

"Is there some way to turn this into a drinking game?" Spook asked.

Even Maestro had to admit that was a nice touch, but he ignored the option.

Emily scooted back against her headboard, white enamel covered with unicorns. "Oh my God, I'm sorry," she cried. "So sorry. . ." And she burst into tears.

"Emily. . ." Turner moaned. "I am not at rest. . . cannot be at rest until I hear your confession. Confession is good for the soul! Confess!" She made more ghost moaning noises.

Spook broke into hysterics and curled up against Muscle, who didn't seem to mind. "Oh, God, she's pretty good at that."

"Yeah, you should have seen her first try." Maestro remembered her sad attempt at subterfuge on their first meeting in this timeline. She'd learned a lot in a short time. Wait—

He'd missed something important. What had the girl said?

"A hiccup spell?" Turner asked, completely breaking character. "Seriously?" She seemed to realize her lapse and moaned a bit to recover. The wind picked up.

"Honestly," Emily insisted. "It was just supposed to embarrass you in the second set. . . not blow you up. I'm so sorry."

Maestro did the math. Ah, Hades. Had it been a freakish accident? A hiccup spell with two love potions and an attraction spell drawing magic her way, plus an amplification spell that wound up the ante on all the ambient energy coursing through the singer's body.

"Ask her why," he said into his Doohickey.

"Why did you do it?" Turner asked. "Oo-ooh."

"Oh, come on." The girl's composure steadied a bit, as if she were simply dealing with the singer herself instead of her possibly vengeful spirit. Kids. "You already had Melvin, and you were only going after Horace because I wanted him. . . and then you were with Jimmy on the side." She made a "pft" sound. "You had half a dozen boys, and I just wanted the one." She started to snuffle again. "I just wanted to embarrass you."

Damn. The whole thing had been an accident.

"Tell her it wasn't her fault," Maestro said into the Doohickey. No point in letting her live a lifetime of guilt for a freakish accident.

"It wasn't you, Emily." The fact that Turner followed his suggestion without question made Maestro smile. He sipped the martini.

"What?" Emily demanded. "Who else?"

Maestro fed Turner her lines.

"It was my own fault," the Galactic cop parroted. "I played with eldritch powers beyond my control. They consumed me."

"Then. . ." The girl seemed confused. "Then why'd you make me confess?"

Maestro continued to feed lines.

"So you can heal," Turner repeated. "You had to admit your jealousy to move beyond it. . . and so I can move beyond it, so you will remember me as a friend."

"She's really good at this," Spook said, rising and crossing to the bar.

Indeed she was. She was almost too human for a Shifter. If

Maestro remembered his xenobiology classes, that could turn into a problem.

"Friends?" the girl in the bed asked. "We hated each other. You were a total bitch to me."

"Believe it or not, being dead gives a girl insight, okay?" Turner improvised. "You need to let go of your crap and move on with your life."

Not bad.

Turner as the ghost turned to leave. She stopped. "About the boys?" she added over a shoulder. "I wouldn't get my hopes too high on either of them."

Emily pounded the mattress. "Oh, damn it. I sorta figured, but. . . my options are kind of limited."

Spook returned with the martini shaker. "If it were still the seventies, all three of them could just give in to nature."

Pointedly keeping silent, Maestro did deign to raise his glass for a refill.

Turner didn't leave right away. What in the world was she thinking? Unseen by the tormented girl, she tapped the Doohickey in her pocket.

The diamond encrusted tiara stolen from Gwen's pillow appeared in Turner's hand.

"Oh, hell no," Maestro muttered.

Turner handed the tiara to Emily.

"Oh, my God, a tiara!" She clapped it onto her head. "Look, I'm a princess!"

Maestro couldn't speak.

Spook took his glass, filled it, and replaced it. "Just how much is that thing worth?"

Maestro sucked down the entire drink in one draught.

Drat.

"I already have a plan to replace it with a fake," Maestro said. "And E.T. never gets another present."

"Can I have it?" Spook asked.

Maestro leveled his ultimate look of utter disgust. Just how much of a little girl was the zombie?

"Hey," Emily said, the tiara worth more than the annual national product of many countries on her head, "you were a total bitch in life, but maybe death agrees with you." She touched the invaluable antique. "Thanks."

Turner teleported out and appeared in the living room.

Emily took the tiara from her head, examined it, and replaced it.

Yeah. Over Maestro's dead body.

He tapped the Doohickey in his pocket and hijacked the teleporter of the Galactic police cruiser in orbit. Let the other kids figure it out for themselves.

Another tap and Emily froze.

He switched out the tiara with a replica and teleported home.

Emily resumed normal time and lay down with a smile on her face, none the wiser.

The trio in Maestro's living room was too busy fussing over drinks to comment on the level of tech he'd needed to perform that little extraction. Sometimes he loved the fact that everyone assumed everything he did was rooted in magic.

Epilogue

Several posters of poor Mr. Snuggles adorned Angie's ancient oak. Beneath the scraggly branches, Maestro held a pet brush covered in ragged snatches of hair. "*Zen monster es dolores perfecto.*" He waved a wand over it to sell the fake spell, then looked up at the cloudy sky and rolled his eyes a bit. "*Ex pepsi versus coke reducto.*" While the words never made much difference, he had to be careful to make them particularly senseless so he didn't accidently cast a spell.

He passed the brush to Turner, the only person present who could do anything with it now that Mr. Snuggles had died. She accepted it with all solemnity and held it behind her back. Would he have a chance to figure out how Shifters actually utilized DNA to copy their outfits?

He dropped his head as if tired. "You need to leave now, Elizabeth."

Angie tugged on his sleeve. "I don't mind if she stays."

"No, no!" Maestro raised one hand dramatically. He'd learned how to con a rube from the Karelas, a family of gypsies that'd adopted him for a few decades back in the day. "Mr. Snuggles does not know her. He will be afraid. He may not heed my call." He pointed to the house and lowered his voice. "Go."

Turner trotted to the house and disappeared around the corner where Spook hid.

Reggie, Maestro knew, sat in an idling moving van up the street waiting for the signal.

Maestro reached up to the sky. "Mr. Snuggles it is time. . . time to come home."

"Mr. Snuggles?" Angie wrung her hands and searched the shrubbery. "Mr. Snuggles are you there?"

A cat meowed.

Angie gasped.

The sound repeated and a blur of orange fur streaked across the lawn and launched himself into Angie's waiting arms.

"Mr. Snuggles!" She scratched Turner's ear as he purred and rubbed against her, missing eye and tattered ear copied to perfection. How did he do that part? That wasn't in the DNA.

"Were you lost, then?" Angie asked. "You were just lost, weren't you? You weren't upset with mommy."

Wow, Turner really knew how to purr.

Angie patted Maestro's cheek. "I don't know how to thank you." She headed toward her house. "If I'd had to go on thinking Mr. Snuggles ran away because of something I did, I'd never have forgiven myself. Because I love this old cat, yes I do. Who's a sweet woozy boozey, den?"

Heh. Heh. Turner glared at Maestro over Angie's shoulder, still purring in spite of his disgusted feline expression.

Maestro scratched the cat's head. "I think *he's* a sweet woozy boozy, den."

Turner swiped at him with one paw. His head morphed into a miniature sabre tooth tiger that opened its jaws and hissed with a growl deeper than a cat that size should have been able to produce.

Angie jostled the cat. "Oh, do you have a hairball, Mr. Snuggles?"

Turner returned to the pure Mr. Snuggles outfit and purred again, but, somehow, Maestro could hear the disdain that somehow bled into the purr. How did s/he do any of that?

A dog barked in the distance. Well, Spook created the sound of a dog barking in the distance, which was everyone's cue. . . right on time.

Turner stiffened in Angie's arm. "Don't worry, Mr. Snuggles, the mean old dog is miles away."

The bark repeated, this time so close even Maestro jumped at the ferocious sound.

Turner emitted a pissed off cat noise and leapt from Angie's arms.

"Snuggle wuggles!" the old woman cried.

The moving van careened down the normally quiet street the exact moment Turner dashed across the lawn.

Maestro felt the subtle tweak of the spell Spook cast to send a turkey dressed in fake fur into the path of the moving van the exact moment Turner streaked past it.

In a screech of tires, the truck hit the turkey with a loud squelch.

Turner squealed loudly at just the right moment, then cut off her cry.

Perfect.

Maestro grabbed Angie and spun her away from the sight of horrible avian carnage.

Angie screamed. She pulled against Maestro's grasp.

"No, Angie, no." He pulled her face into his shoulder. No sense trusting that everyone would execute their parts perfectly. "You don't want to see him like that. Remember him the way he was."

Turner, still in the guise of Mr. Snuggles dashed across the street and behind Maestro's house. Reggie squealed around the corner, where'd he'd likely park the truck and rejoin the team.

"You know he loved you," Maestro said, stroking the sobbing woman's hair. "He was only lost, and you got to tell him you loved him and say goodbye." He patted her head. "This is just a horrible accident, and I will take care of cleaning up. . . of carefully. . ." What the hell came next anyway? "Shhhhh. . ." He wasn't so good at finessing the clients anymore.

Uncomfortable squelching sounds made Spook really, really want to turn around, but Maestro had assured him that watching a Shifter change "outfits" was the height of rude and invasive, so he kept his back turned in spite of his curiosity.

Muscle dashed around the corner and hurried past Spook.

"Eep." For such a big guy, he made really girly noises sometimes.

"What?" E.T. snapped. "I'm only naked. It's not like I'm changing or anything."

Muscle emitted another nervous sound then settled in at Spook's back, his head just above Spook's like a totem pole. Pretty innocent for a late twenties/early thirties dude. How old was he anyway?

"Humans." E.T. appeared at the corner, buttoning her blouse.

Spook grinned. "Now, your mouth says 'human' but I hear you thinking 'monkeys.'" It wasn't literally true, however. . .

E.T. grunted. "What are you, psychic?"

"Well. . . yeah." Spook looked over a shoulder at her—

And there was Muscle, right there where Ross had always been. Good or bad? Hard to say. The poor kid would die one day, too.

"Oh drat," E.T. said with a long, drawn out scoff. "Two of them."

Maestro appeared around the corner.

Spook and Muscle rose.

"Well," their fearless leader told them, "she'll cry for a while, but at least she had a chance to say goodbye."

"That was a really sweet thing you did for her." Spook stepped forward. "Maybe we should hold a funeral for Mr. Snuggles. It'd be a good way for her—"

Elizabeth tapped a temporal dislocation app. It was horribly inaptly named, but it did work. Zombie Lad froze.

"Is that the only way to get him to shut up?" she asked.

The strange large human poked Spook in the chest. As if that would awaken him.

"Possibly so," Maestro said. "It does appear effective."

Elizabeth checked her app. "With just one person, we have about ten minutes on that hold. You want to waste it staring at him or should we make martinis?"

"Martinis," Maestro said without hesitation.

"I thought so." Elizabeth had grown very fond of martinis. She and Maestro headed toward the house. The giant glanced back but followed eventually.

"Ten minutes, you say?" Maestro asked.

"If we're lucky," Elizabeth told him.

As they headed into the house, Elizabeth tapped over to her surveillance app. Outside, a bird landed on Spook's head, chirped a few times, and flew off. She'd have felt bad if it had evacuated its bowels onto him.

"—to feel some. . ." Where was everyone? ". . .closure."

Spook looked around.

Gone. All of them.

Aw, man. Did they teleport? Without him? So unfair. "Way to make a guy feel like the last kid picked for the dodgeball team. . ." Dirtbags. ". . .which I always was."

Someone tapped his shoulder.

He dropped into a crouch in his best Karate pose. "Oo-ee-yah!"

Muscle stood a few inches away with two martini glasses, one held toward Spook.

"Oh." He rose out of the deadly ninja pose. "Martinis."

He sipped. Nice. Muscle made good martinis.

He looked around. Where was the rest of the gang?

Muscle nodded in the direction of the house.

Ah. So Maestro or E.T. had needed to have some sort of sophomoric joke at his expense. Nice. Way to make him feel like part of the team.

Wait. Were they a team?

Muscle sipped his martini and lifted it for Spook to tap.

Spook tapped.

Well, the giant musclebound harbinger of death seemed to like him anyway.

Huh. That had sounded a lot better in his head.

"Thanks." Take your friends where you can get them. Spook had tried to summon a demon because he was lonely. At least Muscle was human, right? Might as well enjoy the martinis while the big guy lived.

Muscle lead him into Maestro's sadly out of date living room where their host and the ET hung out at the bar.

"This is a nice place," Spook said.

"Don't get used to it," Maestro said.

Really? "Do you have to be that way every second of every day?" Spook demanded.

"What?" Maestro scowled. "It's compromised. I don't know how they got past my defenses, but I'm not sticking around to find out."

Oh damn. As annoying as he could be, Maestro could teach Spook so much.

"Where will you go?" Spook asked.

"Don't worry, Hello Kitty." Maestro held out a decanter to refill Spook's glass. "I have a few places in Austin. I'm not leaving town."

Spook sipped. Huh, Maestro had already spelled it for him. Nice. "Good, you make a helluva martini."

Muscle clinked his glass.

"You really are a badass, man." Spook smacked Muscle's shoulder, but DAMN that hurt. He shook out his hand. "Any chance I can get you to show me more of your moves sometime?"

Muscle nodded.

Nice.

Hmmmm.

E.T. twirled her martini with one finger, staring into it as if it held all the answers in the universe. How much could *she* teach him?

Was there any chance. . .?

"Sooo. . ." Spook queried.

"Don't." Maestro sucked down his drink.

"What?" Spook looked around.

The others seemed comfortable and eager.

"We are celebrating success, Spook." Maestro's gaze screamed ennui, but he raised his glass to E.T.. "And hopefully a promotion off this rock for Officer Elizabeth Turner of the Galactic Police. Don't spoil it by trying to turn this into the Scooby Doo gang."

"We did kinda kick ass together," Spook insisted, and E.T. and Muscle seemed to agree.

Before Maestro could rain on the parade, his phone rang. After checking the number, he set it on speaker and held it out.

"This is Maestro," he said. "Tell me your tale of woe."

"Yeah. . . Maestro?" a familiar voice said. "Something just happened."

Police sirens wailed in the distance.

"We have a couple of bodies here," the voice continued, "and I'm pretty sure it's a Steven Spielberg."

The phone beeped, and Maestro held it up. A photo appeared of two bodies laced together as if one had materialized inside the other.

"Although I don't know if it's *Close Encounters* or *Poltergeist*," the man asked. "You busy?"

Maestro met the gaze of everyone in the room.

Oh wow. Would he be a total dick?

Every face was eager to jump in and help.

Wait. Was that a smile? An actual smile on that stoic face?

"Hang on to your panties," Maestro said. "We're on our way."

"We?" the voice asked.

And then life turned into a cool slo mo effect.

They finished their drinks.

They adjusted their coats.

They exited the house, one at a time, but then creating a line shoulder to shoulder.

They walked through the front yard, and a perfectly timed breeze floated anything that would float as they strode to Maestro's intriguing VW microbus.

Booyah! That's just how a team would do it, right?

Fade to black with the sirens in the distance.

Spook felt more alive than he had in years.

Please enjoy this sample from John Robert Mack's novel *Danny Decker and the Horribly Unlikely Space Adventure*, a faux young adult novel available on Amazon. It features Maestro and contains special guest star appearances by Peter Test and Phineas and Bogg. The story is set about six months after the action in *Tales of Mystery and Woe: a comedy.*

DANNY DECKER AND THE HORRIBLY UNLIKELY SPACE ADVENTURE

JOHN ROBERT MACK

"Find a Penny. . ."

With an immense sigh of resignation, Danny Denton Decker turned up the sidewalk to his sadly unterrifying middle school and almost completely failed to notice the coppery glint on the sidewalk at his feet. *Find a penny, pick it up,* said a little voice inside Danny's head.

Danny picked up the penny and, without really looking at it, stuffed it into his pocket.

Hopefully, Mr. Hinkens, Danny's science teacher, would tease him because he was the only boy in class who had *not* signed up for intramural football.

Someone had to tease Danny or torment him in *some* way if he were ever going to have an exciting adventure. He read adventure stories all the time and he knew the score. Science fiction. Fantasy. All the heroes started out as tortured loners no one loved or cared about in any way.

Unfortunately for Danny, his parents loved him and he loved them. Also, while they were too old (or perhaps too young) to use the word itself, he and his older brother actually felt the same way.

Danny was average height for his age but skinny, with bones that stuck out in more places on his body than a body ought to have bones. His hair lay straight and brown and his eyes were green. If anyone googled "boring, average twelve-year-old" he'd undoubtedly find Danny's photo.

He was, perhaps, smart for his age but not enough to make him an outcast. . . or even very interesting for that matter. He even liked his teachers and earned good grades. Yuck.

At one point, he'd learned Tae kwon do from his dad, but he didn't need fighting skills, did he, since Bobby protected him? It was more fun mastering video games, reading, or playing laser tag with his friends in the woods near his house.

Oh spit. That ruined it, too. He actually *had* friends. Real, fun, honest to goodness friends like Torch and TJ who slept over sometimes and surprised him with birthday parties at Lazer Quest, cool presents, and lots of cake and ice cream.

How in the world could he establish the necessary tortured soul on a stomach full of birthday cake and ice cream?

Real heroes needed ghastly, painful childhoods to forge in them the strength to brave terrible horrors in alternate universes and spaceships on the edge of the galaxy. So Danny would never steal a tremendous horde of gold from a blood-thirsty dragon, fight evil alien insects on a desolate planet, or hunt angst-ridden vampires, werewolves, or zombies in an under-saturated urban sprawl.

It was enough to make him scream.

Once, Danny had actually considered antagonizing Bobby so maybe his older brother would terrorize him. Hard to say. Might have helped.

Unfortunately, as Danny had stood in Bobby's bedroom with Socrates the snake coiled around one arm, ready to unleash untold dimensions of reptilian fury on his unsuspecting brother, he just couldn't follow through.

Two reasons.

One: Bobby lay so innocently and helplessly, face down on top of his Star Wars bed sheets in his Fruit-of-the-Looms.

Two: What if the ensuing debacle injured Socrates? Danny's mother would've perished from grief had her favorite snake been harmed.

Okay. . . Danny was doomed. His *mother* raised snakes. His *mother*. You never had fantastic adventures when your mother was cool enough to keep twelve snakes of her very own. It just. didn't. happen.

Had Danny not preoccupied himself with the utter impossibility of embarking on any kind of adventure, he might have noticed the little voice inside his head when he'd picked up the penny.

It had not been, in fact, his own.

This is Why Danny Wears Shorts to Bed

Danny dreamed of strange things that night: a red-haired woman and Old West taverns, images and events foreign to his actual experience. Had he not been awakened by his bed jumping six inches in the air and a foot to the left, he might have wondered about the dreams' origins the following morning.

Instead, he assumed that being thrown into the air and dropped on the floor next to his bed had to be part of a weird dream. Then someone shouted his name so forcefully the only options were Mom or Dad, so he woke up as quickly as possible. How might he explain that the jumping bed could be in no way his fault?

As he forced an eyelid open, all the unusual moments of his dreams slid into obscurity, replaced by the puzzle of who had awakened him in the middle of the night and why. The voice seemed too high for Dad and too low for Mom.

Danny's one open eye spotted Bobby hurrying to the side of the bed in his trademark Fruit-of-the-Looms and black footy socks. His brother's voice packed a force Danny had only rarely heard from his brother. . . and his words made no sense.

"Get up, Danny! The house is on fire and we have to get out." Bobby lifted him to his feet. "We have to get out!"

Bobby looked scared. . . Okay, *terrified* was a better word for it.

Bobby—Danny's big, strong older brother who feared nothing—was terrified.

Spit! In a great number of people, seeing the person you want to emulate cowering in fear would create a feeling of helplessness, but, strangely, in Danny, it had the opposite effect.

Well, Danny Decker said to himself, and it was his own voice this time, *someone better keep it together or we're doomed.*

"You're sure," he said out loud. "Fire? How?"

"There was an explosion. . . Didn't you feel it? I opened my bedroom door. . . It's an inferno out there. . . can't you hear it?" Bobby still held Danny, and, while affection was not uncommon in their family, his grip seemed more a clutch.

Danny listened. Something roared in the distance. Then it happened: one of those moments where time stretched and allowed him to think faster than normal. He looked his brother up and down. What to do? What to do?

This is exactly why I wear shorts and a t-shirt to bed every night, he thought, *and if we both survive this ordeal and Bobby is humiliated by standing in the yard in his underwear in front of all our neighbors, I am soooo going to say I told you so!*

Only six seconds after his brother had asked the question about the audibility of the fire, Danny grabbed the comforter from his bed, snatched his robe from the floor, and dragged his brother into the bathroom they shared where he retrieved Bobby's bathrobe from the back of the door to *his* bedroom.

He pulled brother, comforter, and bathrobes into the shower, cranking the water on cold full blast.

Bobby sputtered and struggled. "What the—?"

"Put your robe on before it gets wet," Danny insisted, shoving the robe into his brother's chest and pulling on his own as the water poured over them. "If it's wet, the fabric will stick to itself and make it hard to pull on. The wet stuff will protect us as we dash through the fire, and your bathrobe will prevent the neighbors from learning details about your anatomy they don't need to know."

Bobby looked at his brother through squinty eyes. "*I'm* supposed to be saving *you.*"

Danny turned Bobby in the shower's spray. "You can save me next time."

They jumped out of the tub, huddled together so they could pull the soaked comforter over the two of them. They rushed from the bathroom and through Danny's room since his was closer to the stairs which would, hopefully, lead them to safety.

"Wait a second." Bobby touched the door with one hand. "It's not hot. We're okay."

Oh yeah, someone had done that in a movie.

Bobby yanked the door open onto a hopeless inferno. Heat washed over Danny, but not enough to hurt. Smoke filled the air, but not enough to choke.

The brothers stepped into the open hall that looked over a railing and down onto the first floor living room.

Two things seemed strange: one, the living room wall—which had always blocked the view of the street and been a pretty solid wall type of thing with a lovely fireplace—had vanished. Completely. Ah, that was why they hadn't already asphyxiated from smoke.

Two, a little dinosaur stood at the bottom of the stairs blocking the escape of Mom and Dad, who held one another on the stairwell. The dinosaur shouted in a language like a really annoyed grackle and gestured at Danny's parents with what looked like a silver banana.

A silver banana?

Dad held a table leg in one hand, as if it might actually be some kind of protection against a silver banana. Mom, inexplicably, brandished some sort of vacuum cleaner attachment.

Oh wait, the little dinosaur wasn't blocking his parents; his parents were preventing *it* from climbing the stairs. They shouted at the dinosaur with rather astonishing language. If so many lives had not hung in the balance, Danny might have laughed.

He experienced another time-condensed moment: the dinosaur at the bottom of the stairs wasn't, in fact, a dinosaur. It was how a dinosaur, specifically something like a velociraptor, would look if it had evolved for a few million years more without a giant asteroid cutting short its evolutionary path. A change in its food supply, over millennia, would cause a velociraptor to shrink. Its brain case would grow, as would its arms, and it would walk upright. Nothing like that could have evolved on Earth.

On Earth. . .

It was an alien. . . and it pointed a weapon at his parents. . .

Danny knew what came next. "Look out!"

. . .too late. . .

There wasn't a beam. No bright blue or red or green light from the weapon to the hapless victims. The little dinosaur simply pointed his silver banana at Danny's parents, squeezed the thing, and Mom disappeared.

The alien pointed the banana at Dad, squeezed, and Dad was no longer there.

No special effects, no glory. . . just gone.

A horrible noise erupted from Bobby's throat when his parents vaporized, loud and horrified and high-pitched. It drew the attention of the alien, who looked up at the brothers, huddled together under a soggy blanket at the top of the steps.

It narrowed its eyes and waved its banana at them as it climbed the stairs.

Briefly, a holographic screen appeared in front of the alien. It said something in grackle and then winked out. Danny had no idea what the device registered, but from the way the aliens' eyes widened and it licked its lips, whatever the dinosaur sought. . . it had found it.

In a weird parallel to human behavior, it threw back its head and laughed in triumph.

That simple action saved the boy's lives.

While the dinosaur laughed, it raised its gun arm without really looking at them.

Bobby grabbed Danny and put himself between his brother and the alien.

Oh, heck no! Danny had read the novels! "Shielding someone with one's body" meant one thing and one thing only: instant and horrible, bloody death.

"You idiot." Danny grabbed his unsuspecting brother, pulled him close, and spun them both. With his back to the alien, Danny planted his feet against the stairs and pushed off as hard as he could.

The brothers launched down the stairs directly at the smug alien who had just finished his triumphant laugh. The collision hurt, and all three of them rolled down the last of the stairs and onto the floor below, but Danny had all four limbs and no one had been vaporized. When his world stopped spinning and crashing, he lay on his stomach, his brother sprawled across his backside, pinning him, and the alien lay prostrate a few feet away.

More importantly, the alien's silver banana lay less than a foot from Danny's hand.

While his brother wriggled around as if trying to sort up from left, Danny regarded the banana and the dinosaur, who glanced around, smacked its holster then locked eyes with Danny, who had the weapon in arm's reach without a clue how to use it.

Just grab the stupid thing, a strange voice in Danny's head said.

Danny grabbed the stupid thing.

Point and squeeze, said the voice.

Danny pointed and squeezed.

The alien vanished.

Problem solved.

Oh. . . wait. . . the house was on fire and Danny's parents were dead.

Danny had just killed an alien that resembled a highly evolved dinosaur.

Brain. wouldn't. work.

Bobby grabbed Danny and pulled him out of the burning house into the yard where a couple of firemen dragged them over to the fire trucks.

"Are you okay?" The firemen gave them dry blankets. "Where are your parents?"

If you tell them the truth, they'll think you're insane, the voice in Danny's head counseled, so he grabbed Bobby by the lapels of the bathrobe he wore only at Danny's insistence.

"We don't know what we saw." Danny pressed his mouth against Bobby's ear. "They were there one second and then they were gone. We didn't see anything else."

Bobby held Danny with anger in his eyes. "But we saw more than that. . . that thing killed Mom and Dad."

And that's the moment it hit.

That thing had killed Mom and Dad.

They were dead.

Horrible pain and anguish are never fun or entertaining to read unless you're messed up in the head, so we're close to the moment we leave the boys. They turned to watch their home burning to ash, one entire corner inexplicably missing.

They were orphans. . .

Orphans?

Realization slammed Danny in the frontal lobe like a cement truck.

"No, no, no, no, no. . ." Danny's legs buckled. "I didn't mean *this*." He fell helplessly to his hands and knees. "I didn't mean *this*!"

He was an orphan.

His adventure could begin.

All it had taken was the death of his parents.

Danny's wails morphed into screams, and Bobby held him close. The fire blazed in the background and the two brothers fell to the ground clutching each other in grief and sorrow. . . and it's really time to let them deal with this on their own.

We'll check in on them again the next day.

The story continues in *Danny Decker and the Horribly Unlikely Space Adventure*, available on Amazon, if not now, then really, really soon.

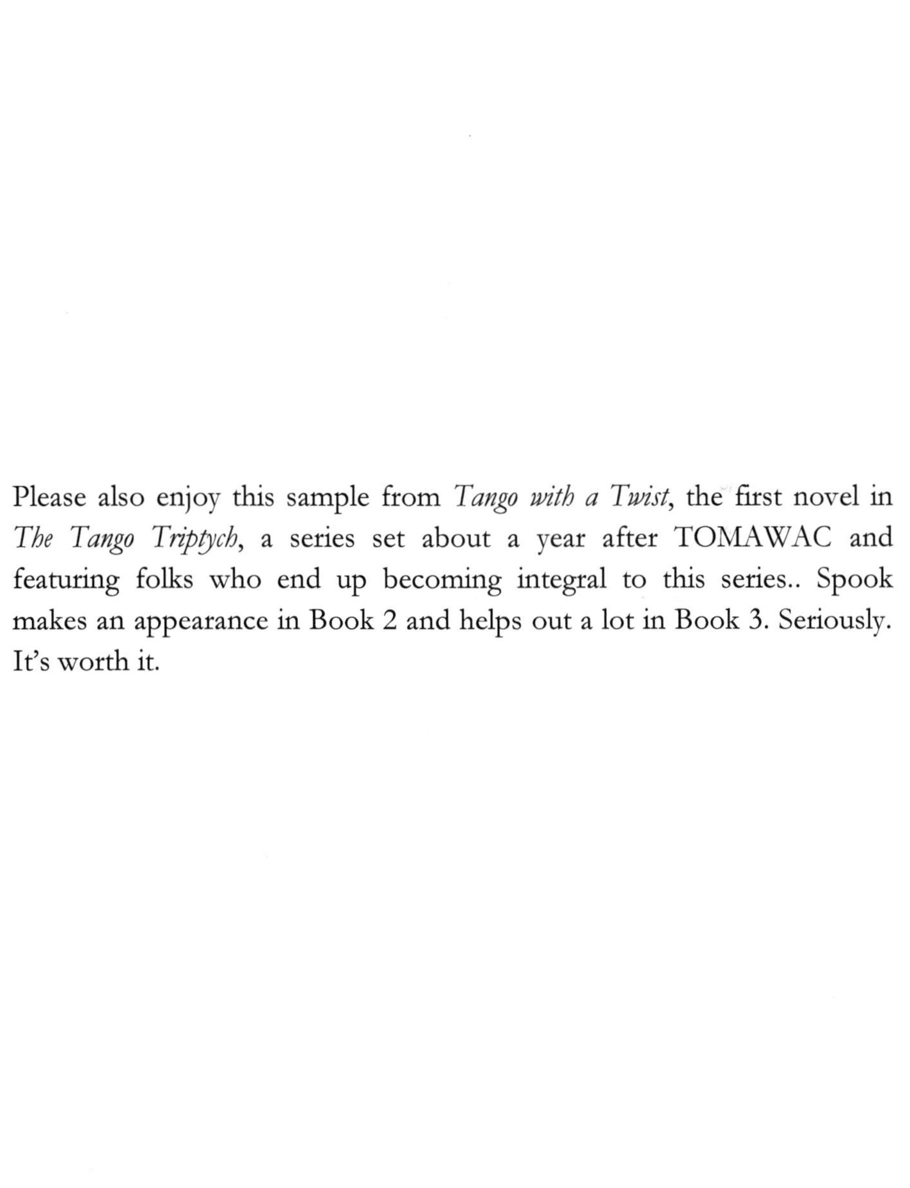

Please also enjoy this sample from *Tango with a Twist*, the first novel in *The Tango Triptych*, a series set about a year after TOMAWAC and featuring folks who end up becoming integral to this series.. Spook makes an appearance in Book 2 and helps out a lot in Book 3. Seriously. It's worth it.

TANGO
with a twist

by
John Robert Mack

One

Dead people. Everywhere.

The cemetery of my dad's hometown was the last freaking place I wanted to visit. I waited quietly in the Texas heat to give him a few minutes to pay his respects and to stretch my legs after the long drive from Austin. Was it wrong of me to avoid the reason we were there by recalling all the nights my girlfriend and I had sneaked into cemeteries to make out? Ex-girlfriend. Monika.

Grackles made that spooky sound grackles make while Dad stared at a rock. Cemeteries are weird. Not because of sparkly vampires or lacrosse-playing werewolves. They're just so damn. . . peaceful. I mean, if not for all the corpses, it would've been the perfect place for a family picnic.

"You can't park that there!" A loud South Texas accent hurried toward us, carefully avoiding the burial plots. He was built like a scarecrow and wore a police uniform two sizes too big. So much for peaceful.

Our moving van filled the dirt road, everything we had left in the world collected inside it. For a moving van, it was tiny. In the cemetery, it seemed like a Sam's Club hearse: *Bury Them in Bulk and Save!* The patrol car now facing it flashed red and blue lights.

"What the hell are you doing with a moving van in a cemetery?"

"Moving." Dad peered at the cop's name tag. "Palatino? As in old Sheriff Palatino? You his grandson?"

Oh, my God, small towns freaked me out.

Palatino adjusted his gun belt. "I'll ask the questions here." He couldn't have been more than a year or two older than me. Twenty at the outside. The acne made him younger. He nodded at the moving van. "Planning on loading up?"

"Loading what?" Dad waved at the nearest block of granite. "A lot of gravestones go missing around here?"

I chuckled.

Palatino squinted at me, then at Dad. I think the squint was meant to be intimidating, but Dad was a forty-something Conan the Barbarian. Except blonde and pale with a crew cut. He stared the guy down. "We're moving here from Austin. We stopped to pay our respects before heading over to my sister's place."

Again with the belt adjustment. "Who's your sister?" The dude reminded me of that Barney Fife guy on some old show my dad had made me watch.

"Macarena Davis." Like the cop would *happen* to know who she was.

The light of recognition sparked in Barney Fife's eyes. "You're the boxing coach?"

"Ex-boxing coach."

Oh, my God. This was *that* kind of town? Note to self: stay away from anyone named Bates. Everything about the cop's demeanor changed. He settled into one hip as if he'd channeled his inner Sheriff. "Had a little trouble with the law out there in the big city, didn't you?"

Dad took a breath. "It worked itself out."

Barney Fife squinted again, then turned his attention to me. "You're a dancer, right?" He looked me up and down. "Your aunt told me you were moving here. She told me a-a-all about you."

I pulled my shoulders back. Dad might've been willing to let this pissant twerp play big man, but I wouldn't.

"You a hot deal up there in Austin?" the cop asked.

I shrugged. I was a world champion. Well, ex-champion.

"You got a name?"

"Ethan Fox." Speaking through gritted teeth was a challenge.

More belt time. "Well, the family who runs the dance studio hereabouts? They're close friends of mine, and if you do anything to mess with any of them, you will answer directly to me."

Dad's hand lifted as if he were about to take my arm, just in case, but then it fell to his side. Yeah. Dad had stopped touching people six months earlier, after he'd had his "trouble with the law."

"It's probably not much compared to those fancy Austin places," the cop said, "but Mrs. Montez throws a *heck* of a Saturday Social, and you need to treat her people with respect."

Kill me, now. Please. Barney Fife needed to be taken down a peg or two—

"Look, deputy. . ." Dad might have been adrift in a world of guilt, but he could still read my mind. "I'll get the van out of here in a few minutes. I wanted to say hello. . ." The sorrow and defeat in his voice pissed me off. "We don't want any trouble." He was a fighter, damn it. "I just wanted to say hello."

The people in the ground, at our feet, were strangers to me, but "Beloved-Wife-and-Mother" had been his sister and "Beloved-Husband-and-Father" had been his best friend.

Palatino pushed his hat back an inch and squinted down his nose at us. He nodded as if he were doing us the world's biggest favor by not running us in. He moseyed back to his car. "Welcome to Dumass, Texas, Ethan Fox."

No, really, that was its name. He'd tried to pronounce it *Doo-mahs*, but get a grip.

When the cop climbed into his car, Dad sighed. "You okay?"

I engaged my fake enthusiasm on supernova. "They throw a *helluva* Saturday Social!" Birds leapt into the air and flew off. "This place fucking sucks." If you notice the number of things in my life with the prefix "ex" you might have more sympathy for the attitude. A shrink would say it was a defense mechanism.

Dad returned to his silent contemplation of granite. He was so depressed, he didn't even bitch me out for being rude.

Deep breath. It's a dance thing. If you're getting wound up, take a deep breath and it'll relax you. Deep breath.

The folks in the ground were my biological parents. Dad had adopted me after his sister and her husband died in a fire when I was only a few months old. I didn't remember them. At all. Well, Dad had told me tons of stories, but I had no actual memories, no flash of an angelic smile with an over-saturated sunny background. No mementos either. No baby blanket with my name on it.

To be honest, this visit was probably harder on Dad than it was on me. He'd been "Dad" for nearly all of my seventeen years, so he was my *dad*, you know? What was I supposed to feel about these strangers who'd brought me into the world?

A concrete angel looked down on me disapprovingly. It was exactly like a statue in the cemetery where Monika and I used to make out.

I missed making out with Monika, and, just so we're perfectly clear, "making out" *is* a euphemism. Feel free to google "euphemism." Most of my friends were adults and anything lower than a B+ meant Dad kept me home from dance practice, so my vocabulary rocks.

I stared out across the trees. Dad wasn't going to say anything about my snide remark. "I'm sorry," I told him. "I'm a douchebag."

"I was going to say, 'little prick.'"

"Now you know *that's* just not true."

He chuckled. Good. He'd always been *that* dad.

A year earlier at the gym, this guy named Jimmy Russo knocked me out. When I'd come to, Dad was holding me. Paternal worry covered his face. "You okay, son?"

"Dad, I'm fine." With all the guys watching, I felt kinda dorky held in my dad's arms. "Let me up."

He tried to kiss my forehead.

"Dad! How old am I?"

"What? Too grown up to kiss the old man?" He pushed his face into mine. "That's it. I want a kiss on the mouth."

"Dad!"

I fought him off, much to the amusement of the guys watching. I fled to the locker room to check for a black eye. When I saw myself in the mirror, I groaned. A penis drawn in Sharpie decorated my cheek. Yeah. He was *that* dad.

Well, he *used* to be that dad. I missed it. A lot.

The call of a grackle brought me back to Dad. . . and the cemetery. . . in Dumass, Texas. The sun beat down on us like it wanted us dead. September in Texas? Fucking hot. He didn't throw a fatherly arm around me the way he would've six months before.

He'd killed a man. It was an accident, but he held himself responsible. That's how we lost everything and why we left Austin to move in with my Auntie Mac. It was the reason he didn't touch anyone anymore, and it was "that thing we didn't talk about." We used to talk about everything. Seriously. *Everything.* Certain people had called him a monster enough times he'd ended up believing them, I guess.

He stared at the rock for a long while. He laid down some flowers.

I tried to feel something and failed.

No, that's not true. I wanted my dad back, but I didn't mean the guy in the dirt. For the first time in my life, I felt like an orphan.

"You okay?" he asked again.

"I'm fine, Dad," I lied. "I'm fine."

David hunched over his tablet watching video of Katy and her best friend Gertrude, whom everyone called Juicy. They huddled together staring at Katy's cell phone. The camera set in the ceiling of the dance studio bathroom was perfectly placed to record both stalls and still see over Katy's shoulder at the vanity. The video had been recorded the day before. David had watched it a dozen times. What was he going to do?

"Oh. my. God." Katy squeezed Juicy, their breasts pressed together. "He can nail six, seven, eight. Eight! Eight turns he can nail."

"Don't bust a tit." Juicy grabbed the cell. "You are so *hot for this guy."*

"I have a boyfriend." Katy snatched her phone. "How many times do I have to

tell you he's gay, anyway? Look at the way he dances. Straight guys do not *move their hips like that."*

"There is that."

Son of a bitch. Katy would never be interested in him now with this new, big city dancer in town. The son of a bitch was good looking too, in that pretentious, pretty boy way Katy was sure to like. So what if he was gay? Girls always fell for the gay guys. What did they call it? Metrosexual?

He didn't have the luxury of waiting for her to dump the quarterback anymore. He had to make his move now. He glanced up. Photos of Katy watched over him from every wall of his bedroom, her face alive in the flickering candlelight.

God, she was beautiful. He would do anything, anything *to make her love him. He'd even googled* "how do i make a girl love me?" *One site had grabbed his attention.*

Simple instructions. Kind of whacked out, sure, but simple enough. Okay, fine, he'd give anything *a try. The blogger was passionate. She'd been certain he would succeed, so certain she'd sent him naked pictures of herself dancing around a fire. So. . . dedicated, right?*

He rushed to the small table in the corner and snatched up the cloth doll with Katy's face pinned to it. He slowly wound a cotton thread around and around the doll, muttering, "Katy and David. Katy and David. Katy and David."

After making sure I knew where Auntie Mac's house was, Dad dropped me off at the dance studio the cop had mentioned. "At least there's somewhere you can dance, right?"

Woot.

"I'll be at the house in a few to help you unpack," I said. The town was so small there was no reason I couldn't walk it.

As he drove off, I felt like a little kid on his first day of school. Don't forget I'd spent most of my life traveling the world on my own, so no big, right? The year before, I took second place at Blackpool, the most famous dance competition on the planet. I took first at World's too, which was almost as cool. All my friends, who were dancers and coaches, treated me like a king. Out here I was just Macarena Davis's nephew. Nobody.

Esmeralda's Tango Emporium lived at one end of a half-empty strip center that may have been posh a hundred years ago, but was now. . . well, the opposite of posh.

And "Emporium"?

I pulled out my cell and googled the word.

Thought so. Not a good name for a dance studio.

I snapped a photo for Instagram and was about to tweet. . . then I shoved the cell in my pocket. Who would read it?

With a deep breath to settle into my cheery dance champion persona, I opened the door and took one step into. . . the saddest, shabbiest studio I'd *ever* seen. A solitary old couple stumbled through something that might have been an ancient version of cha-cha and might have been the hokey-pokey. The music playing was "Sway." No, not the vaguely interesting remake with hot strippers who could sing. The original. And no one was being ironic. A dingy gold chandelier above needed so many bulbs replaced it actually managed to *darken* the room.

The little bell on the door behind me jingled.

"Out of the way, Ken Doll!"

Ken Doll? I glanced at my reflection in the hazy mirror: blond hair, blue eyes, nice teeth. Damn it, she was right. How had I never noticed that?

An elbow in the middle of my back propelled me into an imitation leather bar stool as a teenage cyclone in dance flats barreled past. I watched her from every angle in the studio mirrors as she stomped across the dingy parquet floor carrying more toilet paper than an army would use in a month. Latina, lots of leg in tight jeans, curvy under the t-shirt.

"Hey Tango, wait up." I trotted after her.

In the mirror, she smiled at the nickname. "Whatever you're selling, it can wait until I unload."

Man, she walked fast. "Let me give you a hand."

On the other end of the dance floor, she turned and stopped. "Do I look like I need help, Ken?" She did a double take so subtle nobody but a recently dumped guy like me could've noticed it. "I don't know you."

"I'm new."

Her face relaxed like she'd just recognized a long lost friend. "You're the *dancer*." She backed through the swinging door and vanished.

Was the town *that* small? I'd been there an hour. Tops.

Her voice called through the door. "Come on in."

Okay.

Smile: check.

Suave, masculine dance posture: check.

With a wink at the white hairs still dancing in the middle of the floor, I stepped through the swinging doors into the same storage room that's in pretty much every dance studio I'd ever seen: dark, cluttered and smelling vaguely of old shoes.

Nice. The first familiar thing in town.

Before you judge me for loving a stinky old closet, think of that ancient pair of shoes, the perfect pair that fits like skin and reminds you of every hike or race or ramble. This room was familiar like that to me.

"I guess I can't call you Ken Doll anymore." She stacked TP. "Didn't you win some kind of award at some contest somewhere?"

I hauled out my cell, tapped the screen and held it out to her. "Second at Blackpool." Here, at least, I was in my element. My titles always earned me instant cred at dance studios. "Ten-dance youth champion at World's. How do you know anything about me?"

She took the cell. "Get used to life in a small town. I talked to your aunt last week."

Hmm, small town creepy: check.

She watched the video and one hand went to her mouth.

Stellar. It *was* the best I'd ever danced, and. . .

She laughed out loud, killing my moment of pride. "You have an app of yourself on your home screen? That is so precious!" She held the phone out before the video was even done.

Precious? My masculinity whimpered and crawled away to die. I closed the app. I had to get used to it: out here everything I'd accomplished was irrelevant.

She pulled her t-shirt off and I sort of forgot about the cell. "Is she your BFF, the girl dancing with you in the video?"

Her bra was purple and. . .

Okay screw it, all I could think was, *omigod, tits!* Out of nowhere, a perfect valley of dark skin. I glanced around. Was somebody punking me? Don't get me wrong, I'd been backstage enough to see women in a quick change, but that was different. That was at a competition when I was more worried about forgetting my dance sequences. This was a shadowy storage closet, and internet porn had taught me what happens when hot girls undress in shadowy storage closets.

A heavy, boy's class ring dangled between the lovely hills. It forced me back to reality.

Wait. She was still talking?

". . .and the support group at school is great."

Support group?

"It's a small town, but you're perfectly safe here." She slid on a purple blouse and pulled her long, black hair out from under it. "Are you all right?" She didn't button it right away, which meant only one thing.

"I'm not gay."

She laughed again but this time with less gusto and she did up her blouse self-consciously. "What do you mean, you're not gay?"

I should've known what was up the moment she pulled off her shirt, but I was sort of distracted at the time. "*No. soy. mariposa.*" That's how to say it in South Texan. "Does your boyfriend know you strip in front of gay dudes?"

"How do you know I have a boyfriend?"

"Class ring on a string."

One hand went to the necklace. "Oh." Suddenly, her eyes grew huge and she spouted a litany of Spanish that went way beyond the phrases and obscenities I'd picked up at Austin High. She shoved me clear through the swinging door, where I stumbled a couple of steps and fell on my ass.

She finally reverted to English. "Why'd you let me take off my shirt in front of you, *culo*!"

"Like I could've stopped you."

"You could've turned around."

"I already told you I'm not gay, Tango." I got to my feet. "A hot girl strips in front of me, I'm only turning away if she asks me to."

"Tango's. . . racist. . ."

Ha. She was floundering, and the word "hot" threw her off track. Two points for me. "Then so's Ken Doll."

She planted her hands on hips cocked to one side in a very distracting manner. "You're a teenage ballroom champ with a gay dad and you expect me to believe you're straight?"

And there it was.

I'd learned how to cope: keep quiet and wait for her to figure it out on her own.

Having a gay boxing coach dad had its advantages: complete parental approval for the dancing hobby was at the top of the list. Insistence on boxing lessons to deal with the ramifications of the dance lessons was another. Why everyone assumed like father like son, I'd never understand.

Tango managed better than most. Rather than making it worse by babbling on about how many gay friends she had, blah, blah, blah, she stared at me for a few seconds while the old dancing couple watched the scene, probably wishing they had popcorn.

"Okay, Foxtrot, you get your first three Mexican stereotypes for free."

Several points for her.

"Hi there." I held out a hand. "My name's Foxtrot and I'm new to town."

She smirked. It was a pretty smirk. Damn that class ring.

"Hey there, Foxtrot. My name's Tango."

We shook hands, and I tried to prolong the contact for an extra second or two, but she glanced past my shoulder and retracted her hand quickly. In the mirror, I watched several teenagers enter the studio. She stepped closer and whispered, "The banter is fun, but please don't tell anyone that you know I'm wearing a purple bra."

Understanding that she could get in trouble if someone suspected she wasn't doing her job, I inclined my head in a slow nod and stepped aside so she could greet the group, happy to keep the memory for my own enjoyment.

She strode across the floor and her bearing changed. She stood taller and pulled her shoulders down. Her hips rolled a little more and her steps hit softly. "*Oye chicos*, if you haven't practiced I'm going to kick every single ass."

Holy crap. A coach? I figured she traded janitor service for classes.

There were four girls and five dudes. Oh wait, four dudes and one boyfriend. At least, from the way she latched onto him, I assumed it was his ring on her string. He was tall and shaped like a football player, not a dancer. He had dark hair and eyes and a face that grinned wa-a-ay too much. Seeing a hot chick you like kissing her boyfriend is like watching a *People of Walmart* video. It's gross and makes you squirm, but you can't force yourself to look away.

Wow, was she *ever* going to come up for air?

My dance coaches never did that.

A very tall, white dude with Asian writing on his t-shirt blocked my view. "Hey there, I'm K-pop." His hair was tall too, black streaked with red, and cemented into fun angles like an anime character. Cool.

"K-pop?"

"I really like Korean pop music, so Katy calls me K-pop." He held out a hand.

I craned my neck to see around K-pop's hair.

Yep, she was still sucking face.

"Katy?" I asked, full of innocence. "She told me her name was Tango." I took the offered hand. "You can call me Foxtrot, by the way."

The girl, whose name was still open to debate, came up for air. The fact that she named all her friends was stellar because the names always meant something, like K-pop's. It made them easier to remember, but there were ten people on the crew, for God's sake, and who remembers the names of all seven dwarves?

She introduced them one by one and really fast: K-pop, Taco, Juicy, Shilling, Woody, Cosita, Mono, Ephraim and Boyfriend. Yeah, her boyfriend's name was "Boyfriend," which avoided confusion in the long run, I guess.

And "Juicy"? The girl must have noticed my unspoken question. "I really love Juicy Couture." Ironically, she actually *was* Korean, whereas K-pop was not.

Why did everyone let Katy name them when she herself had no nickname? No clue, but something told me that getting her to accept my suggestion would mean I had arrived.

She took center stage and clapped her hands. "Okay, Foxtrot, now you've met the gang, you can piss off. We have work to do."

Mutters of dismay communicated that the group felt she was being rude to the new guy. The new guy agreed.

"You don't want to sit here and watch." She spoke faster and she gestured more. "We're learning some new choreo. Bo-ring."

Hands in my pockets, I broke for cool. "I don't know. Maybe I can learn a new move?"

That's when it happened: the moment that changed the tone of the whole scene. I swear I heard the sound of a record scratch.

Juicy regarded me, full of wide-eyed curiosity. "Oh? You're a dancer, Foxtrot?"

If it'd been *Glee*, they'd all have turned to look at me simultaneously with a big whip-cracking sound effect. Except for Katy, who was already staring at me with a little extra salsa in her cheeks.

She hadn't told them.

And she knew.

She knew Blackpool.

She knew who I was, and not just from Auntie Mac.

She'd lied.

Closing in and holding her trapped in her subterfuge, I stared her down. "Well, I dance a *little*. I'd *love* to see what y'all can do."

A murmur of excitement at a chance to show off rumbled through the studio, cut off by a sharp whistle from Katy. "No offense, Foxtrot." All the bravado and teacher presence returned. "But you dance *ballroom*." She gestured at those around her. "We're a *crew*."

They fell out.

"Hells yeah," said Woody.

"Ballroom?" asked Ephraim.

Yeah. I had to cope with that shit a lot too. Time to impress the freak out of them. Sure I danced ballroom, but I was more *So You Think You Can Dance* than *Dancing with the Stars*. I mean, I was seventeen, damn it. Back in *Austin*. . .

Well. . . I wasn't in Austin anymore.

Katy settled her shoulders, eyes blazing, all her Latina *La-tin-essss* daring me to ask for a showdown. A few months ago, I would have. Come on, this was my chance for the sexy face-off, right?

Something stopped me. Deep in her eyes, she was afraid.

Of what? Of a hot, blond, Ken doll?

As I looked over her crew, a sick feeling hit my stomach and I took a deep, deep breath, letting all the excitement bleed out of me. So *that's* why she didn't want me there. Why she lied about not knowing Blackpool. Why she made fun of my app.

I held up both hands. "My apologies, Katy. You're right. I should. . . go home and. . . unpack. . . things."

I shook a few hands and bumped a few fists. Everyone was friendly enough, but I saw it in their eyes: I danced ballroom. *Era ñoño.* I was lame. Not a good feeling, but if I was right about the crew, I had to let it go.

As I left, I watched Katy in the mirrors. When you're around mirrors long enough you learn to see the world almost 360 degrees at a time. She acted like everything was same old, same old, but she glanced at me out of the corner of her eye. She wore a mother's look, as if she knew her little kid had just avoided the neighborhood bully. Relief.

Outside, I hurried around the corner and waited. When the music started, I slunk to the glass door and peered inside. The music was faint, but it rocked. Katy's team, however, did not. Half of them were off beat. The choreography was what you saw in the first ten minutes of a movie about the downtrodden dance team who would rise to fame and glory by the end of it.

Okay, there's truly no way I can describe them without coming off as a complete douchebag. . . because they sucked. Utterly.

K-pop really wanted to be a pop-and-lock star, but all his moves reeked of five years ago. Juicy thought she was sexy but didn't realize that an ultra-flexible pelvis just made her look like a slut. It didn't mean she could dance. She couldn't have been worse if she'd been *trying* to look bad.

That's why Katy ejected me. She was smart enough to see the truth and didn't want her friends to know it: out here this crew probably rocked the planet, but anywhere else they were a bunch of wannabes in costumes. She didn't want me to laugh at them and force them to face how little they mattered to anyone outside their Dumass world.

So why stand down and leave when I saw that Katy was afraid? Why? Because that exact same haunted expression stared back at me every time I looked in a mirror. How could I make fun of that?

Six months ago, I probably would have.

Not anymore.

David sniffed the rose and adjusted the ribbon. He wiggled his fingers over the flower and muttered some nonsense from the naked chick's website. He placed it on the windshield of Katy's car and hid in the shrubs across the street. Red was her favorite color and she only liked roses with a strong scent. Unscented roses were a waste of time to her. She'd once told Juicy that a single rose was a romantic gesture, but an entire dozen smacked of desperation.

An hour passed.

Katy ran from the house and jumped into her car. She must've been late for the dance crew's performance. Would she notice the rose? Yes. She climbed out of the car and picked up the flower delicately. She glanced around with a smile that filled David with hot desire.

"Ethan Fox, you naughty, naughty boy." She sniffed the rose and her smile grew.

Son of a bitch! Nothing the naked chick told him to do worked!

Chapter Two

The morning after I met the dance crew, I struggled to hang a punching bag in the garage. *Mumford and Sons* played on the MP3 player that wasn't an iPod because I was too much of a leader to follow a trend. Someone blocked the light of the rising sun. Dad. He didn't offer to help. "How the hell did you sneak that past me?" With the sun behind him, he looked like a gangster in the cheap suit and tie Auntie Mac had bought him.

She'd picked it out too, thank God, so while it was cheap, at least it was stylin'. A little tight around the shoulders, but the shoulders in question were huge.

I managed to hook the bag. "You look good in the suit."

"Please answer the question."

I climbed down and propped one foot on the ladder channeling the emoticon of cool. All the boxing gear, apart from the bag and a pair of gloves, had been left behind in Austin. "You know how I snuck it past you. I paid Mario to do it for me."

"Sneaked," he auto-corrected. "How'd you pay him off?"

"Mario's getting married in a couple of months. He wanted to surprise Molly so I taught him a few waltz steps." I gestured at the heavy bag. "Ta-daa."

It was an argument bound to happen sooner or later, but, hopefully, the revelation about Mario's last minute nuptials would distract him.

"Take it down." He spoke quietly, which was freakier than if he ran around yelling.

"No."

We stared at each other for about a gajillion years before he turned around and walked away. Up until the accident, Dad spent two hours a day, three days a week coaching me. Now, boxing was part of the thing we didn't talk about.

"Have fun jousting dragons, Dad." I called his job hunt "jousting dragons" because there were as many jobs to find as there were dragons.

Deep breath.

After setting *Mumford and Sons* to blast away on repeat, I pulled on the gloves and focused on beating the crap out of the bag. Hitting it hard helped me forget I was lonely and pissed off. It was pure and physical. I lost myself in it: constantly moving and hitting. Always keeping my guard up.

But my mind wandered: Monika's last words to me? You know, when she dumped me.

"After everything we've been through together and everything I've done for you, I just don't know how you can *do* this to me. I *hate* you, Ethan Fox! We're through!"

She'd stalked away and left me in the middle of a busy dance floor that'd fallen silent. About fifty people gawked at me, wondering what I'd do, a circle of vultures waiting to see if I'd break down and cry like a little girl.

"I told her the new make-up made her look like a whore," I lied. In my head, it was funny.

People had been a bit shocked, but they'd returned to their lessons.

I forced my attention to hitting the heavy bag in front of me. "One, four, three, two, three, three." It was a training drill. The numbers represented different punches. The drill was meant to clear my head.

Didn't work.

What had I really told Monika right before her tear-filled parting shot? "I'm sorry, Monika, but Dad lost *everything*, the gym, the house, the cars. We're going to Auntie Mac's because we don't have anywhere else to go." I'd worked hard to keep my voice low so all those people in the studio wouldn't hear. "I can find a way up here on the weekends to practice, but I can't afford the coaching anymore."

"What about the costumes? We can't use last year's costumes."

"There's no way I can afford new costumes now." I'd forced myself to fake a smile. "You're the most beautiful girl out there no matter *what* you're wearing."

Scroll back to her response, and maybe, just maybe, my stupid one-liner won't sound quite so evil.

We'd met when we were eight. I was the only boy in class and she was the top girl, so our coach paired us up for a Fred and Ginger routine. We were so darn cute, her parents begged Dad to pull me out of regular classes so we could stay partners. And so it went. Monika usually got what she wanted. We started dating officially the night she snuck into my hotel room and introduced me to euphemisms at fifteen. It was the weekend we won our first state comp, so two reasons to celebrate, right?

"One, four, three, two, three, three." I focused on beating the crap out of the bag. My aunt's garage existed in a completely different universe. I'd never see Monika again. Was that good or bad?

Something spattered across my shoulders and scared holy hell out of me. I spun and blocked, ready with a powerhouse if I needed it.

The girl silhouetted in the garage door several feet away dropped the extra pebbles onto the gravel drive. Monika? No, she cocked her hip in a very recognizable manner. Katy.

I reached for the ear buds before remembering the gloves, so I smacked myself upside the head at the same time I knocked the buds out of my ears.

"Sorry, Foxtrot. I wasn't sure how else to get your attention."

"Hey." It was about all I could manage. No idea how long I'd been at the bag, but it would be a few minutes before I caught my breath.

"Can I come in?"

I nodded. Wow, she was hot in the early morning light.

She looked me up and down. "Turnabout's fair play, I guess."

Oh yeah, I was shirtless and sweaty. Normally, no big deal. Dancer. Boxer. Google "ethan fox shirtless" with your safesearch on and you'll find pix of me. But with Katy right there in my garage? Utterly different story.

By the way, without safesearch, you'll get an entirely different Ethan Fox.

I dove for snarky. "You stopped by for an eyeful?" Using my teeth, I ripped open the Velcro closures on my gloves. "Shouldn't you be in school?"

"Shouldn't you?"

I slipped into my discarded t-shirt. "Dad figured I'd be training all across the country this year, so I do school online." Had I managed to make that nonchalant? He'd paid in full before we went broke.

She hesitated, closed her eyes and shook her head microscopically. "You're from a completely different planet."

Was that a good thing or a bad thing?

She opened her eyes. "We had a dance gig this morning. The Starbucks' grand opening."

"Starbucks?"

She smirked. "It's a big deal around here."

Wow. I encircled the bag with one arm and leaned my head against it, trying for disarming cuteness while I let her get around to her reason for stopping by.

She raised one perfect eyebrow. "So. . . a boxing ballroom dancer?"

I shrugged. People get around to the point a lot faster if you let them talk.

"I'm sorry about the ballroom crack in front of the crew," she said, "but you took me by surprise. I figured it'd be a few days before you found the studio." She wandered around the garage, touching things and picking them up. It was cute. "I'm a tango dancer. Third gen. The whole dance crew thing is kinda new to me, but I'm the best dancer in town." Her tone wasn't egotistical, just stating a fact.

"Head cheerleader?" I asked.

She made a face as if she'd just sucked the mother of all lemons. "I said *dancer*."

So it was like that. I avoided smiling.

Cheerleaders and studio dancers? No love lost. Trust me.

"Anyway. . . your aunt told me about you because my mom owns the only dance studio in town and she knew you'd make your way there eventually." She picked up a piece of newspaper, smoothed it out and folded it. "I saw your website and stuff." She glanced up. "It's not stalker or anything. I just thought maybe I could offer you a proposition."

Proposition? Now she had my complete interest.

She laughed. "I have a boyfriend, Foxtrot." She held the class ring up with one thumb. "I want to offer you a job."

"Coaching the team?"

She gave me the same face she'd made about cheerleaders. "I saw your coaching videos. You dance great, but your teaching sucks. I want you to show me choreography and *I'll* teach the team. While you've been running around the world dancing like a star, my mom's been training me how to teach."

"I'll do it."

"What? Just like that? No ego about how you're all world-famous and must know more than me about everything?"

"We need the money." Couldn't let her figure out the obvious reason why I'd rather work with her alone than with the whole crew. "Dad isn't going to find a job here any time soon. While it's great that we have a roof over our heads, sharing a bathroom with your dad isn't all it's cracked up to be."

"Too many hair care products?"

My turn to make a face. "Dude, he's a boxing coach. He thinks gel is something you use for a pulled muscle. I *so* get another Mexican joke, now."

Her face wandered from confused to amused. “Fine, but there isn’t enough money for you to move out. I’ll give you what I’m getting, but that’s all I have.”

“It’s more than I’m making now.” Score. Distracted her with the money angle.

The honk of a car horn startled me.

Katy spun around. “Shit, he’s already done tearing down the stage?” She turned back to me. “If anyone asks, I walked here because you lost your wallet when I dropped you on your ass yesterday.” She moved away slowly. “It’s Corey, and I don’t want the team to know you’re coaching me.”

“Corey?”

She lifted the ring again. “Boyfriend.” She lowered her voice. “And while the rose was pretty, please don’t do stuff like that, Foxtrot. I have a boyfriend.”

“What rose?”

She blinked a few times. “The rose I found on my car this morning. Very sweet, but if we’re going to work together—”

“Wasn’t me. Perhaps Boyfriend?”

She chuckled. “We’ve been going out for a year. The roses dried up months ago.” She settled into that hip thrust I liked so much. “It really wasn’t you?”

“I don’t know where you live.”

Ha! She was disappointed. She *liked* thinking it was me, even if she had to tell me not to do it anymore.

Complicated.

Nice.

Boyfriend honked again. Katy jumped. “Whatever. Studio, ten o’clock tonight and I dropped off your wallet, right?”

I pulled it out of a pocket and waggled it in the air for all to see. “Thanks for the wallet, Katy,” I said louder than necessary. “Sure am glad you found it. I was sick worried.”

She tossed me a smirk before dashing down the drive to the waiting car. She didn't wave as they drove off, but I like to think she wanted to. She also didn't kiss Boyfriend hello, so that was nice.

He drove a new Dodge Challenger, which meant he had money but was compensating for a tiny dick. Good news and bad all rolled up in a shiny red package.

I missed my Roadster.

David adjusted his binoculars. In the garage, Fox stripped off his shirt, pulled on gloves and went at the punching bag again. Loud music destroyed the peaceful morning. Inconsiderate prick. The noise was helpful, though, as David slipped out of the bushes, across the street and around the side of the house. He hurried through the gate across the backyard and made his way into the kitchen. He'd been in the house a dozen times already. Macarena Davis was known to hand out leftovers from her restaurant to the local single men, as long as they returned her dishes promptly.

The room at the top of the stairs screamed teenage boy. Clothes littered the floor, half-unpacked boxes stacked up against one wall. A pile of gold trophies filled one corner. David slid one arm under the bed and attached a mic. He tucked a small cloth bag into the frame at the head: bladderwrack, anise, lemon verbena and mustard seed.

Ouch! A static spark hit him as he touched the metal frame.

The naked chick had promised *it would ruin the big city guy's mojo. Promised. And she sent him video of her with her toys, too.*

David didn't know if curses worked, but she'd guaranteed success and if the spell didn't work she'd refund the money he'd spent on herbs. He'd try anything. Amazon had already shipped two books about witchcraft.

He stalled. Witchcraft? Seriously? Is that what he was doing?

Whatever. If it got Katy *to send him naked photos, who cared, right?*

He hurried from the room and down the stairs.

The sound of a patio door sliding caught him by surprise.

He froze. Was Fox coming in or going out?

Indie rock blared out from the backyard. David breathed again. He ran to the front door, but slowed to a casual walk as he exited the house.

I arrived at the studio at eight o'clock rather than ten. Two advantages to a small town: everywhere is walking distance and it's easy to find out when the only dance practice starts.

Music filtered through the cracked glass. My look was a very carefully executed casual: sweat pants and a tank top that showed off my boxing shoulders. I checked to make sure everything was in place. How would I explain being early? *I just thought I'd stop by and practice my lame ballroom moves. What do you charge for floor fees?*

Okay. Showtime.

The studio was no better than the first time I'd seen it. Without sunlight filtering in, it was even shabbier, like something Liberace puked up in 1975. I've said there are advantages to having a gay dad. One downside is accidently dropping phrases like that. Google "liberace living room" and you'll get a good picture of the studio decor. Literally.

Practice was full-on. The "crew" was running—wait. Damn ironic quotation marks. I shouldn't let the sarcasm slip into my voice. Try again.

Practice was full-on. The crew ran a piece with K-pop and Juicy featured up front. They locked with a little popping and K-pop didn't completely suck, but Juicy was awkward. K-pop was more fluid, but slow. Juicy was faster, but she counted the moves out loud. Who did that?

The rest of the crew struggled through a time step in the background, a basic "step-touch, step-touch" thing white boys have danced for fifty years. Shilling moved pretty well, but her timing sucked. Woody had rhythm but moved his pelvis like a dick dancer. Put him with Juicy, upload the video to a porn site and they could raise some serious money. Ephraim and Mono were nearly invisible.

Taco was. . . Bless his heart, Taco just didn't belong on a dance team.

For those of you not familiar with the saying, "Bless his heart" is the greatest Texan contribution to the English language. You can say anything you want about someone as long as you precede it or follow it with "bless his/her heart." As in, "She is the biggest slut on the planet, bless her *heart*." Get the tone right and you have free rein.

The song ended, they struck a final pose and I applauded. "That was great, y'all. How long have you been working on that?"

Big grins all around.

K-pop answered. "Bro, that's our new piece. We started it today."

I excel at fake surprise. "Whoa. Today?"

Katy stomped over. "What are you doing here, Foxtrot?"

I raised my hands, warding her off. "I just thought I'd stop by and practice my lame ballroom moves. What do you charge for floor fees?" Rehearsal always pays off. The crew bought it.

Katy remained skeptical. "Take five, *chicos*."

I lowered my voice as she dragged me to the black leather bar. "I need to see what you have to work with, Katy. If I can't coach them directly, I need to know what they can do so I know what to show you." She wound up to get sarcastic with me, so I disarmed her with a compliment. "You're better than the rest of them. I can't choreograph based on what *you* can do."

She rolled her eyes. "You suck up." She squeezed my elbow really hard and I'd guess my growing excitement was the opposite of what she'd intended. "You can stay, but stop with the surprises and don't you *dare*. . ." The intense glare she fed me had a similarly opposite effect. "Don't you *dare* do anything to insult them."

I nodded. "I'd call first, but I don't have your number." Hopefully, the innocent face worked better than the compliment.

She released my arm and turned away. "Leave thirty bucks on the bar, Foxtrot. It'll cover you for the month."

K-pop wandered to my side. Fist bump. "Bro, you totally need to join the crew. Your shit on YouTube is beast." Big grin. "Total *Beast,* hai?"

Yeah, that wasn't a shocker. I had a routine on YouTube to a song from this Korean band called Beast, spelled B2ST for reasons undisclosed. Coming from one of their fans, it was a pretty big compliment. Those guys could dance.

I leaned closer. "Thanks, bro. But I don't think Katy likes me."

For the record, I'd never called anyone "bro" before.

He nodded sagely and the red streaks in his anime hair bobbed in the dusty light. "Let me work on the coach, bro." Another fist bump. Katy shouted his name and off he trotted.

He needed to be my new best friend. Everything about him screamed sidekick. Also, he was nicer to me than anyone else I'd met.

Speaking of which. . . a heavy arm fell across my shoulders. A deep voice said, "Hey, 'Foxtrot'," forcing me to check punctuation. See, that's why I rehearse. He didn't actually make the air quotes, but I heard them. It was Boyfriend, and I could tell he was working hard to keep his voice dark and menacing. "I see you staring at Katy, bro. I need you to stop."

Seriously? Do guys say "bro" anymore?

"Come on, Boyfriend." My response flew out of my mouth before I could stop. There was no lisping or mincing, but it was an Emmy-worthy performance. "Look at that outfit. And her hair? Perfection. How can I *not* look at her? OMG."

Lol.

I'm not proud of that moment, and if Dad ever found out. . . at least he'd likely touch me again. You know, to smack me. But I had to make sure this goon didn't see me as a threat or he'd *never* let Katy work with me alone.

"Wait a minute." His face ran the gamut from confused to stupid, back to confused and settled on stupid. Game show themes ran through my head. "Katy said you're straight."

My hip pushed out in a perfect copy of Katy's and I imitated her eye roll. To avoid an utter stereotype, I didn't put my hands on my hips. "I'm a teenage ballroom champ with a gay dad, how in the hell could I possibly be straight?"

Why did I do it? I can only guess I figured he might think I was funny and perhaps a little creepy and he'd want to leave me alone. Yeah. That didn't work.

Boyfriend's face lit up like I'd just offered him a free spoiler for his Challenger. "Bro!" He led me away from the group while I dealt with the whiplash from his change in attitude. "Next week is Katy's birthday, and I have no-o-o idea what to get her. You totally have to help me pick out something awesome so she doesn't break up with me."

I raised an inquiring eyebrow.

He grew sheepish. "We've been having a few problems."

In the mirrors, I saw Katy look around and spot us. From her expression, she was utterly perplexed as to why Boyfriend was suddenly my new BFF. She saw me watching her watching us and looked away abruptly.

My innocent face is my best. I have that open honest expression that helps me get away with murder. I gripped his arm with all the companionable *bon ami* I could manage. "Of course, I'll help you. We can't let Katy break up with you. . ." Wait for it. ". . . bro."

Fist bump.

Practice resumed. I had to remind myself that I'd promised not to insult the crew. Katy glanced at me a few times, obviously judging my reaction, but I'm so good at using the mirrors she couldn't have known when I was watching.

Their technique was shoddy. I mean, only one or two could smoothly pull off a double turn, which should've been easy after the first few months of dancing. Half of them had bad posture, and Taco, bless his heart, was never going to get the new bit. Then K-pop pulled him aside while Katy worked on something else. The skinny Korean wannabe drilled with Taco over a dozen times until he managed to—almost—nail it.

K-pop raised his arms and whooped. "You rock the world!"

Taco could barely dance through the move, but K-pop celebrated as if it were the most amazing accomplishment in the world. For Taco, maybe it was.

They rejoined the group. Everybody high-fived them and pushed ahead to the next section.

When Monika and I had practiced in Austin, we were *serious* about it. We were always preparing for the next comp or performance. Even with the other dancers at *our* studio there was competition. We never, ever laughed or joked with them. If another couple earned higher ranks, Monika wouldn't speak to me for a week.

The atmosphere at the Emporium was more like Dad's gym: a bunch of folks having fun. It was about spending time doing what they loved rather than being the best in the world. That was so not my norm. It wasn't even my occasional.

I wasn't there just to stalk Katy anymore. Watching the team practice was fun. But when it reminded me of the good times I used to have with my dad, I decided to head out. It was too confusing.

Everyone waved and said goodbye. K-pop and Boyfriend made a point of bumping my fist. Katy kept her back to me as I left, but she used the mirror to watch me all the way out the door.

Ethan's story continues in *The Tango Triptych*, available on Amazon. He and many of his friends are featured in future episodes of *Tales of Mystery and Woe.*

I hope you enjoyed these samples. If not, remember they were free.

Acknowledgements

This series, more than any other, has had moments inspired by the people I love the most. The Alpaca Consortium was inspired by Sarah Mathews when I asked why intergalactic travelers would waste gas money visiting a worthless hunk of rock like ours.

The exploding singer came to me when my buddy Andrew and I watched a sad, pathetic band playing to an empty house during SXSW. The opening action was exactly as it happened, and as I sipped my drink and felt sorry for the poor girl behind the mic, I had a vision of her exploding because that would be the only thing that would have received any sincere applause. I filed it away.

The complications between Maestro and Spook owe much to moments with my adopted family, especially Ryan and Chris, who taught me so much about both love and detachment.

Maestro's house is a real place where I lived with my favorite roommate, Jace. If you ever find it, place a bottle of something really nice on his porch, but leave him the hell alone.

Dan will find himself all over the place throughout the entire series.

Aisha, who was originally cast as E.T. for the video series, has informed everything I've written about her since.

Maestro was originally envisioned as an ideal of myself, but working with Travis has forever rendered the character in his image.

As always, thanks to Lauran Strait for making me really examine my word choices and write like a big boy. I hope I finally made it good enough.

Yes, Bitter Sweets is real, although renamed. Keep looking.

About the Author

John Robert Mack originally conceived of TOMAWAC as a stage play. After a couple of readthroughs, his friends convinced him it should be a screenplay. A producer found and lost (as happens more frequently than we'd like to believe) and he decided to translate the series into novels. He is teaching dance in San Antonio Texas while he waits for the world to beat down his door for the novels. He's written plays, novels, and stuff for a really long time. No pets or children to speak of, but he has three nephews and myriad other adopted family members who make all this hard work worthwhile. Namaste.

57856041R00135

Made in the USA
Charleston, SC
24 June 2016